A Beckoning Hellfire

A Novel of the Civil War

J.D.R. Hawkins

Printed in the United States of America.

Library of Congress Control Number: 2020902600

ISBN   Paperback   978-1-64803-077-2
             eBook   978-1-64803-078-9

Westwood Books Publishing LLC
11416 SW Aventino Drive
Port Saint Lucie, FL 34987

www.westwoodbookspublishing.com

Title: A Beckoning Hellfire: A Novel of the Civil War (The Renegade Series)
Author: J.D.R. Hawkins
Publisher: Westwood Books Publishing
ISBN: 978-1648030772
Pages: 249
Genre: Military Historical Fiction
Reviewed by: Jack Chambers

Hollywood Book Reviews

The realities of war are often far more brutal and harsher than the stories and imagery the governments of a nation will make it out to be. The search for glory and heroism will often outshine everything else, but those who find themselves in the midst of war will find more cruelty, fear, and bloodshed than any sense of glory they were promised. To find a means of preparing for war is far less likely the more one focuses on the morality of our world. As Sophocles once said, "War never takes a wicked man by chance, the good man always."

In author J.D.R. Hawkins's *A Beckoning Hellfire: A Novel of the Civil War*, the second book in *The Renegade Series*, the author takes readers into the dark realities of war and vengeance through the eyes of David Summers. The story finds David thrust from his farm in Northern Alabama and into the heart of the American Civil War on the battlefields in Virginia and Pennsylvania. The news of his father's death in the Battle of Fredericksburg rocks David to his core, and he goes in search of vengeance against the people he blames for his passing. Yet as time goes on and the war looms large over him, he begins to lose the bloodlust that drove him forward as the battles wear on him physically and mentally, leading to a haunted look at the human cost of the American Civil War.

As a reader who has had the pleasure of reading several books in this historical fiction series, I was immediately drawn into the author's familiar yet always engaging focus on historical accuracy and cinematic writing style. The emotional and psychological weight of the Civil War has never felt more profound, as the author does an excellent job of showcasing both sides of the war and the many different realities of those fighting on the frontlines of battle. The atmosphere was definitely heavy, and the haunting tone the author's writing struck was a great way of highlighting the plight of the common man who fought in this war, rather than focusing on the historical figures or wealthy landowners who fueled the war behind the scenes.

This is the perfect book for those who enjoy historical fiction reads, especially those that enjoy historical fiction that focuses on American History, in particular the American Civil War. The balance the author found between the historical accuracy and the rich character development was great to see, as David's evolution throughout the narrative was the heart and soul of this narrative. The reader gets a true sense of the horrors and weariness that overcame the average soldier during the war, and made for a well-rounded reading experience.

Thought-provoking, adrenaline-fueled, and historically entertaining, author J.D.R. Hawkins's *A Beckoning Hellfire: A Novel of the Civil War* is a must-read historical fiction novel and a great entry into the author's *The Renegade Series*. The haunting imagery and detailed accuracy of the battles and death that many soldiers experienced during that time puts a real human element into this fictional story, and will leave fans eager for more of the author's incredible work.

A Beckoning Hellfire is Poignant, Beautiful and Thoroughly Researched!

J. D. R. Hawkins does it again! A Beckoning Hellfire follows the same family as in her previous book, A Beautiful Glittering Lie. When the family receives devastating news, David is set on enlisting, and going into war against the North. He and his best friend, Jake, join up in the Cavalry Regiment. David leaves his family behind, and Jake leaves his family and fiancee, as they go off to finally get a taste of the adventure they had been craving.

The experience is far from what either of them pictured, and it gets worse when they have to be in different regiments. Driven onward by his faith in God, thoughts of his father, and the memory of those who took their last breaths at the hand of the North, David fights with every fiber of his being.

Hawkins should come with a "Tissues Needed" warning label, since she keeps breaking my heart. Her novels are poignant, beautiful, and thoroughly-researched. As with her previous book, I was drawn in from the very first sentence of A Beckoning Hellfire, and regretted how quickly I can read. I didn't want it to end!

I love the way Hawkins develops her characters, and portrays their personal growth and the coming-of-age of David. With her novels, you're doing more than just reading; you're having an experience. I highly recommend this to everyone that likes fiction, even if historical isn't usually your cup of tea. Students would also benefit greatly from this being adapted as part of the curriculum.

Hawkins should be nicknamed 'Arachne' for the beautiful tapestries she weaves of the Civil War. Without a doubt, 5/5 stars. I would give more but, alas, there are not enough stars on the scale.

E-Book Review Gal

Civil War/History Lovers Need This Book

What a great read! The author covers the history so very well and adds brilliance as she brings you into the human side of war. The characters are vivid and well defined.

The story is exciting and thought provoking throughout. It questions the validity of war as well as the necessity. By using one main character, you almost feel as though you are a member of his family.

It ends in a manner that screams for a sequel. (Don't peek).

She has written a prequel, "A Beautiful Glittering Lie" and I'm about to read it.

By Raymond H. Mulle
Vine Voice

A Unique Civil War Tale

After having read a thoroughly engaging Civil war tale in A Beautiful Glittering Lie, I was certainly interested in reading the sequel.

David Summers is heartbroken after hearing the news of his father Hiram's death in the Battle of Fredericksburg. This motivates him to convince his best friend, Jake, to go with him and enlist in the Confederate army, more to avenge his father than for idealism. As with his father, he and Jake find that the war means nothing more than horror, suffering and cruelty.

Again as in her first book, Hawkins recounts the human side of this tragic war. The young men in the story all too soon are thrown into battle. The author gives the reader a realistic view of the horrors of the battlefield, along with the characters' reactions to all that happens around them.

Historical facts that mix with a look into how the war is seen from the eyes of a young soldier, this is what makes this book so unique.

By Elaine Bertolotti
Author of Florence and Me

ACKNOWLEDGMENTS

I would like to express my sincere gratitude to the following people. Without their assistance, guidance, and support, this book would not have been possible.

Brandy Station Foundation
Brandy Station, Virginia

Civil War Life—The Soldier's Museum
Fredericksburg/Spotsylvania, Virginia

John M. Coski
Historian and Director of Library & Research
The Museum of the Confederacy Richmond, Virginia

Cris Crisfield
Rocky Mountain Christian Church, Niwot, Colorado

Decatur Public Library
Decatur, Alabama

Shelby Foote
Author

Fredericksburg and Spotsylvania National Military Park
Fredericksburg/Spotsylvania, Virginia

Gettysburg National Military Park
Gettysburg, Pennsylvania

Jennifer L. Jones
Chair, Military and Diplomatic History
National Museum of American History
Smithsonian Institution, Washington, D.C.

Bob Linier
Firearms expert, Loveland, Colorado

Longmont Public Library
Longmont, Colorado

John McClure
Virginia Historical Society

David Miller
Associate Curator, Military and Diplomatic History
National Museum of American History, Smithsonian Institution
Washington, D.C.

My Family
For their ongoing support

Teresa Roane
The Museum of the Confederacy, Richmond, Virginia

Bill Sumners
Director and Archivist
Southern Baptist Historical Library and Archives, Nashville, Tennessee

For Jeremy

Table of Contents

But what a cruel thing is war. To separate and destroy families and friends and mar the purest joys and happiness God has granted us in this world. To fill our hearts with hatred instead of love for our neighbors and to devastate the fair face of this beautiful world...My heart bleeds at the death of every one of our gallant men.

—Robert E. Lee, letter to his wife, December 25, 1862

Chapter One

"Here it is! Come quick!"

David sauntered across the dead grass toward his little sister. Amused by the way she was jumping up and down like a nervous flea, he couldn't help but grin. Obviously, she was too excited to care that her petticoats were showing from under the brown coat and green calico dress she wore, or that her long auburn hair had broken free from its bondage as her bonnet slid from her head and dangled down her back.

"Which one, Josie?" he asked, stifling a snicker.

She planted her feet and pointed to a small yellow pine near a cluster of sweet gum and ash trees. "Right here!" she exclaimed.

Glancing down at the sapling, he gave her a crooked smile. "Well, that's a mighty fine tree, but ain't it kinda scrawny?" He estimated the pine to be three feet tall at most.

Josie frowned at her older brother, who had one eyebrow cocked from under his slouch hat. His hands were tucked into his brown trousers, and his linen shirt hung loosely on his tall, lanky frame. "No," she said, " it's jist right. We'll string some corn on it, hang some nuts and berries on it, and it'll look right smart in the corner of the front room."

With a shrug, he said, "All right. If you reckon this is the one."

She nodded, her bright blue eyes reflecting her elation.

David relished the moment, for he knew Christmas was her favorite holiday. He had only heightened her anticipation on the way out to the woodlot by reminding her what would happen that evening, how Santa would be stopping by later when she was sound asleep. Of course, he had no explanation as to how eight tiny reindeer could pull a sleigh all the way to Alabama. Josie promptly informed him that she wasn't a child any longer. She was all of thirteen, and didn't believe in those farfetched stories anymore, but he knew better. She would be lying in her bed tonight, listening and waiting.

"Well, go on now, cut it down!" Josie insisted.

He put his thumb and forefinger to his lips and gave a high, shrill whistle. Noticing how the gray sky was growing darker, he looked over at the edge of the clearing where they stood and saw the underbrush rustle. Suddenly, two hound dogs bounded out of the trees, followed by a gangly young stallion.

"Come on, Renegade. Over here," he called out to the colt, who responded by cantering to him.

Josie giggled at the sight. "Your dumb horse thinks he's a dog!"

"He ain't dumb. I'll wager he's a lick smarter than you are, li'l sister," David teased.

The horse blew and stomped his front hoof.

"Why, that's the most ridiculous thing I ever heard of. And not only is he dumb, he looks right silly, too. He can't decide if he should be spotted or palomino!"

David observed his horse for a moment. Renegade's face was piebald. His dark chestnut coat was highlighted with white spots and patches concentrating on his underbelly, and his mane and tail were light flaxen. He had white socks up to his knees. His unusual eyes were brownish green. David remembered how he had heard that a horse with strange-colored eyes like Renegade's was considered sacred and chosen by the Cherokee Indians. Several people had noticed the strange coincidence, and his other sister, Rena, also frequently commented that he and his horse had the same colored eyes.

"I reckon he knows what he is," David remarked. "Besides, he's unusual, and that makes him unique."

"Oh, he's unique all right," Josie said, giggling again. She pulled her hair back from her face and replaced her bonnet.

David untied a saw from a leather strap attached to Renegade's saddle. He knelt down, quickly sawed through the little tree's trunk, picked it up, and tied it across the saddle's seat. His two black and tan dogs sniffed around the tree's sawed off stump. Suddenly, they both lifted their noses into the air with their ears pricked. They bolted across the open clearing, baying at an unseen curiosity as they disappeared into the woods.

"Caleb! Si!" David hollered after the two hounds. "Well, there they go," he observed wryly. "All right, Renegade, take it on home." He patted his horse on the shoulder.

Renegade nickered softly, shook his head, and trotted off in the same direction as the two hounds.

Josie gasped. "Look, David! It's startin' to snow!" She tilted her head back and stuck out her tongue, trying to catch snowflakes on it.

He chuckled.

"Come on, you do it, too," she coaxed him.

He obliged his little sister by imitating her.

Josie laughed, spinning around with her arms extended while snow fell silently down around them.

"Oh!" David clasped his hand to his face. "One fell in my eye!"

Josie giggled.

He couldn't help but smile, although he was careful not to let her see, and snorted to cover up his delight. "Well, I'm right glad you think it's so funny." He looked at her, trying to keep a straight face. "Come on, Josie, girl. We'd best be gittin' on back."

He allowed her to go ahead of him as they started on the bridle path that cut through the woods.

"Let's sing Christmas carols!" she said. "That new one we heard last year. Jingle Bells!"

"You start," he prompted.

"Dashin' through the snow..."

He joined in. Their voices grew stronger in unison.

"In a one-horse open sleigh..."

They came to an empty field, and trudged through, stepping over mud puddles while they continued singing.

"Jingle bells, jingle bells, jingle all the way..."

Their house stood quaintly at the far end of the field. Smoke circled from its two chimneys, dissolving into the gray sky. The sweet smell of burning hickory reached out, inviting them closer. From a distance, the structure appeared to be two separate cabins sitting side by side, but upon closer observation, one could see that they were connected by a covered breezeway. Each section contained two rooms and a fireplace. A wide flat porch on the front of the split log building served as an entryway. The tin roof, which seemed to expel heat in the summertime, also managed to repel snow during winter months.

The cold, damp air encroached upon brother and sister. As they sang, their breath escaped, floated out across the fields, and vanished in phantom gusts.

"Oh what fun it is to ride in a one-horse open sleigh!"

On the last note, Josie's voice jumped an octave. They laughed at their grand finale and walked around to the front of the house, where

Renegade was waiting patiently for the tree to be removed from his saddle. A buckskin horse stood beside him.

"Whose horse is that?" Josie asked.

"It looks like Bud Samuels' horse."

David and Josie looked at each other, wide-eyed. "Pa!" they both exclaimed.

Josie sprang onto the porch, burst through the front door, and went inside while David untied the small yellow pine. He set it aside, pulled the saddle from Renegade's back, and removed his bridle.

"Go on into the barn, Renie," he said. "Or you'll be one big ole snowball in a minute."

The colt blew and trotted around the side of the house.

David carried his tack into the breezeway. He placed it on a horizontal board, which was supported by a plank on each end. Collecting the tree, he heard the sound of Bud's voice coming from inside.

"I had some trouble gettin' here," Bud was saying as he entered. "But I convinced the Home Guard to follow me home so's I could show them my furlough paper."

David produced the tiny tree. "I know it's small," he said with a grin, "but Josie insisted, and..." The sight that befell him inexplicably filled him with dread. His smile faded. He looked around at the faces before him and let the tree fall onto the wooden floor. Warmth from the fireplace did nothing to relieve the chill that grasped him. "What is it?" he asked.

"Come in, darlin', and close the door," his mother said from her high-backed chair, which sat near the empty corner they had readied for the Christmas tree. Her brown skirt encircled her like a puddle. Her dark brown hair, streaked recently with gray, was parted in the middle and contained in a white cotton hair net. She clenched her hands in her lap, and her lips were pursed. The flickering firelight accentuated the grooves on her face, which, for some reason, David had never noticed before.

After closing the door behind him, he looked at Rena, who was sitting beside the hearth. She vacantly stared back, her violet eyes welling up with tears.

"Rena?" he asked her.

She looked away and hugged Josie, who had taken the chair beside her. David walked across the room to their neighbor, Bud.

"It's a pleasure to see you again, Mr. Samuels," he said, shaking the man's hand. "How's Pa? Is he comin' home for Christmas, like he wrote?"

"Have a seat, David." Bud's eyes filled with concern. He scratched his straggly, graying beard. Obeying the command, David slowly sank into a chair, keeping his eyes fixed on Bud's face.

"I'm afraid I have bad news." Bud cleared his throat, then slowly, deliberately said, "Your father's been killed at Fredericksburg." He looked down at the floor. "A little over a week ago. I know he was lookin' forward to seein' y'all. I'm...immensely sorry."

He pulled a folded piece of yellowed paper from his coat pocket. The gray coat was torn and tattered in places, not at all like the beautiful piece of clothing that had been provided to him nearly two years earlier. His trousers and the kepi he held in his hand were weathered, too.

"Miss Carolyn, Hiram wanted me to give you this here letter...in the event of his death." He solemnly handed her the note.

Squeezing her eyes shut, Carolyn held it to her mouth. Tears streamed down her weathered face. "Thank you, Bud," she finally said. "You've been a good friend to my Hiram. I know he appreciated you dearly."

Bud nodded. "Please let the missus or me know if there's anything we can do," he offered, and walked toward the door.

"I surely will." Carolyn wearily stood, followed him to the door, and walked him out.

Bud placed his kepi on his head, untied his horse, mounted, and galloped off down the lane. The rhythm of hoof beats faded.

Turning from the doorway, Carolyn somberly gazed at her children. Her two daughters came across the room to hug her. The three of them burst into tears. Carolyn gazed at her son, who was sitting motionless across the room, his handsome young face drained of color, his hazel eyes growing a darker brown.

"David," she said, her voice filled with the sorrow that had now overtaken the room.

He looked over at her, his face blank with grief-stricken shock. Finding no comfort in her anguished expression, he glanced up at the ornately-carved mantle clock, the one his father had given to her as a wedding gift. It read ten minutes past five. Beside it sat a framed tintype of his father, adorned in Confederate glory, ready to march off to victory, but now he was never to return. David's eyes wandered, and he noticed things he'd taken for granted before: the raised oval portrait of his paternal grandmother on the wall, the paintings of flowers his mother liked so well that hung on the opposite wall, the fieldstone fireplace that his father had built, and the pine furniture that had been there ever since he could remember. Somehow, all of it seemed irrelevant.

Moving numbly, he rose and walked across the room to pick up the little tree he had dropped earlier. A tiny pool of water remained where it had fallen. He carried the tree outside, leaving a trail of moisture that splattered onto the floorboards. The cold winter air, uncluttered with snow, barely whispered, its breath deathly quiet and still. Dusk was rapidly approaching.

David hurled the tree as hard as he could. It landed with a rustled thud out in the yard. Without pausing, he walked into the breezeway past his mother and sisters and grabbed a kerosene lantern. He carried it outside, lit it, and threw it at the pine. The glass shattered upon impact. Kerosene trickled out onto the tiny branches and within seconds, flames engulfed the little tree. He stoically watched tongues of fire consume the sapling. Slowly, he turned to face his mother and sisters, who were standing on the porch, watching him while they wept.

"I reckon we won't be celebratin' Christmas after all," he said, his voice raspy with distress.

Impending darkness engulfed his heart. Feeling the need for solitude, he walked around the house toward the barn, vaguely hearing his mother call out to him. The sky opened, releasing icy rain. He stomped past the pigpen and the chicken coop. Upon reaching the old wooden barn, he went inside and blinked several times before his eyes adjusted to his dim surroundings. He caught glimpses of shadows dancing off the walls and up around the rafters. A pungent combination of dry, clean hay and musty wood enveloped him. The rain rattled down upon the barn's tin roof and sounded like a thousand tiny drums. Three cows studied him with soft brown eyes. One mooed a welcome as he walked past them.

Sidestepping bales of hay stacked near the stall door, David paused to shake off cold drops of moisture that clung to his shirt, and ran his hand over the top of his head, wiping the rain from his dark brown hair. A large Percheron, standing in the stall next to Renegade, gazed at David with his ears pricked.

"Hey, Joe Boy," David said softly to the tall white gelding.

The draft horse sniffled at David's pockets, but seemed to lose interest, and shuffled to the other end of his stall when David didn't offer a treat like he usually did. Renegade looked up from his fodder and nickered softly. David walked over and gently stroked his muzzle.

"I'm sorry I put you through all that trouble of bringin' home a tree."

Anguish and anger welled up inside him. Searing-hot tears streamed down his cheeks. His hatred seethed. His grief was overwhelming, and he could hold it back no longer. Sobs escaped him. He grasped onto his horse's mane, burying his face in Renegade's neck. The colt stood quietly, seemingly to console him.

Several days later, a sepulchral ritual commenced. Dreary rain persisted, becoming a bone-chilling drizzle. A small group gathered around a symbolic gravesite, the dirt left undisturbed since there was no body within. The grave was designated by a pine marker that David had carved. Mourners in black stood with heads bowed under ebony umbrellas while the pastor spoke.

"Forasmuch as it has pleased Almighty God in His wise Providence to take out of this world the soul of our deceased brother, Hiram Summers, we therefore commit his body to the ground: earth to earth, ashes to ashes, dust to dust, lookin' for the general resurrection in the last day and the life of the world to come, through our Lord Jesus Christ, at whose second comin' in glorious majesty to judge the world, the earth and the sea shall give up their dead, and the corruptible bodies of those who sleep in Him shall be changed and made like unto His own glorious body, accordin' to the mighty workin' whereby He is able to subdue all things unto himself. I heard a voice from Heaven sayin' unto me write, from henceforth, blessed are the dead who die in the Lord, even so sayeth the Spirit, for they rest from their labors."

The pastor requested that all recite the Lord's Prayer in unison, then the crowd chanted, "Amen."

Carolyn reached out to her daughters, who carried her from the gravesite. They floated off with their faces veiled, their bodies swathed in black bombazine. The mourners dispersed until only one remained, who stared blankly at the pine headboard.

Hiram Summers
Beloved Father and Husband
Born May 11, 1821
Died December 13, 1862

Drizzle fell upon his uncovered head, and his shoulder-length hair hung in icy locks. He stood there, paralyzed, not sure what to do next, not wanting to do anything but stand there in the rain, wishing it would stop, but not wanting it to, because the rain seemed to drown his heartache and numb him into disbelief. Feeling as if someone was there with him, he could see his father's face, almost imagine the sound of his voice, and he shuddered.

"Come on, David. You can't stand out here in the rain all day. You'll catch your death of cold."

Recognizing the familiar voice, he responded, "I don't care, Jake," and was glad the rain hid his tears.

The young man moved closer, holding an umbrella over David's head. "Let's git on back to the house," Jake said softly.

"It's all my fault."

"What is?"

"Pa's death. If it wasn't for me, he never would've gone. He would've stayed here to tend to the farm."

"You don't know that," said Jake. "You can't blame yourself."

"I'm the one who wanted to jine up. He went in my place and made me promise to stay here. If it wasn't for me pushin' the issue, he might've jist let it go." Squeezing his eyes shut, David muttered, "This is God's way of punishin' me, for wishin' Owen Ridgeway was dead."

"That ain't why," Jake said, his voice low and soothing. "And don't go blamin' yourself for Owen's death. He brought it on himself."

The two of them knew it to be true. Their schoolmate had been a turncoat, enlisting with the Yankees instead of the grand Confederacy. Owen had not died nobly. He had succumbed to God's wrath, and the boys knew his death by disease was justifiable. Still, David felt responsible somehow. He finally looked up from the makeshift grave. He didn't care if Jake could see he'd been crying. He waited for Jake to tease him about his sensitivity, but was grateful when it didn't come. They walked together in silence, away from the wrought-iron fences. Reaching the waiting wagon, they climbed up onto the seat.

Jake took the reins and snapped them. "Git up, ole Stella, gal," he coaxed.

The wagon lurched forward as the coal black Morgan slowly plodded down the puddle-riddled, muddy road.

"Stella don't take much to gittin' up her speed," David observed, but his voice was filled with sadness.

"She jist don't like the rain," Jake replied. "Her old joints stiffen up in this here weather."

As they came within sight of the Summers' saddlebag house, Jake signaled for his horse to trot. "It looks like all of Morgan County is here," he said.

"Reckon Pa had a lot of friends." David drew a heavy sigh.

Stella came to a stop near the front door. The two boys climbed down and went into the house. Black bunting traditionally covered the windows. Regardless of the dismal décor, the aroma of food enticed them.

"I don't know about you, but I'm starvin'!" Jake quickly walked through the crowd toward the food.

David hesitated, but soon wished he hadn't.

"I'm so sorry about your pa, David."

The condolences continually came from friends and neighbors as he slowly made his way through the gathering.

"May we all meet beyond this vale of tears," said Mrs. Samuels, a middle-aged woman with a soothing voice and a warm smile.

Unwittingly, David felt a twinge of jealousy. It wasn't fair that Mrs. Samuels got her husband back, when he would never have his father back. "Yes'm," was all he could muster.

The pastor approached him. "I'm sorry for your loss, son, and I wish your father peace to his sleepin' dust."

David nodded, grimacing slightly at the words. "Thank you, Pastor," he meekly responded. Making his way through the gathering, he overheard two elderly gentlemen.

"There's been many a funeral this past week or so," one remarked.

"I've heard tell as many as half a dozen from this county alone died fightin' with Hiram," the other said.

David came upon his mother, who embraced him. She looked up at him with her hazel eyes, but the large eyes that had always arrested him were now swollen and red. He felt his heart tighten like a fist.

"Your pa is with the angels now." She forced a smile. "And with our dear little Elijah."

David stifled a sob. He kissed his mother on the cheek, wishing for some way to relieve her suffering. Rena and Josie came across the room, and the entire family embraced.

"New Year's Eve is the day after tomorrow," Rena said in a melodic voice that sometimes made David's heart flutter. "Next year can only git better for us, because this horrendous war will be over."

"Hiram wouldn't want us to mourn him. We should be celebratin'," their mother said, wiping a tear from her eye.

David opened his mouth to say he didn't feel like celebrating, but swallowed his words when he saw the sad, forlorn expression on his mother's face. "You're right, Ma," he replied, and looked at his two sisters. "Pardon me while I go find Jake."

Edging his way through the crowd, he glanced at the open doorway to his parents' room. Mourners gathered around the big bed, mumbling. He felt invaded by their presence, and wished they would at least allow his mother enough privacy to leave her room alone. Managing to make his way to a long table set against the back wall, he found his best friend piling food onto a plate.

"Look at all this!" Jake exclaimed, his brown eyes gleaming. "There's enough food here to last y'all a week! Fetch yourself a plate!" Jake eagerly devoured a biscuit.

"I ain't very hungry." David looked at the table covered with apple and cherry pies, fruitcake, ham, fried chicken, chitlins, red-eye gravy, biscuits, black-eyed peas, sweet potatoes, hominy, cornbread, collard greens, oysters, and dried fruits. He was overwhelmed by his neighbors' generosity, since he knew that money and provisions had grown increasingly rare. Despite his sorrow, he found his mouth watering at the sight, so he reluctantly picked up a plate and began filling it.

"Come this spring, I'm fixin' to jine the army," he blurted, surprising himself by verbalizing his plans. "I've been givin' it some thought since Pa died. Seems like a good way to pay those Yankees back for what they done." He gave his friend a sidelong glance. "And I want you to come with me, Jake."

Nodding in agreement, Jake said, "Mister Lincoln don't realize what he's doin' by tryin' to put an end to our peculiar institution and settin' all the niggers free." He popped a sweet potato into his mouth, chewed it twice, and gulped it down. "I can't wait to kill me some Yankees!" His grin dissolved. "But I ain't legal to go. Not like that would stop me, but I don't know if I should leave right now, what with spring plantin' comin' up."

David thought for a moment. "Well, if you're fixin' to go, best do it now before the war's over." He shoved a slice of ham into his mouth.

"That could be any day now," said Jake.

"So we should jine up right away."

Jake shrugged. "I'll think on it a spell."

Frowning, David devoured a biscuit. "I hate leavin' my poor ma and sisters to fend for themselves, though."

"My folks can help them take care of y'all's farm," Jake said. "Or they can send Percy and Isabelle over to do it. That is, if they don't run off come the first of the year with all the other darkies."

"I promised Pa I'd stay and take care of this place, but I can't do it now. After all, the Good Book says 'an eye for an eye.'"

"That's the spirit!" Jake chuckled. He jovially punched his friend in the arm. "When are you, er, we, fixin' to leave?"

"Reckon we ought to wait till after my birthday. That way, Ma can't rightly object." He picked up a chicken leg. Pointing it at his friend, he said, "I'll tell her in a few weeks, after things have quieted down some," and took a bite.

"Well, that's when I'll tell my folks, too, "said Jake, "and Callie."

David glanced around the room, his eyes darting across the crowd of familiar faces. "I thought she would be here," he said with a rueful expression.

Jake gave him a fleeting glance before focusing his attention back to his plate. "She was there at the funeral. I reckon you didn't see her. She had to git on home, but said for me to tell you that she was...er, how'd she put it...sensitive to your pain." He shoved a forkful of greens into his mouth.

David shook his head. "She won't take lightly to your leavin'."

With a shrug, Jake replied, "It ain't like I'll be gone forever." He grinned, and grabbed another biscuit.

David finished his snack. He looked up and noticed his mother talking to a familiar face. The sight made him bristle.

"Look what the cat dragged in," he said to Jake, who followed his gaze.

"Kit Lawrence?" Jake took a bite of fried okra. "I ain't seen him around in a while."

"I was hopin' we got rid of him," said David. "But it looks like he found out about Pa's death." Setting his plate on the table, he made his way through the crowded room to his mother.

"Not now, Kit," she was saying. Noticing her son's approach, she added, "We'll discuss it another time," and shuffled off.

"Mr. Lawrence," David forced himself to say respectfully.

"Sorry about your pa, son," Kit Lawrence said in a raspy voice. His breath reeked of tobacco and whiskey. "I can't tell you how much this cuts me to the quick."

David recoiled. "If you're fixin' to say I told you so, then save..."

"That ain't why I'm here," he said, giving what David perceived to be a genuine, sorrowful expression. "My intentions haven't changed. I promised your pa when he left that I'd look after y'all, and that's what I aim to do."

Wanting to lash out by telling him his intentions weren't desired, David decided to interrogate him instead. "Where have you been for the past few months?"

"Up in Kentucky. I have a business partner up there. We've been, er, sellin' wares to the army."

"Oh?" David raised a skeptical eyebrow. "What kind of wares?"

"That ain't none of your concern, boy." Kit's familiar scowl returned. "In fact, I have to be gettin' back. You tell your ma I'll come callin' on her later on." He turned and sashayed out the door.

David was tempted to keep the message from his mother, but decided to relay it to her once everyone had gone. She merely nodded before shutting herself in her room.

The thought of Kit Lawrence butting into their affairs made David's blood boil, but he knew the final decision was his mother's. After all, Kit was supposedly his father's best friend from childhood. A certain honor came with that, he supposed, but he didn't see how any of them owed Kit anything. He had turned his back on Hiram by failing to enlist with him; by telling him his convictions were wrong. He didn't even show up to send Hiram off. No, David decided, none of them owed Kit Lawrence a damn thing.

January slowly gave way to February. The war subsided, taking an unnerving pause since the Battle of Murfreesboro in Tennessee around New Year's. Union soldiers re-occupied nearby Huntsville, which only enraged many of Morgan County's residents further. David learned of the invasion one day during a visit to the blacksmith. Resentment and hostility simmered throughout the county. In David, it was ready to boil over.

"Mrs. Fletcher's son has gone off to fight, too. Left in the middle of the night," John Moss said as he lifted Renegade's right front hoof. He was a short man with a bushy blond beard and piercing blue eyes. David often wondered how he could manage the taller horses, let alone get up on one.

"Is that a fact?" he responded. "Ain't he only fifteen or so?"

"Yessiree," said John, while prying off Renegade's old shoe. "They're all fixin' to leave, sayin' the war's nearly done." He let go of the colt's hoof, walked over to a stack of horseshoes near the furnace, and selected one. Clamping the shoe with a pair of tongs, he set it over the flame. "I reckon you'll be followin' right behind him, won'tcha, David?" He picked up the glowing shoe, set it on an anvil, and pounded on it with a hammer, causing sparks to fly.

"I reckon I will," David said, not sure if John heard him or not. He hadn't cared a copper about secession before, but now the war was too close to home. The Northern invaders had taken his father, and all he could think about was his own vendetta.

John set the shoe into a barrel of water, causing it to hiss as steam spewed into the air.

"Your ma know about this?" a baritone voice boomed behind him.

David turned to see Bud Samuels standing in the doorway, holding the reins to his buckskin horse.

"Bud," John greeted him. He picked up Renegade's hoof again and nailed the new shoe in place.

"She will soon enough," David replied. "I'm leavin' the day after my birthday."

Bud entered the shop. He tied his horse and removed his hat. "Well, I know how she'll react. But I'll tell you this much. Your pa would be right proud." He sat down at a small wooden table that was set off to the side for waiting customers.

David took a seat across from him. "Thank you, Mr. Samuels." He paused for a moment. Deciding to give in to his curiosity, he asked, "What was it like at Fredericksburg?"

"Cold," said Bud. "Mighty cold." He reached over to a small tin pot on the table, held a cup under the spout, poured dark liquid into it, and took a sip. Suddenly, his eyebrows creased together in a scowl. "What in tarnation is this?" he coughed.

"Ersatz coffee," said the blacksmith.

"What's in it?" croaked Bud.

John looked over at them from the furnace. "That there's got chicory, corn, goober peas, and acorns in it. Oh, and my own secret ingredient."

"What would that be, John?" Bud asked. "Chicken crap?"

David chuckled.

The blacksmith grinned, exposing numerous gaps where teeth had once been. "Now, if I told y'all, it wouldn't be a secret." He commenced to pounding on another horseshoe.

Bud scratched his beard. Setting his cup down on the little table, he sighed.

"What else happened in Fredericksburg?" asked David. "Did Pa say anything before..." Sadness interrupted his question.

"He said he loved y'all. And that he was proud."

"Proud? Of what?"

"Fightin' for the grand ole Southland. And of you. He talked about you all the time, David. How much of a man you'd become, and how you didn't put up a fuss about runnin' the farm when he left."

"Reckon it was my responsibility," David replied. His mind wandered back to the day Bud and his father joined up with the 4th Alabama Infantry Regiment, "The North Alabamians," and had gone off to fight in Virginia nearly two years ago. He glanced over at John, who smiled at him, and picked up Renegade's rear hoof. "Anything else?"

"Well, somethin' strange happened after the battle." Bud glared up at the ceiling.

David followed his gaze, but didn't see anything unusual. He looked back at Bud, who still had his face upturned.

"That last night, the sky lit up, and all different colored lights flashed across through the haze. We reckoned it was God tellin' us He approved, bein's we won the battle and all. It was wonderful." Bud flashed a toothy grin.

David wasn't sure if he agreed with Bud about receiving God's approbation. If that were so, then why was it God's will to take his pa?

"Are you fixin' to go back to the fight, Bud?" John asked, while working on Renegade's last remaining hoof.

"Yessir. Soon as the weather breaks." He stood up, and David did the same. "I ain't supposed to be back to Virginia for a couple months." He looked at his cup and winced before setting it down on the table. "What I wouldn't give for some real coffee," he sighed.

"And sugar," said John.

Suddenly, a loud bang caught them off guard. They turned to see a young man enter.

"Summers! Damn!" he roared, glaring angrily. He stomped toward David. "I've been lookin' for you." He gave David a harsh shove.

"Whoa, young'un!" Bud said, placing himself between the two. "What's goin' on here?"

"Tom!" David reacted. "What the devil's gotten into you?"

Tom glared at him, his dark blue eyes penetrating. "It's because of your pa," he said, his anger turning into a sob.

"What is?" David exchanged glances with Bud.

John walked over to assist, a forging hammer in his hand.

"He promised my daddy that he'd be there to protect him, but he didn't!" Tom tried to take a swing at David, who dodged his fist.

Wasting no time, Bud intersected by grabbing Tom's arm, and whirled him around. "I reckon it's time you leave till you cool down some," he said sternly.

David's hazel eyes grew dark. He gaped at his attacker. "What are you talkin' about?"

"You know damn well! You heard him, same as I did!" Tom was panting now, sweat beading on his forehead and running down his reddish-brown sideburns. He stood wringing his hands, struggling to control his rage.

John came closer with the hammer. "You heard Mr. Samuels. It's time you high-tailed it, boy." He motioned with the hammer toward the wooden door, slightly ajar, and swaying in the cold breeze.

Tom drew a heavy, quivering sigh. He glanced around at the gathering, and rushed out, leaving the door open behind him.

Turning toward David, John asked gruffly, "You know what that was all about?"

David gave a solemn nod. Tom had reminded him of the day their fathers attended a sending-off ceremony in Huntsville, four days before they left for the war. "I remember now," he said. "Pa told Mr. Caldwell that he would look after him, jist like all the fellers did. They all gave the same vow. Don't you recall, Mr. Samuels?"

Bud scratched his beard. "Yeah, of course I do. We all took that oath...that we'd look after each other and all."

John shook his head, distraught. "Well, it's a darn shame, that's all." He returned to his task.

"Did Tom's father die, Mr. Samuels?" asked David.

Bud scowled, which was indication enough.

When John had finished shoeing Renegade, he led the colt over to David and handed him the reins.

"Thank you kindly, Mr. Moss," David said. "Ma will see to it that you git paid once the crops are in."

"God speed, young'un," said John. "And take care of that horse."

"Yessir." David turned to face his father's best friend. "Well, Mr. Samuels, good luck to you," he said, setting his slouch hat on his head.

Bud reached out to shake his hand. "And to you, son. I hope we meet again in this here life."

David hadn't thought about that possibility. He soberly nodded.

"And watch out for those varmint Yankees when you git to Huntsville," Bud warned. "I don't know if they're still up there, occupyin' the city."

"I will," David replied.

Clicking his tongue against the inside of his cheek twice as a signal to his horse, David led Renegade out of the shop. On the walk back home, an eerie feeling came over him, one that refused to let go. It was the same sensation that had haunted him since Bud spoke his ominous words about meeting again in this life. Tom's appearance and the thought of all that death made David shudder.

With the advent of warm weather, David spent his days reading the *Farmer's Almanac* and planning out which crops to plant, but he was fully aware that he wouldn't be the one to plant them. The weeks seemed to drag on endlessly. His only reprieve was to visit Jake and persuade him to enlist.

By mid-March, school resumed, so David escorted his sisters to their one-story schoolhouse, the same building that was transformed into a storage facility for harvested cotton in the autumn and vacated during summer and winter months when the weather was too hot or cold. He had graduated two years before, just after his father left for the war, and had spent his time fulfilling his promise to tend to the farm while his father was away. When Hiram left, no one thought the war would last this long, and everyone hoped it wouldn't last much longer. But David hoped it would last long enough to see his intentions through.

As he walked the two miles back home, he whistled softly to himself, wishing he had brought along his trusty steed to shorten his travel time. A soft breeze weaved through the budding trees around him. He glanced up from the road just in time to see an incoming rock. It whizzed past him and slammed into a nearby tree with a thud.

"What the hell?" He walked over, picked it up, and pulled off a tied-on piece of paper. "This is for what your pa did to mine." He crumpled the paper in his left hand and threw it on the ground. Looking around, he hollered, "Come on out you coward! I know you're out there!"

"I got more rocks and I'll use 'em!" a voice shouted back.

David recognized it. "Caldwell! I ain't got nothin' to do with whatever my pa promised yours!" He was itching to fight, but his adversary remained invisible, making him feel awkwardly vulnerable. Trying to call him out, he said, "Can't we jist put this behind us?"

Tom laughed. "Not on your life! The way I see it, you're the next of your pa's kin to pay for his mistake." Another rock whooshed by, this time plummeting into the underbrush.

David's temper flared. "Fine! If that's the way you want it, you've got a fight on your hands!" He stomped off down the road, expecting a rock to slam into his back, but it didn't come. Rounding a bend, he bolted toward home.

A week before David planned to leave, he decided to break the news to his family. He had waited as long as he could, since he was apprehensive about the event and knew they would try to talk him out of it.

His mother set steaming bowls of Hopping John in front of each of her children, who had gathered around the table. Josie grabbed a spoon and went to take a bite.

"Josephine Summers, you wait till we say grace," her mother firmly scolded her.

"Sorry, Ma." Josie set the spoon down.

Carolyn seated herself. She folded her hands, rested her elbows firmly on the table, and glanced around, waiting until her brood had all closed their eyes. "Lord, thank you for this food which we are about to receive. Bless this family, and give us a prosperous year. We pray in your name, Amen."

"Amen," her children echoed.

Carolyn passed a plate of fried cornbread to Rena.

"I don't see how we can prosper this year, Ma, what with the Yankees breathin' down our necks, and now a tax-in-kind bein' imposed on us," David remarked, swirling his spoon around in the bowl of bacon, rice, and sarsaparilla stew. He scooped up a purple-hulled pea, an onion, and some red peppers, but let them fall back into the thickness.

"The army is entitled to whatever we can provide them," said Carolyn. "If they want us to tithe a tenth of everything we grow, then that's what we'll give them."

"But what if we have a bad crop this year?" asked Rena. She looked across the table at her brother.

"The Good Lord will provide for us, dear," Carolyn said confidently.

Rena watched her brother swirl his spoon around without taking a bite. "David, ain't you hungry?" she asked.

Josie snickered. "That would be a first." She grinned at her brother before shoveling another spoonful into her mouth.

David hesitated. "There's somethin' I want to say to y'all." He let go of the spoon and looked directly at his mother. "I'm fixin' to jine the army."

Carolyn immediately stopped eating. He felt like he had put a knife into her heart by the way she glared at him.

"David, I need you here," she said softly.

"I have to go, Ma." His voice grew defiantly stronger. "You know I do."

"No, you don't, David," Josie said in a high pitch. She reached across the table, grabbing hold of his wrist. "You don't have to go."

"Well, I want to, then. I'm fixin' to go and that's final." He took a deep breath. What had been building up inside of him for weeks had finally been released. The whole episode made him irritated. His mother was about to protest, he knew she would, but he had to make her understand.

"When?" She stared at him with her big hazel eyes.

Feeling his anger subside, his lower lip quivered slightly. "April third," he said, his voice softening under his mother's gaze. "The day after my birthday."

"That's next week!" Josie exclaimed.

"What about your plans to go to Auburn?" asked Rena.

David snorted. "I can't go to college now. Not with all that's happened." He looked down at his bowl and shrugged. "Besides that, Auburn's closed, and we don't have the money, anyways."

An awkward silence engulfed them.

"I ain't hungry anymore," Rena sobbed. She hurried out of the room.

David watched her leave. Guilt swept over him, but he couldn't waver. He had a duty to fulfill. "Jake's comin' with me," he mumbled.

"Oh, he is, is he?" his mother asked.

"Yes'm."

"Do his folks know about that?"

"I reckon so." He glanced over at Josie, who was still eating, but staring at him blankly.

"What about the crops? Have you considered that?" His mother set her spoon down on the table. "It's more than we can manage, David. You know we have over a hundred acres out yonder."

"I know, Ma," he said, his voice softening even more. "Jake's folks will help out, or their slaves will."

"Did you speak to them about it?" Carolyn frowned.

He stared at his bowl. "No, but I'm fixin' to...tomorrow."

His mother sighed, picked up her spoon, and took a bite. He reluctantly did the same. The mantle clock ticked repetitiously, accentuating the quiet.

"I'm done, Ma," Josie announced. "May I be excused?"

Carolyn nodded, so Josie rose from her place at the table and departed to the adjoining cabin.

"I'm done, too, Ma." David said. "May I be excused?"

"You can help me with clearin' the table. I ain't done with you yet."

David clenched his teeth. Under normal circumstances, he usually evaded clearing the table, since he considered it to be women's work. This was his mother's way of showing her disapproval, he knew.

19

Avoiding eye contact, he stood, gathered the dishes, and followed her out the back door. His two coonhounds, who had been waiting patiently, sprang to their feet, their tails wagging furiously.

"Caleb, you ole mutt. Si, you scoundrel," he greeted them affectionately. He scooped the leftovers into their dish and patted his hounds in an effort to postpone the confrontation with his mother, but finally forced himself to face the inevitable. Leaving the dogs to eagerly devour their food, he entered the small wooden kitchen building. Heat from the cook stove engulfed him; the smell of fried bacon still lingered. He set the empty bowls down next to the wash basin near a burning kerosene lamp. As he turned to leave, Carolyn grabbed hold of his forearm, compelling him to look at her.

"I know I can't talk you out of this, because you think it's your duty and you want to do it for your pa." She stared deeply into his eyes.

He slowly nodded, and bowed his head. It became apparent to him that his sagacious mother had known his intentions all along, for she could always read his thoughts and feelings.

"David, look at me when I'm speakin' to you," she instructed.

He timidly obeyed.

"That horse of yours will die of a broken heart if you don't take him along. And besides that, he knows how to git out of his stall, and he'll jist go chasin' after you." She gave him a sad smile. He faintly smiled in response. "Jist promise me one thing." She held tightly onto his arm. The flame flickered, punctuating the uncomfortable, sudden stillness.

"What's that, Ma?" he asked quietly.

"That you and Jake will git in with the cavalry. I'd feel a whole lot better if you did."

"But, Ma, how will we kill any Yankees if we're in the cavalry?"

She frowned. "I reckon you'll find a way."

David chuckled, but seeing his mother's hardened gaze, quickly let the smile fade from his lips. "I don't know if ole Stella can make the journey," he said.

"Ole Stella will do jist fine. Now, you promise me." She grasped tighter onto his forearm to the point where it was starting to hurt.

"All right, Ma. I promise."

She released her grasp. "And you make sure Jake promises his folks. I know ya'll think it's one big romp, but I can't lose you." She turned away, stirred the cinders in the wood-burning stove, and started heating up water for the dishes.

"Ma, I'll be all right."

He gave her a quick peck on the cheek. His mother didn't react. He turned, exited out of the kitchen, and glanced back. She was still facing away from him. Sauntering across the yard, he passed the well and the two outhouses and went into the house. Respectfully, he tidied up the table for her before retreating to his room. He could hear his sisters' muffled voices seep through the wall as he plopped onto his bed and positioned a down pillow under his head. The entire episode had left him exhausted and emotionally drained. *Tomorrow will be another day,* he reasoned to himself and closed his eyes. Lying across the bed with his feet hanging over the edge, he drifted off.

The will of God prevails. In great contests each party claims to act in accordance with the will of God. Both may be, and one must be, wrong. God cannot be for and against the same thing at the same time. In the present civil war it is quite possible that God's purpose is something different from the purpose of either party – and yet the human instrumentalities, working just as they do, are of the best adaptation to affect His purpose.

President Abraham Lincoln
"Meditation on the Divine Will," September 2, 1862

Chapter Two

Dawn soon disrupted David's sleep. Groggily, he pried himself from his refuge and walked outside. Bright sunshine temporarily blinded him. The shrill crow of a rooster startled him, jolting him into alertness. As he commenced feeding the livestock, he greeted the chickens and sheep with the names he and his sisters had chosen for each one.

He fed the pigs their slop. They started to fight over the filled trough, so he picked up a long stick and whacked each one on the rump as they squealed, grunted, and darted away on their short, stubby legs.

"Pork Pie! Ham Hock! Break it up!" he commanded.

They dispersed, but soon mingled back to the trough with the other hogs.

He dropped the stick, pulled two apples from his coat pockets, and proceeded to the barn. His horses nickered to him as he entered, and he realized the cows weren't inside the barn, which meant his sisters had already milked them and turned them out. He gave each of the equines an apple, led them out to the pasture, mucked their stalls, and rationed out their grain and hay. By the time he had completed his chores, it was nearly midmorning, so he went into the summer kitchen and fixed himself a bowl of grits. He carried the bowl into the house and sat at the table in silence. It was so quiet that he thought everyone else must be outside. Hastily, he cleaned up and retired to his room. A hard-covered book beckoned to him from his dresser, so he picked it up, lay back on his bed, and thumbed through the pages.

"Whatcha readin'?"

He looked up at the sound of her soft, lilting voice. Rena stood in the doorway that connected their two rooms.

"*Ivanhoe*," he said, sitting up.

"Haven't you read that thing at least twenty times by now?" she teased, and gave him a smile.

He shrugged with a grin, unable to resist her sweet smile. Even when they had tormented each other as children, they always ended up laughing.

Moving toward him gracefully, Rena sat beside him on the bed. She hadn't yet tied her hair, so it hung down past her shoulders, shimmering in amber hues and framing her ivory face. Her violet-blue eyes glistened. She looked down, her long, dark eyelashes resting delicately upon her ruby cheeks.

"You're really fixin' to go, ain'tcha," she said.

"Yeah, Rena. I am."

She folded her hands in her lap. "I'll miss you," she said quietly.

A tranquil feeling swept over him, one that happened sometimes when he heard her voice. It softened his heart and calmed him, like an angelic phenomenon. "I'll be back before you know it," he reassured her.

She hugged him. Placing a soft kiss on David's cheek, she stood and moved elegantly toward the doorway before turning back to face him. "You know, David, we've always been close. I hope that feelin' never leaves us."

He grinned. "It won't. I love you, li'l sister." They had shared their thoughts, hopes, and fears through the years, and he knew he could always rely on her sympathetic ear. The memories began flooding in, remembrances that he would cherish forever.

"I love you, too," she said in her melodic way. Turning lithely, she glided out of his room.

A strange, quiet emptiness squeezed David's heart. He shook off the awkward feeling and glanced down at his book, but decided he was too fidgety to linger. Surveying the room, his eyes rested on his guitar, which his father had so painstakingly created for him. But even playing that seemed unappealing, for the desire to sing and strum had left him since Christmas. He impatiently arose, walked out of his room, hurriedly grabbed his coat and hat from the coat rack which stood next to the door, and yelled, "Ma, I'm ridin' to Jake's." As he opened the latch, he paused, but got no response.

Closing the door behind him, he hesitated on the porch and looked out at the barren, rolling fields that were beginning to green up. Torn between his family obligation and his longing to escape it, he was still determined to uphold his decision. A mild breeze blew around him. He put his thumb and forefinger into his mouth and whistled. Within moments, Renegade appeared from around the side of the house. David retrieved a saddle, blanket, and bridle from the breezeway.

"Come on, ole pard," he said to the colt. He threw the blanket and saddle across his back. "We've got some business to 'tend to."

Renegade nodded his head as he stood patiently.

David cinched up the saddle, took hold of the bridle he had slung over his shoulder, placed the bit into Renegade's mouth, and slid the head-piece behind his ears. Stepping into the stirrup, he swung himself up onto his horse.

"Git up!" he clucked with a slight kick of his heels.

At the command, Renegade lunged into a gallop, kicking up clumps of mud behind him. David reached the end of the lane, turned onto the road, and slowed Renegade to a trot. The air was still. Renegade's hoof beats clomped so loudly that they seemed to be the only thing audible. No birds chirped in the trees, no frogs croaked from the ditches. Not even a fly buzzed. David pulled the young stallion to a walk, suddenly overcome with an eerie sensation. A terrifying thought struck him. What if the witch he'd seen as a child was lurking about?

A figure emerged from the trees. David's heart leaped into his throat. The sudden movement startled Renegade, who reared and whinnied in fright. David regained control. He forced himself to look at the interloper.

"Damn you, Caldwell!" he roared, relieved that it was someone he recognized. "You spooked my horse!"

Tom giggled. "I was hopin' he'd throw you off!" He walked toward them. Renegade, still skittish, pranced around, tugging on the reins.

"I told you before, I ain't got nothin' to do with that vow my pa made," David said, trying to contain his patience, along with his horse. "Why can't you jist let bygones be bygones? I lost my pa, too, you know."

With that, Tom's smile faded, and for a moment, he looked remorseful. But his face immediately contorted into a grimace. "Serves you right." He stood there, staring.

David stopped Renegade from prancing. He considered jumping down and slamming his fist into the intruder's face, but thought better of it. His anger ebbed, giving way to pity. Renegade impatiently pawed at the ground and blew.

"That's a right awful thing to say, Tom," he finally said. "I know you don't mean it. And I wouldn't say such a thing to you. Tell your ma I'm sorry for her loss."

Tom's complexion brightened to match his crimson hair. A tear rolled down his cheek, but he quickly brushed it away. "You're lucky I didn't bring my gun," he muttered. Turning toward the deer trail he had emerged from, he disappeared into the woods.

David frowned. He had known Tom since childhood, and understood how he had worshipped his father. Like him, Tom was the only boy in his family, so Mr. Caldwell had doted on him. Now Tom would have to find his own way in life.

"All right, Renie, let's be on our way."

He turned his colt and headed down the road. After riding at a canter for a couple miles, he pulled back. Renegade slowed to a trot. Horse and rider passed the Ryan farm, crossed over Cotaco Creek, and continued through Apple Grove. Turning onto a lane, they descended a hill. Snuggled in the valley amidst magnolias and ancient oak trees, an old white farmhouse stood, surrounded by outbuildings. The house resembled a smaller version of a plantation big house. Renegade trotted up to the veranda and stopped.

"Well, if it ain't Massa David!" a stout black man greeted him upon his arrival. He grabbed hold of the reins as David stepped down from his spotted horse.

"Hello Percy. How are you on this fine day?"

David was very fond of Percy, whom he'd known since he and Jake were children. The man was half a foot shorter than David, with a smile that could warm anyone's heart. His head was nearly bald. His large, dark eyes twinkled like bright stars in the night sky. David wondered on occasion, and had even asked Percy once, why he was always so happy even though he was a slave. Percy replied that the Kimball farm was a far better place than the plantation where he was born. He was with his family, and that was all a man really needed.

"I'z mighty fine, sir. Bless you fo' askin'." Percy tied Renegade to a post. "Massa Jake is in da house. You go on inside." He smiled, and gestured with his weathered hand, flinging it in the air toward the direction of the house.

"Thanks, Percy," David said, returning the smile. He removed his hat, walked up the steps, crossed the veranda, and went in through the front door. To his dismay, there sat his mother, sipping iced tea with Mrs. Kimball. They turned their gazes to him as he entered.

"Ma, what are you doin' here?" David asked, his eyebrows furrowing.

"We were jist havin' a little talk." Carolyn set her sweet tea down on the parlor table.

"Where's Jake?" he asked.

"Have a seat, dear," Jake's mother said. "He'll be right back." She was a handsome woman. It was apparent that Jake had inherited his good looks from her.

David did what he was told. Both women kept their eyes glued to him. Growing apprehensive, he sat in an overstuffed chair with his feet spread apart and his elbows resting on his knees. He nervously twirled his hat around in his hands, staring at it as it spun.

"Your mother has informed me of your plans to go off to war," Mrs. Kimball remarked.

David nodded, his eyes still fixed on the hat. "I'll be eighteen next week, and I ain't fixin' to wait till I git conscripted," he said confidently.

Carolyn chuckled. "They don't enforce that around here," she said. "You know that good and well."

He looked up at her. "Ma, we already discussed this." He glared at her.

A lissome black woman entered. David recognized her immediately as the woman who managed the Kimball's household. She wore a long white apron over her faded black skirt, and a white scarf tied around her head set off the ebony sheen of her hair and the amber hue of her eyes. David thought she had the most beautiful eyes he'd ever seen—that is, for a Negro woman.

"Can I gitcha somethin' a drink, Massa David?" she inquired.

"Tea would be fine, Miss Isabelle," he replied with a slight smile.

"Yessir." Percy's wife floated out of the room, as phantomlike as she had appeared.

The back door slammed, and approaching voices grew louder. Jake entered the parlor, followed by a girl his age. They both smiled upon seeing him.

"David!" the girl said. She came up to him and took hold of his hand. "We haven't seen each other for a spell." Her blue eyes sparkled. They matched the color of her dress, David noticed, and her blond hair was tied up with sky blue ribbons.

"Miss Callie," he cheerfully greeted her.

"We were jist discussin' my son's plans," Carolyn said. She pulled a corncob pipe and a plug of tobacco from her pocket, stuffed a piece of the brown herb into the bowl, and lit it.

"What plans?" asked Jake. He looked at his friend with a puzzled countenance, one that almost seemed exaggerated.

"Ma is here to tell y'all of our impendin' departure," David said.

"Your departure? Why, whatever do you mean?" asked Callie, fluttering her long eyelashes. She was a belle in every sense of the word, even though she hadn't grown up on a plantation. Her cousins lived on one, and that was good enough for her.

David glanced at everyone. They all gazed back at him, waiting for him to speak. He drew a breath. "Jake and I are..."

"What do you mean, Jake and you?" Mrs. Kimball broke in. "You don't plan on bringin' him into this, do you?"

He glanced at Jake. "Well, I...uh..."

"He's seventeen, David, and too young to be leavin'," she insisted.

"Yes'm, but..."

Callie burst out laughing hysterically. "Oh, darlin', I can see you leavin,' but Jake? Why, he has no reason to go! That would be preposterous." She reached up and patted David's cheek.

He glowered, confused by her reaction.

Jake simpered at him. "When are you leavin'?" he asked, his eyes gleaming.

David frowned. He glanced around at their faces. Everyone was smiling at him. He realized Jake hadn't informed his parents as promised.

"The day after my birthday," he said, disappointed in his friend.

"Well, my dear, we are all so proud of you for wantin' to go off and defend us," Mrs. Kimball said.

David uncomfortably replied, "Thank you, ma'am."

"And we certainly hope there aren't other motives for your actions," his mother injected.

"No, ma'am," he lied.

Isabelle entered the parlor and handed David a glass of tea. She smiled politely before giving a small curtsy. Turning toward Jake's mother, she said, "Now if it's all right with you, missus, my li'l Toby's a-waitin' on his dinner."

"Yes, Isabelle, by all means, tend to your child," Mrs. Kimball said, giving the beautiful ebony woman permission to flutter out of the room. "Why, she has become radiant, hasn't she?" Jake's mother said. "Ever since she had her young'un."

She pulled a fan from her pocket and began fanning herself, even though the room didn't seem all that warm to David.

He thought back, recalling the union. Jake's father had purchased Percy at a slave auction in Memphis when David and Jake were small children. Never having encountered anyone of darker skin before, David was intrigued by Percy, so he constantly interrogated him about his origins. The young slave finally confided in him. When David told Jake's father how Percy had been torn from his mother at a young age and forced to work in the fields, Mr. Kimball laughed.

"They're all like little children," he informed. "And they have an imagination to go with it."

Some years later, Jake told David how Percy had been meeting up with a black girl who lived on a plantation in neighboring Lynntown.

"He said he saw her one day while she was out walkin' cotton," Jake explained, "and he's been sneakin' over every night to meet up with her."

After discussing Percy's situation, David convinced Jake to tell his pa. Mr. Kimball, being a kind-hearted man, purchased the young slave girl. The two lovers were joined in matrimony and had been living in bliss as man and wife on the Kimball farm ever since.

David remembered the ceremony four years ago on the front lawn. Apple blossoms floated down around them like pink raindrops, and a number of slaves from Isabelle's old plantation were allowed to attend, making the occasion that much more festive. Once the lovers exchanged their vows, they jumped over a branch, signifying their union. Although the marriage was counterfeit, since nuptials between slaves were not recognized, the occasion was moving, nonetheless.

"I must say, they are a happy li'l family," said Caroline.

"And he's the most adorable little nigger child I ever did see, what with those big brown eyes and that sweet li'l laugh," Callie remarked.

She looked over at David, making him feel uneasy with her talk of babies.

Carolyn patted the empty chair's seat beside her. "My dear Callie, tell me all about your trip to Montgomery. Were you able to visit Jake's sister and her husband?"

Taking her cue, Callie rustled across the room, and sat next to her. "Why, yes, I did. Jenny took me shoppin', and she bought me a wonderful bolt of fabric for a new dress. How she could afford it, though, I haven't a clue. Why, a yard of fabric these days costs three dollars and fifty cents!"

The women chattered on. David impatiently looked over at Jake, and tilted his head to one side, motioning for him to follow.

"Pardon us, ladies," said Jake.

The two boys exited the parlor. As they walked through the back of the house, they heard singing coming from an adjacent room. The voice was soft, slow, melodic, and so profound that it stirred David with emotion. He paused for a moment to listen.

"Swing low, sweet chariot, comin' fo' to carry me home. Swing low, sweet chariot, comin' fo' to carry me home."

The boys went out the back screened door and onto the whitewashed veranda.

"That's Miss Isabelle singin', ain't it?" David asked.

"Yup. She sings to her baby. Some song she learned when she was a little girl on the plantation," Jake explained.

David seated himself in a cane chair. "Where's your pa?" he asked.

"Down at the smokehouse. He and Percy slaughtered a hog this mornin'." Jake sat down in a chair next to David. "I'm glad Percy's here to help, since Pa's leg is flarin' up."

David knew of the injury Jake's father had acquired in the Mexican War, and how he had even seen it once when Mr. Kimball pulled up his pant leg, revealing a mangled limb supported by two metal beams running down each side and secured around his ankle.

"The moon was in the right place last night for butcherin'," Jake said.

The sound of Jake's voice brought David back. He looked at his friend, half grinned, and slightly shook his head. To him, those beliefs were superstitious, except for what he had read in the *Farmer's Almanac*, but Jake swore by them, and by all the astrological signs and indications as well. David had to admit that, most of the time, Jake's predictions were accurate, except for the most ridiculous ones. He snickered as he recalled them.

"If you kiss your elbow," Jake had told him, "you'll turn into a girl." On another occasion, Jake informed him that "if the first corn silk is red, you'll be healthy, but if it's white, you'll be sick." David's favorite, however, was, "If you pull a horse's tail and seal the hair in a jar of urine, it will turn into a snake overnight."

He took a sip of tea sweetened with molasses. "Do you think Percy and Isabelle are liable to run off?"

Jake shook his head. "I overheard them talkin', and Percy told her they have no business up north, and this is their home, so I reckon they'll be stayin' on. It seems all Mr. Lincoln wants to do is tear our families apart." He sighed.

David told him about Tom Caldwell's ambush on the way to his house.

"Maybe we could put glue on his saddle," Jake suggested." That would teach him!"

They chortled.

David said, "That would only make matters worse, and after all, he is still a friend. I 'spect he'll come around." Pausing for a moment, he asked, "So, why haven't you told your folks yet?"

"About what?"

David groaned, and took another sip, still dry from his ride. "About your comin' with me, that's what."

"Oh, I have."

"It didn't sound that way to me."

Jake chuckled. "Reckon they didn't take me seriously. Don't fret about it." He leaned back in his chair, and said dreamily, "Jist imagine. Next week, we'll be on our way to Richmond."

David raised a skeptical eyebrow at him.

"That is, if the army will let us go up that way," he continued.

"Ma made me promise to join up with the cavalry," said David. "I don't know 'bout you, but it seems like a mighty fine notion to me."

David was hell-bent on going all the way up to Virginia to enlist in the cavalry. He wanted to join up with the infamous J. E. B. Stuart, the "Cavalier of Dixie," whose "Black Horse Cavalry" had already ridden around the Union army twice, making a mockery of their general, George McClellan. He thought that maybe, just maybe, if he was lucky enough, he could put a sword through the loathsome Yankee who had murdered his pa.

"We'll jist have to let the recruitin' fellers know we mean business," said David. "If there's a will, there's a way." He took another sip. "I reckon I know why you haven't said anything to your folks. It's because of Miss Callie, ain't it?"

"Could be."

Have you proposed to her yet?"

"I have," Jake said, expressionless. He ran his fingers through his collar-length, dark brown hair.

"And?"

"And..." A wide grin spread across his face. "She accepted!"

David snickered. "That's right dandy news. Congratulations!" He patted Jake's shoulder.

"As soon as we return from the war, we'll have a weddin'," Jake said enthusiastically.

"I knew she would accept." David smiled. "And you were troubled for nothin'."

"You've known her as long as I have, so you know how she is. She can make you believe one thing, and then tell you another."

"Well, now you know her feelin's are true," he assured.

The screen door slammed shut. They turned to see Callie standing behind them, radiant and shimmering in her hooped blue silk gown. "What would you two boys be talkin' about? It wouldn't have anything to do with li'l ole me, now, would it?"

Jake stood, put his arm around her waist, and kissed her on the cheek. "I was jist tellin' him our good news, sweetheart."

Callie laughed. "Why, yes, David. We are relyin' on you to be Jake's best man." She smiled slyly.

David arose. "I'd be honored," he responded, smiling back.

"We haven't told anyone yet," Jake said, "except you."

"I'll keep it a secret," said David.

"Oh, Jake, darlin'," Calle crooned, turning her face to his, "please go in and fetch me my shawl."

Jake mooned over her. "Of course, Callie," he said.

His countenance was that of pure adoration, dripping with too much sweetness for David's taste. He watched Jake's performance with one eyebrow cocked, and for a moment, looked away so they wouldn't see him frown. It was obvious Jake wouldn't be enlisting with him after all.

"Oh, and I believe your mother wishes to speak with you," Callie added over her shoulder as Jake opened the screen door and went inside. She turned back to face David. "I would like to have a word with you privately," she informed him.

"Yes, miss," he responded.

A strange, awkward pause ensued. She moved closer to him. He could feel his face flushing.

"Do you remember last summer, when we were at the fishin' hole with Jake and your two sisters?" She turned her head slightly to look at him out of the corner of her eye.

He nodded. This was making him uncomfortable. Callie reached out and grabbed hold of his hand. He felt like she was cornering him.

"Do you recollect what happened after they all left, and it was jist you and me remainin'?"

"Yeah."

Regardless of how badly he didn't want to remember, he couldn't help but think back to the event. Jake had volunteered to escort Rena and Josie home. David made fun of the way Callie's hair looked, she splashed him, he splashed her back, and then she swam right up to him, clasped onto his head with her hands, and planted a big wet kiss straight on his mouth. He recalled how shocked he was, completely taken aback, this coming from the girl who was supposed to be Jake's. He remembered protesting, telling her that he had to leave, that Jake loved her, and that Jake was the one she should be doing that to. But to his surprise, she laughed, amused by his bewildered embarrassment. She informed him that if anything were to ever happen to Jake, he would be her next choice. Reliving the moment in his mind made him feel even more awkward now. He looked down at his feet.

"David, I want you to know that I love the both of you," Callie said. She reached out and pulled his chin up, forcing him to look at her. "And you know I intend to marry Jake. But if he decides to go off to war, and somethin' should happen to him..."

"Callie Mae Copeland," he interrupted, "don't you be thinkin' that way."

Callie looked deeply into his eyes. David blinked. She drew closer.

"If anything should happen, promise me you will return to take his place."

"I don't reckon he's fixin' to go."

"He ain't made up his mind yet." Her penetrating stare bore into him. "Promise me you'll come back to claim me as your bride."

He felt his resolve melting. "All right, I promise," he reluctantly agreed, knowing it was the only way to escape the confrontation.

"Now then, don't go conversin' with any poor white trash while y'all are in the army, 'cause I want y'all to come back to me untainted." She grinned. "And let's not be tellin' Jake about our li'l ole rendezvous," she said playfully. Letting go of his hand with a wistful sigh, she said, "I do believe all this romantic talk has given me a fit of the vapors." She fluttered her hand in front of her face, simulating a fan. Turning to enter the house, she glanced over her shoulder and smiled sweetly, yet cunningly.

He knew she had gotten her way and felt like he had just made a deal with the devil, although Callie was no demon. She did like to manipulate, though, he pointed out to himself. If it came down to it, he would take care of her because he loved her, too. Besides his two sisters, she was the only girl he had ever kissed.

On the day of his birthday, David routinely tended to his chores, then went to his room and proceeded to pack. He unpacked and repacked, indecisive as to what he would need. The weather was warming up, so he wouldn't need a coat, but he did need extra drawers and socks, as well as another homespun shirt. He opted against the stiff-soled shoes he wore for church and special occasions, deciding to wear his riding boots instead. He collected a towel, comb, toothbrush, and long-handled shaving razor, and shoved the essentials into saddlebags. For Renegade, he packed a hoof pick and a curry comb.

Deciding to leave his guitar behind, he reasoned that he wouldn't be gone for very long, so therefore, wouldn't need any extras. He picked it up and strummed a few chords, remembering the day his father had given it to him. It was two years ago, on his birthday. The recollection hurt and angered him. With a sigh, he set the instrument aside and placed the saddlebags on the floor in preparation for his departure the next morning. He spread the clothes he planned to wear across his dresser and set his boots down on the floor in front of them, imagining how soldier-like he would appear in the garb.

Once satisfied, he laid on his bed daydreaming, but the afternoon seemed to drag, so he left his room and found Rena, who suggested he go for a final ride around his familiar homeland. Just before dusk, he returned, and saw her enter the yard to greet him. She informed him that she had done his evening chores as a birthday present. He grinned and thanked her, handed her the reins before ambling across the yard to the breezeway, and entered the front room.

"Why, there you are," his mother remarked. "Where have you been off to?"

He shrugged. "Jist out for a ride," he said, deciding he didn't want to elaborate by telling her he was saying goodbye to the landscape. Regardless of how she acted at the Kimball's, he knew she was troubled by his leaving.

She glanced at the mantle clock, which read half past six. Setting her porcelain cup of sassafras tea down on the little table beside her, she rose from her chair. "There's somethin' I want to give you, son."

David stared at his mother. She rarely called him "son," and it got his attention. "Yes'm?" he asked.

She hesitated for a moment. "I've been ponderin' this for a spell, and I want you to have it." She pulled at her wedding band until it came off her finger. "Dang rumatis," she muttered. "I'll have to git some pokeberry to calm it."

She handed the ring to him. He stood dumbfounded, so she grabbed hold of his hand, rotated it upward, and set the ring in his palm.

He stared down at the sacred band. "Ma, I can't take your weddin' ring," he half whispered in awe.

"You know this here's a family heirloom. It's only fittin' that it should be passed down to you."

"But, Ma..."

"Your pa is with our Lord and Savior now, David. I have no further use for it," she reassured him.

He looked up at her, his eyes filled with sadness and uncertainty, and gazed back down at the ring in his hand. It was a beautifully simple, thin band of yellow gold about a quarter of an inch thick. Five tiny diamonds were spaced across the top of it. The ring had once belonged to his paternal grandmother, and to her mother before that, who brought it with her when she emigrated from England.

"I don't know what to say," he finally uttered.

"I want you to have it for good luck. And when you find the right girl, you can give it to her."

At a loss for words, he hugged his mother tightly. They held each other for a moment before he gently pulled away.

"Thank you, Ma," he said graciously, and kissed her cheek.

"You're welcome, dear. Happy birthday. I love you." She smiled.

He put the ring on the little finger of his right hand. It fit snuggly, which he was thankful for. The last thing he wanted was to have it fall off without his noticing.

"I love you, too," he responded, smiling back at her.

"Now go fetch Josie, please."

"Where is she?"

"I believe she's out yonder in the kitchen."

He did what he was told. Igniting a lantern to light his way, he sauntered across the yard in the moonlight, his dogs at his heels. The kitchen was dark, but he pulled the screen door open anyway and entered.

"Josie?" he called out. "Are you in here?"

Silence responded. A cricket chirped from outside. A loud bang came from across the room, nearly causing him to drop the lantern.

"Surprise!" voices exclaimed as candles were lit. The kitchen grew bright with illumination. Numerous people stood before him, smiling and clapping in his honor. He recognized the Kimball's, Mrs. Samuels, Sadie Caldwell, several other neighbors and friends, and of course, his two sisters. His mother entered, and lovingly squeezed his arm.

"David, this here's your sendin' off party," Rena said with a smile, "and I baked you a cake for the occasion. Oh, and for your birthday." She motioned to a pound cake surrounded by gifts on the counter.

"We didn't have enough sugar to make frostin'," explained Josie, "so I hope you don't mind."

David gazed around the room in happy astonishment while everyone cheered.

"Let's dig in!" exclaimed Jake. He helped himself to the first piece.

David took the plate his mother offered. "This is a wonderful surprise," he stammered.

The smell of freshly baked cake made his mouth water, but he courteously waited for the other guests to partake. Then, not bothering with a fork, he eagerly shoved a large piece into his mouth.

"My goodness," his mother remarked, "I'll surely miss your ravenous appetite."

Mrs. Kimball chuckled.

The guests each offered a small token for David's journey, things they thought he would need, which included a few small candles, matches, liniment, some peppermints, a new journal and a carbon pencil for writing home, and a small bag of apples for Renegade.

"I have somethin' else for you." Rena reached behind her, retrieving a package wrapped in brown paper from the countertop. As she handed it to her brother, she said, "I hope you like it."

"We thought you could use it up north," said Josie.

David grinned, tore the wrapping off, and opened the box.

"A pistol!" he exclaimed, wide-eyed. He set the box on the table and pulled the handgun out. "A Colt Army."

He turned the weapon over in his hand. It was heavy, with etching on the cylinder, a long, cold barrel, and a walnut stock. The weapon was about fourteen inches long and weighed maybe three pounds, but it felt at ease in his grasp, like it was meant to be there.

"Where'd y'all git this?" he asked.

"Bud wanted to be here to give it to you himself," explained Mrs. Samuels, "but he was feelin' poorly. He wasn't certain if the cavalry had enough pistols to provide, so he wanted to give you that one there, and said he can git himself another when he reenlists."

"And that its aim is true," said Josie, to which the audience chortled.

David wondered how many Federals Bud had killed with the spectacular pistol, but his curiosity was quelled when Mrs. Samuels spoke.

"He wanted me to tell you that he got it off a dead Yankee. Just before he left Fredericksburg to come home."

David admired his gift once more, but this time, a surge of repulsion entwined with his appreciation. How many Confederate soldiers had been shot with it? A jolt of revenge flashed through his veins, and he knew he would turn the gun on the one who shot his father. Perhaps that was what Bud intended as well.

Another thought crossed his mind, and a brief feeling of relief swept over him. He had been planning to take the shotgun, but now he could leave it with his mother, just in case she needed it to fend off wild animals...or Yankees. They had come to the farm before, and this way, she would be safe.

"And here's the holster to go with it," Carolyn said as she pulled the leather strap from a cupboard where she'd hidden it.

She handed it to her son, who smiled appreciatively.

"There's more!" Josie exclaimed. She reached behind her to the countertop, recovering the gift she had constructed for him. "Open it!" she chirped, her hazel eyes gleaming.

"Careful Zeke!" Jake teasingly warned, calling David by his pet name.

Placing the gun down on the table, David took the small, unwrapped box from his sister and opened it. Puzzled by the contents, he set the box down to examine them.

"I scrounged up a few things I thought you might need for your trip," Josie explained. "There's tooth powder, soap, a housewife, a new pocket knife, a lookin' glass, so you won't cut yourself shavin', and a Testament. And look..." She took the miniature Bible out of the box, unfolded its dark leather flap, and opened it to reveal a small, cloth Confederate flag, the Southern Cross. "I even made you this here bookmark." She handed the Bible to him.

"Why, thank you, Josie," David responded, his heart filled with gratitude. "Thank y'all very much," he said to his guests. "I know I'll be puttin' these things to good use."

Rena stepped up to him and kissed him on the cheek. Josie followed behind her, then kissed his other cheek. To his embarrassment, the gathering cheered.

"We have sweet tea and lemonade for anyone who's thirsty!" Rena announced. The guests began to mingle. They took turns hugging David and wishing him well. Jake stood in line, and when he reached the honoree, he stuck out his hand.

"You ain't comin' with me, are you," David stated, expecting the answer.

"Reckon I ain't quite decided yet," he replied.

"Well, if you are, then be here at dawn, or I'm leavin' without you." Jake grinned.

"Where's Miss Callie, anyways?"

Glancing around, he said, "Oh, she ought to be here any minute."

The boys continued talking. Eventually, the party started winding down, and guests began to depart. Jake's eyes narrowed on something behind David, so he turned to see. Tom Caldwell approached. Preparing for a confrontation, David and Jake stood their ground.

"Fellers," Tom said upon reaching them. He nodded his head in greeting.

"Caldwell," they mumbled in unison.

"I'm here to apologize for the way I've been behavin' as of late," Tom said. "It's come to my attention that I've been…irrational."

David and Jake looked at each other.

Tom seemed humble enough, so David replied, "Well, thank you kindly, Tom. I knew you'd see things differently once you simmered down some."

"You were right all along," said Tom. "It ain't my place to blame your pa. After all, I wasn't there, and I didn't see what went on."

David nodded in agreement.

"So as a gesture of goodwill, I'd like you to accompany me to my place, for a…goin' away present." Tom stared at him, slightly smiling.

David frowned. "You couldn't bring it here?"

"Naw. It's too big to carry." He patted David's upper arm, albeit a bit too roughly. "Fetch your horse and come on."

"I'll wait here for Miss Callie," Jake said. "You go on ahead, and we'll be there directly."

"No need to hurry, Jake," Tom said quickly. "Let David enjoy his surprise a spell before y'all git there."

Jake glared at him.

Sadie, Tom's younger sister, took notice, and quickly made her way across the room. "Why, Mr. Kimball, I hear tell that…" She looped her arm around Jake's and led him away.

Tom motioned for David to follow, so after dismissing himself from the party, David obliged. He retrieved Renegade and rode him out to the yard where Tom was waiting. The redhead spurred his horse, so Renegade followed. Cantering down the road for a mile, they came to the Caldwell dwelling. A dog barked a warning welcome.

Tom dismounted and tied his bay gelding to a post. He said overzealously, "Your surprise is in the barn."

David stepped down from his steed. "Stay here, Renie." He glanced at the house, noticing that all the windows were dark. "Is your ma asleep?"

"She ain't here," Tom replied as he disappeared into the barn.

David stopped abruptly. Something wasn't right.

"You comin'?" Tom called out.

Looking back at his horse, who shook his head and snorted, David hesitated. He decided he was being suspicious for nothing, so he scoffed it off and walked across the yard to the decrepit barn. The outbuildings appeared neglected, even in the dark. He assumed it was because Tom's father had been gone for so long, and apparently, Tom was too lazy or incapable of keeping up the place. The war had visibly taken its toll on the Caldwell's. He entered the barn, but couldn't see in the dark.

"Tom?"

The black-lacquered carriage rumbled along the uneven dirt road, jostling its occupants.

"Father, I do believe that's David's horse up yonder."

Mr. Copeland glanced across the seat to his daughter. "Are you sure? I thought his surprise party was at the Summers' house."

"Well, that's his stallion. I'd know that horse anywhere." She gathered her skirts. "Drop me off here."

"Callie, darlin', are you sure you want to walk down there in the dark with that purty li'l dress on?"

"Oh, this ole thing? Why, of course, Daddy. I want to be in on the surprise, too." She stepped out of the stopped vehicle. "See you later!"

"Tell him we send our well-wishes darlin'." Callie's father snapped the reins, prompting the two bay horses to trot off.

Callie hoisted her skirt up to her knees and tramped toward the Caldwell's home, which sat just off the road. The rumble of the carriage faded, giving way to what she thought were loud voices. *The party must be goin' gangbusters without me*, she thought. Exasperated, she picked up her pace.

Something flew out, hitting him in the face. "Ow!" David reacted, drawing back to see Tom standing in front of him with his fist clenched. Before he could retaliate, two others attacked from out of the darkness and pinned his arms behind his back.

Tom chuckled. "Surprise!" he mocked sarcastically. He walked over to a lantern that was propped on a bale of hay, and lit it. "Now I can see you bleed," he growled, his voice so filled with angst that David hardly recognized it. Walking back over, Tom planted a fist into David's abdomen, causing him to buckle over in agony. The captors laughed, amused by their brutal punishment.

"Git off me!" David yelled through clenched teeth.

Another punch to his gut doubled him over in anguish.

"Hit him again, Tom!" one of the attackers prodded.

David glared at the boy through his suffering. In the glowing lamplight he recognized Matthew Baker from school. Groaning, he said, "It don't matter what you do to me. I can't change the past."

"Maybe we should stop now," another old schoolmate, Barney Matchless, said.

"Don't be a sissy, Summers," Tom taunted. "You can take more, can't you?"

He punched David in the stomach again, and David cried out in pain. Tom flashed a satisfied grin, but the smile quickly faded, and his face became clouded with anguish again. His gaze flickered to the side. David watched him quickly move toward a wall of farm tools. Tom returned holding a heavy chain. David's eyes grew wide with horror.

You ain't really fixin' to use that, are you?" he asked in disbelief.

"I don't reckon you should, Tom," said Matthew.

Tom's sinister snicker answered David's question. He yanked the chain in the air like a whip, trying out his aim a few times.

"Hold him steady, fellers!" he said with a sadistic smile.

"No!"

They wheeled around to see Callie standing in the doorway. David broke free. He lunged at Tom and hit him hard. Tom dropped the chain, and David grabbed it. Tom attacked him. David turned and lashed out with the chain, hitting Tom in the knees. Tom cried out and fell, writhing on the floor while he swore and held his bleeding kneecaps. His thrashing knocked the lantern over and it fell onto the packed dirt floor with a crash. Hay quickly ignited as fire spread through the barn. David stood motionless with the chain in his hand, stunned.

"David!" Callie shrieked. "Behind you!"

Barney and Matthew attacked. David lifted the chain, but Barney yanked it from his grasp and threw it across the floor. Matthew tried to hit David in the face, but David managed to duck the punch.

Tom continued to screech, curse, and roll around. "I can't stand!" he yelped. "Goddamn you, Summers! You crippled me!"

41

Callie's repeated screams for them to stop went unheeded, so she decided to intercept and attempted to come between them, but Matthew effortlessly pushed her aside. Disgruntled, she huffed, crossed her arms, and stomped her foot.

Barney threw a sucker punch, which David dodged, and it landed squarely on the bridge of Matthew's nose. Matthew hollered and backed away, holding his nose while blood spurted out between his fingers. Callie cried out in disgust. No one had noticed that the fire had climbed up the back wall and was now creeping overhead across the rafters. Suddenly, a beam broke loose and fell, crashing onto the straw-covered floor. Sparks ignited, spreading like molten lava in all directions.

Realizing the fire's intensity, the attackers sprang to their feet and scurried out the door like frightened rats while David panted to catch his breath. He looked over to see that Tom was caught between the wildfire and escape. Smoke quickly thickened the air, spiraling up toward the ceiling.

"Help!" Tom yelled. "Damn it! Somebody help me!"

"I'll git you out, Tom!" David stumbled about, trying to find a pathway through, but the smoke was so thick that his eyes burned, making it difficult to see through his tears. He coughed uncontrollably, gasping for air.

Callie grabbed his arm. "David! We have to git out while we still can!" She tugged his arm as hard as she could until he was finally persuaded. They staggered out of the burning barn to the sound of Tom's shrieks. Matthew and Barney had vanished.

"Should we go fetch help?" she asked.

"There ain't anyone here who can help us."

They stood staring at the barn, coughing and gasping for breath, sweat running down their faces while ashes drifted up into the sky. The roof suddenly collapsed, sending embers flying. They both jumped in reaction and backed away toward Tom's horse and Renegade, who was still standing where David had left him.

"Let's go," she insisted.

He couldn't take his eyes from the barn. Flames licked higher into the night, casting eerie, dancing shadows across the barnyard. The barn's timbers crackled and exploded from the heat.

"We can't go," he said. "We can't help, and we can't go." His voice cracked, like he was choking back a sob.

"We have to fetch help," she said, and climbed up onto Tom's gelding. Renegade pranced, ready for a race. "David, I mean it! We have to go *now*!"

He looked up at her, a blank expression on his face, and slowly shook his head. "This can't be happenin'," he said. "Why did he do that?"

"*Come on!*"

The panic in Callie's voice jolted David into reality. He suddenly knew they needed to leave, so he climbed into the saddle. Renegade burst into a gallop, with the gelding and Callie right behind. They rode hard for half a mile until she insisted they stop. David pulled back on his colt, and Callie drew up beside him.

"I can't ride that fast anymore!" she wailed.

"I'm right sorry, Miss Callie. I jist wanted to git away from that place."

"Should we fetch your ma?"

David sighed. The last thing he wanted was to bring his family into it. "I dunno. By the time we git back, the barn will be gone...and what's left of Tom."

Callie groaned. They stared at each other in silence for a minute.

"Well, what should we do then?" she asked.

"If we fetch Ma, she'll make sure I don't go anywhere while they investigate what happened, and who knows how long that could take."

"David! You mean to tell me you're still fixin' to leave?"

The sound of her voice riddled him with guilt. He looked down at the ground. "I have to, or I'll never git the chance to avenge Pa's death."

"You'll be in a heap of trouble if you leave."

He shook his head. "I'm in trouble either way." He looked back up at her, unable to see her face in the dark. "I'll have to leave at first daylight, 'cause I know they'll be comin' after me," he said. "Barney and Matthew will lay all the blame on me."

"I was there and I saw what happened," she consoled him.

"Miss Callie, no offense, but you're a girl. They won't believe you." He paused, waiting for her to protest, but she refrained. "They'll drag me through a trial, and it's our word against theirs, so that won't prove my innocence." His anger rose so profoundly that it nearly made him cry, but he forced down the emotion.

"You don't know if that will happen," she said.

"I can't take that chance. Miss Callie, promise me you won't say a word about what happened to Ma."

She glared at him. "I promise," she half-whispered.

He gently kicked his horse, and Callie followed. They reached the Summers' farm, dismounted, and walked over to the well, where they hurriedly washed the ashes and sweat from their faces. They went in the house to find Caroline, who informed them that all of the guests had dispersed, including Jake, who had gone to look for Callie.

"Where have y'all been?" she asked. "And how did you git your faces all wet?"

"I'll tell you later, Ma," he said, fully intending not to.

He and Callie went back outside, climbed up onto their mounts, and rode off while Caroline watched from the doorway.

Knowing that they hadn't passed Jake on their way, David took a side road to avoid the Caldwell place. They travelled toward Callie's house, and rounding a bend, they saw Jake up ahead on Stella.

He turned to see them approach. "Oh, there y'all are!" he said as Renegade and the gelding came to a halt. "Whose horse is that?"

Callie slid down. "I came across David. Somethin' happened, Jake. Tom...is dead." She started to cry.

"What?" Jake frowned. He dismounted and encompassed Callie with a comforting hug. "What do you mean?"

"I killed him." David barely recognized his own voice, husky from breathing in smoke.

"They ambushed him," Callie went on. "I saw the whole thing. The barn burned down with Tom in it!" She howled.

"Now, calm down, honey," Jake soothed.

"I have to go. Tonight." David said stoically. "They'll be comin' for me."

"What are you talkin' about?" Jake fired back.

Callie proceeded to explain, and although Jake tried to dissuade him, David was adamant. He was leaving with or without him.

"I'll wait until just before sunup," he said. "If you ain't there by then, I'll see y'all when I git back." He turned Renegade and rode off without even a goodbye.

Upon his return home, he learned from his mother that his sisters had both gone to bed. Tom Caldwell's uncle and two other men had stopped by, asking questions.

"What did you tell them?" he asked.

"That you were with Callie. I told them you were leavin' for the war tomorrow. Did you go over to Tom's?"

"Well, I..."

She yawned. "Never mind. I'm tuckered out." She kissed his cheek, smiled, and went into her room.

David went to bed, but sleep evaded him. Tossing and turning, he listened to the silence outside his bedroom window, waiting for the sound of hoof beats from his pursuers, but all he could hear was a distant great-horned owl. His mind raced. This wasn't how his grand departure was supposed to be. Without even participating in the war, he had already committed murder. But it wasn't a Yankee he had killed, it was a friend. He didn't understand how Tom could have turned on him, and how he, in turn, could have turned on Tom. He didn't trust himself because of it. His heart thumped wildly in his chest. He could still hear Tom's screams. Profound guilt crept over him, consuming him.

I shouldn't have gone in that barn, he thought. *Then Tom would still be alive.*

Heaving a heavy sigh, he arose and quietly accumulated his belongings, deciding not to tell anyone he was leaving. He wanted to spare them in case the sheriff came to arrest him. If he was captured before he reached Virginia, they would find out soon enough. Without a word, he stole out to the barn, fed Renegade some oats, and led him around to the front of the house, where he sat on the porch step with his packed gear, holding loosely onto his horse's reins. Darkness still engulfed the valley. He yawned, listening to a whippoorwill call from across the barren fields. The night was unseasonably warm. He waited as patiently as he could, but time was running out, and he grew more anxious with each passing minute. The sky gradually lightened to the east. He was about to give up, but suddenly, a rider turned onto the lane, so he untied Renegade, and mounted.

"Say your goodbyes?" Jake asked upon reaching him.

"No time for that now. Besides, I don't want to wake them," he replied.

"Well, reckon we best git a move on," said Jake. "Before they catch up to us."

The boys turned their horses and trotted down the lane. When they reached the main road, David pulled Renegade to a halt. He looked back over his shoulder. The little house stood quietly; smoke curled up into the dark grey, early morning sky from its two chimneys. It looked small, sitting there in the glen surrounded by empty fields. A strange, sad exhilaration came over him as the thought crossed his mind that he might not ever see it again. He nudged Renegade and caught up with Jake, who had slowed Stella to a walk. David's throat tightened, and he wondered if he had made the right decision after all, but he knew he couldn't stay. Not now.

"Your pa would be proud."

Bud's words echoed in his head.

Not so proud if he knew what I was runnin' from, he thought to himself.

But going off to war was what he was meant to do. He would run away for now, fight for his father's honor, and deal with this whole mess when he returned...if he returned.

This great strife has awakened in the people the highest emotions and qualities of the human soul. It is cultivating feelings of patriotism, virtue, and courage. Instances of self-sacrifice and of generous devotion to the noble cause for which we are contending are rife throughout the land. Never has a people evinced a more determined spirit than that now animating men, women, and children in every part of our country. Upon the first call, the men fly to arms; and wives and mothers send their husbands and sons to battle without a murmur of regret ...

—Jefferson Davis, Inaugural Address
February 22, 1862

Chapter Three

The sun broke free from the horizon, slowly rising up until it eventually became so bright, the boys had to tilt their hats to the right sides of their heads to shade their eyes. They followed the road as it meandered over steep hills and deep valleys through the Appalachian countryside, past homesteads, thickets, and tilled fields.

After they had ridden for a while, David asked, "So what made you decide to come along?"

Jake grinned at him from beneath his slouch hat. "Someone has to be around to keep you out of trouble," he teased.

"You mean *more* trouble," David remarked.

They passed through Oleander, Morgan City, and Lacey's Spring, quiet towns that barely stirred, and regularly checked to see if they were being followed, but they didn't see any indication. Their journey lasted all day.

When twilight at last approached, the boys found an abandoned old shed on the banks of the Tennessee River. They had discovered it the previous year when they heard that Yankee soldiers had invaded Huntsville, so they had come to the city to have a look for themselves. Unfortunately, their escapade was discovered, and David's horse, which was actually his mother's, was confiscated.

Since that time, the Federals had been driven out, but from what John Moss the blacksmith said, it didn't sound like it had stayed that way. The boys bedded down for the night, commenting on the mild weather, and without further conversation, fell asleep. At sunup they mounted and rode toward the bridge.

To their relief, Confederate sentries were posted on either side. Allowed to pass, the boys crossed over the Tennessee River, their horses' hooves beating rhythmically upon the wooden bridge. David was reminded of a legend he'd been told, how the Cherokees called it "the singing river," because their medicine men claimed voices sang from the depths. He listened carefully, straining to perceive a melody through the rushing water and hoof beats, but he heard no voices.

As David and Jake rode closer to Huntsville, more wagons appeared on the road. The drivers tipped their hats or waved while they passed, and the boys gestured a greeting as well, although they were somewhat apprehensive. They frequently looked back for followers but saw no one. After traveling eight miles, they reached Huntsville.

Unlike the last time they were there, Huntsville's residents had returned to their homes and the streets were filled with people hurrying about their daily lives. Shop-keeps stood outside their storefronts, children ran alongside the road, and old men sat on porch chairs, watching Jake and David ride by. Wagons lumbered along, horses neighed, a dog barked, and metal clanked. Two women, perched on wooden stools under a magnolia tree, dipped tobacco with sassafras brushes. Jake asked them if a friend, Emily Levinsworth, and her family had returned to Huntsville. The women merely shook their heads. David heard a fiddle playing a melancholy tune and recognized the ironic melody as "Johnny's Gone for a Soldier." The music floated through the air, intertwining with people's voices.

Jake pulled up to an elderly man and asked for directions to the recruitment office.

"It's right down that a way, sonny. Past Court House Square," the old man said, pointing a crooked finger.

The two boys turned their horses and continued down the bustling thoroughfare to the courthouse, which was regally situated at a busy cross-section and surrounded by steps leading up to it on all four sides. David glanced over to see Jake gawking at a group of girls in bonnets and colorful dresses, who were standing in front of the Spotsworth Apothecary. He grinned at Jake, who pulled the slouch hat from his head and waved it in the air. The young women giggled in response.

Arriving at their destination, David was surprised to see that the office looked like just another storefront. He'd expected it to be more prominent. Down a few buildings from the recruitment office's entrance, a three-piece band consisting of a fiddler, banjo player, and drummer performed a dragging rendition of "Dixie's Land." David summed them up to be amateurs at best.

A sign posted next to the door of the recruiting office read *Conscription to Anyone Over 18*. The national flag of the Confederacy, the Stainless Banner, hung from a pole bolted to the outside wall near the door. The flag rippled in the breeze like it was waving for them to come inside. The riders dismounted and tied their horses to a rail. Removing their hats, they stepped onto the wooden walkway, their boots clunking against the pine boards as they walked.

"What if he asks if you're eighteen?" David said.

"Well, reckon I'll have to make him believe I am." Jake jutted out his chest.

Suppressing a snicker, David followed Jake inside and glanced around the room. No one else was waiting to sign up; it was just the two of them standing in the middle of the room surrounded by cabinets and bookcases. A bridle hung from a peg next to an unlit wood-burning stove that squatted against the wall. The window was undressed, and the wooden floor was unswept. An empty coatrack stood between the door and window. A picture of the president, Jefferson Davis, hung above the filing cabinets next to the Bonnie Blue Flag. Behind a thick, umber oak desk sat a lean man in a gray officer's uniform. He was busy writing something on a piece of paper and kept his eyes downturned. Holding up an index finger, he finished writing his thought, picked up the paper, and set it on top of a pile.

Placing his pen in the inkwell, the captain looked up at them. He folded his hands on the desk in front of him. "Are y'all here to sign up?" he asked.

"Yessir," they replied.

"Are y'all of legal age?" He had a long, blond moustache that reached to his chin and wiggled when he spoke. His light brown hair was short, and he had a bald patch on the top of his head. His eyes were beady, penetrating, yet gentle and tired.

"Yessir," David said, quickly adding, "We came up here from Morgan County," so that the captain couldn't tell he was lying.

"Morgan County?" the captain asked. He stood, pushing his chair behind him with a screech. David noticed that he had a bit of a paunch. "Alabama?"

"Yessir," replied Jake.

"Why'd y'all come all the way up here?" the captain inquired sternly.

"The recruitin' office down there is only open Monday through Thursday, and we jist couldn't wait," Jake fabricated.

The captain looked skeptically at them but then relaxed his expression. "Aw, what the hell," he sighed. His brow creased. It became apparent that the man was tired of war, and of recruits coming through his command.

Jake cleared his throat. "Where are all the other fellers who are signin' up?" he asked, indicating by the quiver in his voice that he was either nervous or excited or both.

"Oh, we've been plenty busy this mornin'. Y'all jist came durin' a lull is all."

The captain turned away and flipped through a stack of papers piled on top of the cabinet behind him. He pulled one from the stack and placed it to one side of his desk, then pulled a second sheet from under a stack on the desktop and shoved it in front of Jake and David.

"Sign here," he said

Jake reached over and withdrew the pen from the inkwell. He scanned down the page until he found an empty line and scrawled his name. With a grin, he handed the pen to David, who took it in his left hand and dipped it in the well. There were a series of exes aligned down the page, one occupying nearly every line. Signatures intermingled with them, but most were not legible. David signed his name beneath Jake's and replaced the pen.

The officer pulled the sheet of paper toward him and read what they had written. "Y'all are required, as soldiers of the Confederate States of America, to give an oath of allegiance. Raise your right hands and repeat after me."

Jake and David lifted their hands into the air, palms facing the captain.

Reading from the document he had retrieved from the cabinet, the captain said, "I, state your name."

"I, Jacob Arthur Kimball." Jake looked at his friend, who hesitated.

"I, David Ezekiel Summers," he uttered.

"Do solemnly swear or affirm that I will bear true allegiance to the Confederate States of America." He paused, and the boys repeated the words. "And that I will serve them honestly and faithfully against all their enemies and opposers whatsoever." He stopped again, letting them echo his words. "And observe and obey the orders of the President of the Confederate States, and the orders of the officers appointed over me." Once again, he broke for their recital. "Accordin' to the rules and articles for the government of the armies of the Confederate states."

Both new soldiers repeated the last phrase, and put their hands down.

The captain took two sheets of paper from the top of a pile on his desk. "These are y'all's enlistment papers." He picked up the pen and started scribbling on one of the sheets. "Keep them on your person at all times."

He asked Jake his height, place and date of birth, and did the same with David, who gazed down to see his name and brief description handwritten in the provided spaces, along with the date and the captain's signature, which he was unable to decipher. The captain had them sign their documents before handing them each a copy.

"Sir, do we git uniforms?" Jake asked.

"Sorry, we're out," the captain said. "Have been for months." He looked them over and added, "Besides, y'all are mighty tall. Doubt we could find clothin' to fit."

"Sir, we have our own horses, and we want to jine the cavalry," said David.

The captain looked at him quizzically. "Do y'all have saddlebags?"

They nodded.

"How about firearms?" the captain asked, passing a fleeting glance at the pistol David wore.

"I brought my shotgun," Jake replied.

"And I have a pistol," David said, pulling the Colt .44 from the holster on his hip.

"Why, that's army," remarked the captain. "Where did you git it?" He looked at the boy, but then said, "Never mind. All right, Private Summers."

"Do we git sabers?" asked David.

"You will, when y'all ride into Tennessee and find General Wheeler."

"We're headed for Virginia," David informed him with as much confidence as he could muster.

The captain looked hard at him, making him feel self-conscious. "It's standard procedure for soldiers to receive their provisions from the quartermaster once they've arrived for duty. But since you boys have a ways to travel, I'll issue some things y'all will need along the way. Follow me."

He walked through the back door into another room. It was dark and musty, but glimmers of light shone through spaces in the wall boards, enough so they could see stacks of army gear. The captain stepped around the piles, picked up two accoutrements from each one, and carried them over to the new recruits.

"Y'all are each hereby issued a tin cup, boiler, utensils, canteen, shelter tent, and gum cloth."

He handed the articles to them as he spoke, and walked past them into the front room. The two new troopers followed.

"There's enough Yankee cowards around here to keep y'all occupied," the captain said.

"Yessir, but we have a need to be in Richmond," said David. The urgency in his voice caught the officer's attention, and his expression softened.

"Well, if that's your intention, then so be it." He scratched the bald spot on his head, pondering the situation. "I reckon you boys will run off to wherever it is y'all intend to go, regardless of orders or assignments. Catch the Chattanooga train. It leaves in..." He pulled a chained watch from his pocket and clicked it open. "...about two hours. If y'all reconsider and decide to stay closer to home, then jump on the Louisville and Nashville train, which departs in three hours, and meet up with Wheeler's men." He paused, engulfed in thought, as if making sure he had mentioned everything he was required to say. "Pay is thirteen dollars every month, issued in Confederate currency, and forty cents per day for the use of your own horses. Dismissed." He glared at them, but his countenance softened, and he sighed. "Now salute your superior officer."

David and Jake glanced at each other, and gazed back at the captain. Both put their hands to their foreheads, but each one raised the opposite arm. They bumped elbows, clumsily holding onto their gear as they did so.

The captain returned the gesture. Noticing Jake waver, he sighed again. "Keep your hands straight, elbows out, shoulders back. Hold this position until I release my salute."

He held his hand to his brow, frowned at the two troopers with some misgiving, then let his hand fall. David and Jake relaxed.

"May the good Lord go with y'all...to wherever that is," the captain muttered with a nod. Sitting back down behind his desk, he picked up the pen, dipped it in ink, and began scribbling.

The boys again exchanged glances and departed the dusty room, walking out into bright sunshine. As Jake strapped his cavalry gear onto

Stella's saddle and mounted up, David hesitated. A current of guilt rushed over him for causing his friend to lie. He looked up at Jake.

Jake grinned. "Let's git on over to the depot, Private!" he said.

Attaching his newly acquired gear to the saddle straps, David untied Renegade and stepped up into the saddle.

They trotted toward the train depot, which was fortunately only a few blocks away. When they arrived, they went inside to purchase their tickets with money David had been saving for months. With tickets in hand, they walked out of the depot and led their horses to a nearby field to graze.

Jake reached into his coat pocket. Withdrawing the contents, he opened his hand to reveal two buckeyes. "I got one for each of us," he said. "Pa says the Injuns use 'em for good luck." He plucked one of the horse chestnuts from his hand and set it in David's outstretched palm. "I reckon this will tide us over till we git back home."

He smiled, a flicker of remorse reflecting in his eyes. David knew he was thinking of Callie. Jake's sad smile suddenly gave way to a huge grin that spread across his face, and David couldn't help but smile back. They started to chuckle, then laugh, until their excitement grew into whoops and hollers.

A shrill whistle ruptured the air, cutting through it like a dagger. The horses shied and stomped, gazing at the approaching entity with their ears pricked. David and Jake looked down the track.

An enormous black locomotive thundered toward them. It slowed and whistled once more. Tugging a trailing succession of passenger and box cars, it eased up to the platform. Enormous wheels connected by a heavy side rod slowed their rotation. The locomotive ground to a halt. Spewing steam, it moaned like an overworked field horse, sighing deeply upon completion of its exhausting task.

David and Jake led their horses over to the platform. The conductor stepped off his perch from outside the engine to assist passengers as they shuffled past. Some were dressed in finery, others in everyday garb. A group of men in derby bowler and stovepipe hats ambled by, complaining about the economy.

After the last passenger had stepped off the train, the conductor noticed the two young soldiers standing there, staring at him. "You boys ridin' to Chattanooga?" he inquired.

"Yessir," Jake said. He strode up to the long-coated man, and held out his ticket.

"Y'all bringin' those horses?" the conductor asked, scratching his forehead under the bill of his black hat.

"Yessir," Jake responded again.

David approached and stood beside his friend. He offered his ticket, but the uniformed man waved it away.

"Hang onto those until y'all are seated. The train doesn't leave for a while yet. We'll have to situate your horses in a cattle car. Follow me."

He strode down the length of the train. The boys followed, leading their clomping steeds behind them. The conductor stopped at an open boxcar.

"Y'all drag that plank over here," he instructed, pointing to a heavy wooden plank lying at the end of the platform.

Jake and David handed him the reins and dragged the plank over to the car. On the count of three, they heaved it up into the opening.

"Lead 'em on up. I'll be back," the conductor said before walking away.

Jake led Stella into the empty car. David followed with Renegade. Sunshine leaked through the cracks between the car's slats. Fresh straw covered the floor.

Returning with two assistants, the conductor walked up into the car and pulled one of the outside doors shut. David reassuringly patted Renegade while giving him a handful of oats he'd pulled from a saddlebag. He followed Jake down the plank, and heard the other side door slam shut behind him. Glancing back, he saw the two Negro assistants step down the plank. They pulled the heavy board from the car before replacing it to the edge of the platform.

"Much obliged," David said.

One of them slightly nodded, but the other glared angrily, causing David to wonder what he'd done to offend the man.

"See you boys in..." The conductor checked his pocket watch. "...a little over an hour." He and the two Negroes walked away.

"Looks like we have some time to kill," said Jake. He jerked his head to the left. "Let's head this way."

They walked down the thoroughfare, observing all the happenings along the way with vast intrigue, since they hadn't frequented the big city often. So many people in one place was a novelty to them.

Jake stopped in front of a hotel window. "You hungry?" he asked, gazing in at the diners.

"Sure am."

They went inside and easily found a table since the afternoon crowd had thinned. A few patrons glanced over at them, but most didn't pay any attention. The boys seated themselves.

A burly maid approached. "What can I git you fellers?" she inquired in a gravelly voice.

"What's the specialty here?" asked Jake. He leaned over to David and said, "My pa told me to always ask that."

"Nothin' much special 'bout it," she replied. "Jist plain ole cookin'. I'd recommend the pork chops, though."

"We'll have that, if you please." Jake looked at David, who nodded his agreement.

They sat quietly while glancing around and whispering about their pursuers, their predicament, and their previous encounter with the Captain. Twenty minutes later, the food arrived, mildly warm. The gravy had congealed, but nevertheless, they devoured their meals quickly, hardly speaking while they did so. They were almost too excited to eat, let alone speak, and in solemn reserve, they wanted to escape the scene before their pursuers caught up to them. Upon finishing their meals, they paid the stocky woman and went outside.

A small crowd had gathered down the street. Curious as to what the attraction was, they decided to investigate, and upon closer review, realized it was a photographer.

"I know Ma would like to have a photograph of me," Jake said, "and we can have one made up for Miss Callie, too. Come on!"

He grabbed his friend by the arm, pulling him toward the tent. A sign hung from the side of it that read:

Photographs
3¢

They made their way through the group of onlookers until they reached the photographer.

"What can I do for you boys?" the man asked. He was a young man in his twenties, clean-shaven, and dressed in a fine suit. He pulled a plate from a boxy contraption that resembled an accordion and stood beside him on a tripod.

"We've jist jined the cavalry, so we want our beloveds to have a remembrance," Jake proudly announced. He smirked and stuck his chin out.

"Is there a way you can send these back to our kinfolk?" asked David.

The photographer smiled. "Yessir. Jist leave me their names, and I'll see to it that they git your likenesses. Now come on in!"

The boys followed him into the large canvas tent. David visualized entering a circus tent like the ones he had read about, but once inside, he observed that instead of wild animals, photographic apparatuses, including a variety of chairs, rolled tapestries, and props of every sort, cluttered the interior. The young photographer requested that Jake stand in front of an oil painting which covered the back inside wall of the tent. Noticing the artwork vaguely resembled orange hues of fall foliage, David wondered why the cameraman needed a backdrop, when there were plenty of leafy trees outside.

"Hold perfectly still," the photographer instructed.

Jake placed his hand inside his shirt front, imitating Napoleon's famous pose. David had seen so many other proud Southern soldiers posed like that in ambrotypes displayed by his friends and relatives. After a pop, a puff of smoke, and what seemed to be an eternity, the photographer announced he was finished. Jake relaxed, slumping with a sigh.

"You should've posed with your shotgun," David pointed out.

"Damn!" Jake responded. With a quick glance at the photographer, he corrected himself. "I mean, darn."

The photographer chuckled. Looking at David, he said, "You next."

Imagining his likeness next to his father's proud image on the fireplace mantel, David smiled. "Thank you, sir." He walked over to the painted canvas as the photographer motioned to the designated spot. Removing his hat, David brushed his hand through his thick, long hair, threw his shoulders back, and positioned his pistol across his chest. Tempted to grin, he resisted, knowing that it wasn't proper protocol.

"Hold still until I tell you," the photographer said. He bent down and pulled a dark cloth over his head, becoming coalesced with the camera.

A pop and a flash came, followed by a long wait. David stood frozen in time before the photographer released him.

"Now one of both of us," said Jake, "for Miss Callie."

He looked at David and winked. They stood like statues in front of the canvas, both straight and still without poses or props, their hats held in their hands, their lips straight, and their eyes wide. Once finished, they waited outside while the photographer developed the negatives. He exited the tent a short time later.

"I reckon y'all were fixin' to be immortalized as frightened rabbits," he said with a laugh when he handed them their tintypes, "but these here look mighty good."

The new troopers paid him in Alabama currency, then snickered and teased each other while they gazed down at the encased photographs clutched in their hands.

"You look like a monkey with a gun!" Jake mocked.

David snorted. "Well, you sure don't look like Bonaparte," he jabbed back. "More like a hog with heartburn!"

"Write down your information," the photographer said, "and I'll see to it that these tintypes reach their destination."

The two new soldiers reluctantly gave up their prizes and wrote down their addresses.

A gruff voice from across the street said, "Have you seen two boys fittin' this description?"

David glanced over to see Mr. Matchless, Barney's father, talking to another gentleman in a top hat. Matthew Baker's pa and Tom's uncle, Joseph Caldwell, were with him.

"Jake!" David half-whispered, elbowing his friend. He gestured with a slight nod toward the four men on the other side of the street.

"Thanks kindly, mister," Jake said to the photographer, quickly ending their conversation. He turned and weaved his way through the crowd. David followed, glancing back over his shoulder to see that their escape had gone unnoticed.

"That was close!" David said, and stopped in his tracks. "What if they've been to the depot lookin' for us?"

"We didn't give anybody our names," said Jake, "so they won't know who we are or where we're headed. They've most likely been to the recruitin' office, though."

"I reckon we should hide out till the train's fixin' to leave. Then jump on."

"Good idea."

As if by providence, the conductor yelled, "All aboard!"

David and Jake went around to the side of the depot. Peering around the corner, they saw their three pursuers run up onto the platform. They yelled at the conductor, motioned toward the passenger cars, and searched underneath. The boys looked at each other. A bell clanged for a few seconds. The steam engine shrieked loudly, its whistle ear-splitting.

"C'mon," said Jake. "Follow me."

He crouched down, and when the men turned their backs, bolted toward the train. David followed. They ran around the far end of the train to the side opposite the depot. Finding the cattle car their horses were in, they heaved the door open. The locomotive blew one long, last whistle. It lurched. The cars behind the engine clanked and groaned, knocking into each other as they were jerked into motion.

The boys ran to catch up, careful not to trip over the rails. David hurled himself up, grasped the side of the door, and climbed in. He held his hand out for Jake to grasp, but the train was chugging faster. Jake nearly stumbled. He caught himself, burst forward with all his speed, and grabbed hold of his companion's hand. David heaved, pulling him up into the boxcar. They steadied themselves and slid the door shut while the train pulled away from the station.

David thought he was going to pass out. He fell to his knees.

Jake slapped him on the back. "I'm mighty glad you didn't leave without me!"

Unable to contain his relief, David burst out laughing, and Jake did the same. After their fit of laughter subsided, David sunk down into the deep straw and gazed through the slats at the rolling countryside, letting his mind wander. He thought back to the day his father left for the war, aboard a train adorned with the Stars and Bars, surrounded by a cheering crowd. Men had generously given money to the soldiers, and ladies had bestowed flowers and kisses on them. None of that fanfare had awaited the two new recruits this time. They didn't even have their own seats.

"Here we go!" Jake exclaimed.

"I reckon so," David said with a grin.

The iron horse increased its speed, steam penetrating the air as it rhythmically chugged down the track. With it, a strong tug pulled at David's heart, and he realized something he'd been denying himself: this could be the last time he'd ever see Alabama again. He already felt homesick.

After an hour passed, the rumbling on the rails lulled them to sleep.

A shrill whistle jolted David awake. "Jake," he said, nudging his friend. "We stopped."

Jake sat up and looked around. "We must've stopped for water." He turned to Stella and patted her neck. "Wait here, ole gal," he said.

David stroked Renegade's muzzle, watching Jake make his way to the sliding door.

"Let's git on up to our seats," he said.

With much effort, they pulled the door open, and when they saw no one was watching them, they jumped out. Closing the door, they walked up toward the passenger cars. They saw several empty seats in one, so they climbed up the three iron steps to the landing and went inside. No one seemed to notice their delayed arrival. Hastily, David claimed the window seat, and Jake plopped down next to him. They started to snicker, then chuckle. It was like they were in church, expected to behave since they were in a public place, but unavoidably attracting attention. Their chuckles were contagious, not only to each other, but to the elderly couple seated across from them.

After several minutes, the train pulled away, leaving the water tower behind. David and Jake couldn't stop exchanging glances while they grinned at one another, trying in vain to retain their composure. If anyone had asked them what was so funny, they wouldn't have been able to answer. It was the exhilaration in their hearts that bubbled out into hilarity.

David looked down the length of the passenger car, watching seated patrons sway from side to side with the motion of the moving locomotive. One young woman a few rows down struggled to keep her two children in their seats. The car was filled with couples, families, and business partners, but no other soldiers, or at least, none he could distinguish. After a few minutes, the conductor entered. He slowly made his way down the aisle, punching tickets. Looking up, he noticed the two troopers.

"Now where'd you boys come from?" He sneered, amused by their expression. Obtaining Jake's ticket from him, he punched it. "Why, y'all look as excited as those two young'uns back there," he remarked. The man had a profound, distracting chin cleft, which David unwittingly stared at as the conductor spoke. "Since you boys don't know where to board the train, I'd be willin' to bet y'all ain't never ridden on one before." He reached across to take David's ticket.

"I did once when I was a young'un," said Jake, "but he never has." He tilted his head in David's direction.

The conductor handed David's ticket back to him. "Hang onto those. Y'all will need them to switch trains in Chattanooga. We'll be there in three or four hours."

"Thank you, sir," David said. He looked over at Jake, who unconsciously pinched his chin in an attempt to make it resemble the conductor's. David couldn't help but snicker. Feeling a hard gaze upon him, he glanced at the elderly woman sitting across from them and flashed a polite grin, but she didn't flinch.

"If y'all ain't fixin' to go to Chattanooga, then where are y'all headed?" she inquired. Her wrinkled face was downturned in a frown.

"Virginia, ma'am," said David cordially.

"Virginia? What the hell's in Virginia? You got relatives there or somethin'?"

"No ma'am," he replied.

"Leave the poor boy alone," said the clean-shaven elderly man sitting next to her. "These fellers don't need to be reportin' to you." The man thrust out his hand. "I'm Josiah. This is my wife, Martha." He shook each of their hands.

"How do you do," Jake said to the man, then turned his gaze to Martha. "Ma'am. I'm Jake, and this here's David."

"Pleased to meet y'all," Josiah said earnestly.

"David, you still have not answered my question," Martha said.

She and her husband were dressed in everyday drab-colored clothes, except for the brightly red-feathered hat she wore. She pulled the pins from it as she spoke and placed it in her lap. David wasn't quite sure if he should take this woman seriously or not, but since they would be riding together for quite some time, he felt obliged to converse with her. For some reason, she ignored Jake, who was fortunate enough to be avoiding her interrogation.

"We've jined up with the cavalry," he explained.

"The cavalry?"

"Yes'm."

"In Virginia?"

"Yes'm."

"You ain't stayin' in Chattanooga?"

"No, ma'am."

"Well, why the hell not?" she pried.

David swallowed. "It's a long story," he said. He looked at Jake for support, but his friend just snorted.

"Is that a fact? What'd you do, kill somebody?" She cackled. David tried not to appear guilty. "You want to kill some damn Yankee tyrants, don't you?"

"Yes, ma'am," he replied.

"Well, the more you pick off the better. We'd all be better off if those Yankee cowards would jist stay up north where they belong!"

"Calm down, Martha, dear," Josiah said, patting her hand. He shook his head, like he knew what was coming, had heard it all before, and couldn't do a thing to prevent it.

"Why, those Yankees are the most vulgar, lowdown, obscene creatures that ever walked the face of the earth," she went on.

"Reckon I agree, ma'am," David replied.

"I never did see such a lot of crude, money-hungry thieves in my entire life. They're the scum of the earth, they are."

"Yes'm," said David with a nod.

The old woman's talk started to sink in, and his hatred once again began to simmer. He had managed to keep it in check for a week or so, but every time he was reminded of what the Yankees had done and what they were capable of, he became more enraged.

"I hope you kill a hundred of them," said Martha. "At least a hundred of them. Maybe more."

"I'll do my best, ma'am."

"Why, of course you will, because you're a good boy. You're the best blood of the grand ole Southland, that's what you are."

"Thank you, ma'am." David grinned at the compliment.

"Call me by my Christian name. I'm old enough to have earned it."

"Yes'm. I mean, Miss Martha...ma'am."

Jake poked him in the ribs with his elbow, stifling a laugh.

David moaned softly, uncomfortable with his predicament. He wished he could trade seats with Jake, although that might appear too obvious, and he knew Jake would never agree to it. He looked out the window, watching the rolling hills of Appalachia drift past.

This is fixin' to be a very long ride, he thought to himself.

While the train chugged along, Martha chattered on, complaining about the weather, the Yankees, inflation, the slaves running off, the war, and why the hell it wasn't all over by now. Someone just wasn't doing his job, she was sure of it. If she was in charge, things would be very different.

David smiled and nodded politely, all the while thinking, *It's probably a good thing she isn't in charge.*

Jake had dozed off with his head on David's shoulder, and therefore, had abandoned him. Not that he'd been any help, anyway, but now David was by himself, faced with Martha's confrontation. She wasn't at all like the women back home. They were far more subdued than this.

After what seemed to be twice as long as it actually was, the train whistled and began to slow. David shoved Jake, causing his head to fly over to one side. Jake awoke with a snort. David wished he'd fallen out of his seat; that would serve him right.

"What the hell's goin' on? Are we slowin' down, David?" the old woman asked.

"Yes'm, Miss Martha, ma'am," he replied. Calling her by her first name was far too awkward.

The passengers all gazed out the window as the train clanked, groaned, slowed, and whistled before finally coming to a halt.

"Now where the hell will y'all be stayin' till the train leaves in the mornin'?" she asked, pinning her gaudy hat back on her head.

Her husband leaned over to avoid being poked in the face by the intrusive head garment.

"I don't know, m...m...Miss Martha," David stammered. "Right here at the station, I reckon."

"We have to stay with our horses," said Jake, rubbing the sleep from his eyes.

Miss Martha looked at her husband, who simply nodded. They had obviously been married so long that they could read each other's minds.

"I insist y'all come to my sister's house this evenin' at eight o'clock sharp for vittles and a warm bed. Hell, it might be the last indulgence y'all git for a long time," she said.

David hesitated, not sure if he could take any more of Miss Martha's company. "I don't know if we should impose."

"Nonsense," she growled. "It's the very least we can do for our boys goin' off to the fightin'." Reaching into her handbag, she extracted a piece of paper and a stub of a pencil, and scribbled something down. "Here's the address. There's plenty of room in the stable for your horses. Now don't disappoint me."

She winked at David, stunning him with her gesture.

"We'll be there at eight, Miss Martha," Jake promised. Grinning widely, he snatched the note from her. He looked at his friend and exaggerated a wink.

David knew his friend had seen Miss Martha's wink and, of course, couldn't resist teasing him about it. They waited for the passengers in front of them to file out. As they stepped off the train, Josiah and his wife walked off in the opposite direction, for which David was grateful. His ears were ringing and his head throbbed. He and Jake headed toward the back of the train to collect their horses.

"She really took a likin' to you," Jake observed. He broke out hysterically.

"It ain't funny, Jake," David grumbled, disgusted with the way his friend could flirt with any girl their age and attract attention, but all he seemed to be able to do was attract old women.

Jake apparently thought the same thing, for he said, "She jist wants to have a young soldier around to keep herself occupied."

"Well, why the hell didn't she keep herself occupied with you?" All of Martha's references to hell had rubbed off.

"Because you're more adorable than me." Jake puckered his lips and made kissing noises.

David retaliated by punching his friend, who naturally hit back. Knocking each other off their feet, they were soon wrestling around in the dust. They both started laughing and stood up to see a crowd gawking at them.

"Come on," said Jake. Let's fetch the horses."

The two boys proceeded to the end of the platform, dust from their clothes trailing behind them. They found a long, narrow piece of thick wood. Summing it up to be wide enough, they set it against the doorway and pulled the sliding side door open. Stella nickered a greeting. David spoke softly to Renegade and coaxed him down the ramp. Jake followed with Stella. They led their mounts to a trough near the depot, continuously taunting each other while their horses sucked in water.

"Nice of you to fall asleep on me," David muttered.

"Seemed like as good a time as any," Jake replied.

The boys led their horses over to an empty field. Retrieving picket pins from their saddles, they uncoiled the long ropes, stuck the spikes into the ground, and tied the ends of the ropes to their horses' halters before letting them lose to graze.

Jake threw himself down on the new spring grass. David sat beside him, but soon his head grew heavy, so he fell back on the sweet-smelling softness, watching daylight fade from the sky. Exhausted from the long day, he wouldn't have minded taking a nap, but Jake made that impossible. His excitement spewed out about how he couldn't wait to see Richmond and see what it was like to be in the army, fighting Northerners. David just responded with grunts, trying to keep his eyes from drifting shut.

"I wonder what Miss Callie's doin' right this minute," Jake sighed.

David looked over at him. Jake's face was shadowed by the growing darkness. A profound sorrow suddenly filled David's heart, and he wished he had left his best friend at home after all. Now, because of him, Jake was an accomplice to murder. No righteous acts of heroism or patriotic duty on David's part would ever change that. His selfishness had caught up to him. His guilt was immeasurable.

Listen, young heroes! Your country is calling!
Time strikes the hour for the brave and the true!
Now, while the foremost are fighting and falling,
Fill up the ranks that opened for you!

"An Appeal," Oliver Wendell Holmes, 1862

Chapter Four

Jake extracted a watch from his trouser pocket. He clicked it open and looked at the clock face. "I reckon we should be headin' over there." Rising to his feet, he pulled up a long stalk of grass and stuck the root end into his mouth.

"Over where?" David asked sleepily.

"Miss Martha's, of course."

"You can't be serious. You want to take her up on her offer?" David slowly sat up, relieved that his headache had subsided.

Jake smiled. "Sure do. It beats sleepin' on the hard ground."

Glancing at the pocket watch Jake held in his hand, David asked, "Where'd you git that?"

"Oh, this? Pa gave it to me."

David took the silver ornament Jake handed to him and gazed down at the beautifully ornate eagle engraved on the top, its wings outstretched, and its beak parted. Clicking the watch open, he discovered a little gem tintype of Callie on the inside of the lid. She looked stunning, her hair pulled back from her pallid face and her eyes wide and reassuring. The flash must have reflected in her blue eyes, because they were a very pale grey, almost white. He handed back the watch.

"I brought this, too." Jake withdrew a cloth bag from his trouser pocket and handed it to his friend.

Pulling the drawstring open, David peered inside. "Tobacco? Whatcha need this for?"

"Jist in case."

"In case of what?" David asked as he gave the pouch back.

"Well, we can use it for barter," Jake explained, shoving it back into his pocket. He pulled the blade of grass from his mouth and tossed it.

"Come on, Zeke," he said, using the nickname he'd chosen for David long ago, a shortened version of his middle name.

David hated it but any protest on his part only made Jake use the nickname more often. David often thought of addressing his friend by *his* middle name in an effort to return the harassment, but it wasn't nearly as effective. Every time David called him Arthur, Jake stuck his chest out and strutted around, pretending to be King Arthur. Then he referred to David as "Sir Zeke." There was no way he could outdo his friend, so he finally gave up trying and just suffered through it.

"Let's git on over there," Jake said. "It'll be a hoot."

He walked across the field to retrieve the horses. David stood, knowing he had to give in. Jake gathered the picket ties and brought the horses back, handing David the reins to his horse. A wide grin spread across Jake's face.

"Maybe if you're lucky, Miss Martha will give you a little kiss for dessert."

David snarled and kicked at him, startling the horses, but Jake dodged his kick.

"You're dancin' around like a fool court jester!" David observed, but Jake ignored him.

After tying the picket pins to their saddles and mounting up, the two boys trotted into the quieting city, stopping a few times to ask for directions. They finally reached their destination.

Jake pulled the watch from his pocket again and popped it open. "Only twenty minutes late," he remarked with a shrug. "Purty good for not knowin' our way around."

They dismounted and tied their horses to a hitching rail draped with deep purple morning glories. Jake climbed the steps and tapped the doorknocker twice, then skipped back down to stand next to David.

After a few moments, the tall, whitewashed door opened. A lean black man in a white apron looked down at them standing conspicuously at the foot of the steps. He snorted at the two wide-eyed soldiers.

"Miss Martha, your boys are here." The man held the door open but didn't move.

"Your boys?" David asked under his breath. "Jake, what've you gotten us into?"

They listened as footsteps approached. Miss Martha appeared in the doorway. "What the hell? Oh, it's you two. Come in, come in," she commanded, motioning with her frail arm.

"Ma'am, our horses..." Jake pointed out.

"Henry will take them," she said.

Henry didn't look too happy about his assignment, but he gathered the reins and led the horses around the side of the house while Jake and

David ascended the stairs. They stepped past the old woman and came inside. She closed the door behind them.

"Follow me."

She shuffled by, leading the way down a long dark hallway decorated with unlit sconces and oil landscape paintings. The house smelled strange, like burnt embers and old people.

"So are y'all from Huntsville?" Jake asked.

She stopped and partially turned toward the wall. It seemed like too much effort for her to rotate her small body completely around to face them.

"Hell, no," she said. "I was only there for a visit. I wouldn't be caught dead livin' there." She continued down the hall. The boys exchanged skeptical glances.

This is fixin' to be a very long evenin', David thought.

"Our guests have *finally* arrived," Miss Martha snidely announced as they entered the dining room.

A long table stretched across the length of the rectangular room with empty wooden chairs pushed up against it. Tapered candles in silver candlestick holders adorned the white tablecloth, along with two settings of white bone china plates, silverware, and water-filled crystal goblets. The fireplace emitted a warm glow, and flickering candlelight from the table invited them closer. As they drew near, an elderly woman appeared like a ghost, startling the boys.

"We've been expectin' y'all!" she exclaimed, smiling. She was obviously younger than Martha, but the resemblance was striking.

"My sister, Mattie. This here's David and...and..." Martha scowled.

"Jake," he said.

"Yeah," she growled in an irritated tone. She flailed her hand in the direction of the table. "Have a seat."

Mattie smiled and followed her sister out of the room. David noticed that she seemed to have all of her teeth, which he found unusual for a woman her age. He and Jake took seats across from each other at the oblong table.

"I don't know about this, Jake," David half-whispered.

Swagged burgundy velvet draperies completely covered the long windows. Intricate porcelain figurines adorned the white marble mantle. A dark cherry table beneath one of the windows displayed rows of daguerreotypes, people David assumed were relatives. Two small crystal ashtrays were positioned in front of the photographs, and several lavish landscape oil paintings covered the walls.

"It's a free meal. Quit complainin'," Jake said.

The two women entered, carrying plates of food.

"We already ate, but we'll keep y'all company," Mattie said as she set a plate of sliced roast beef in front of them. She seated herself at the head of the table.

Martha set down a plate of peeled white Irish potatoes. "This'll have to do," she said, placing herself on the chair next to David.

"Thank you," said Jake, remembering his manners. Looking at Mattie, who nodded at him, he bowed his head and hurriedly said, "Lord, bless this food which we are about to receive. Amen."

"Amen," David echoed.

The boys grabbed their forks and shoveled cooled food into their mouths as quickly as they could chew and swallow.

"Where's Mr. Josiah?" David asked between mouthfuls.

"He's retired to quiet repose," Martha replied with a sigh. "Said to tell y'all hello."

The boys continued eating while Martha ranted about the war.

"I tell y'all this," she said. "If those damn Yankees come here, they'll be in for a heap of trouble."

"Did you hear about the Jenkins' boy?" asked Mattie matter-of-factly. "Came back with only an arm and a leg."

David and Jake exchanged glances across the table.

"Oh, and Mr. Haviland's boy," Martha remarked, "came back with half his face blown off."

Jake coughed. David winced. He ate as fast as he could, hurrying to finish before the conversation became more perverse. He noticed Jake doing the same.

"You boys done already?" Mattie asked. "Let me fetch y'all some more."

"No! No, ma'am," Jake said, holding up his hand. "We're plum full."

"Thank y'all very much," said David, grateful for the meal, regardless of the conversation.

Martha slowly pried herself from her seat. "Come into the parlor then. We'll have a nice glass of brandy."

Mattie stood and smiled down at them. The two soldiers looked over at each other, hesitating.

"This way," she reassured.

Jake trailed behind Mattie, and David felt compelled to leave the table and follow. They entered an adjoining room, decorated similarly to the rest of the house, except for a colorful tapestry rug depicting the Taj Mahal, which covered the wooden floor. The fireplace had already been stoked.

Henry's one step ahead of us, David thought.

"Take a seat," said Mattie.

He started for a velvet chair, but Jake dodged ahead of him and sat down in it. He snickered as David looked around. Mattie was already in the other velvet chair, and Miss Martha was on the loveseat. The only available place left was beside her. David glowered at Jake and seated himself next to Martha.

"So, do y'all have any children?" Jake inquired.

David grimaced. He was so exhausted that his head hurt, and he knew Jake had just invited another topic of conversation. Martha pointed to a small table in the center of the seating arrangement, one dressed with a lace doily and supporting four cut crystal snifters of reddish-purple brandy. The boys each took a glass upon her invitation.

"All mine are dead and gone," Mattie answered. "But I do have a grandson in the army. He's out West fightin' heathens."

"What about you, Miss Martha?" Jake asked.

"Not any more. What the hell are you askin' me that for?"

"Well, I..."

"She's old and crotchety. Don't pay her any mind," Mattie said.

"I ain't old. Hell, I'm seventy-nine years young."

The two elderly women continued to chatter, bantering back and forth, exchanging their opinions about the war, the Confederacy's leaders, local heroes, and the weather. Jake chimed in every chance he got. Henry appeared with a snifter and refilled their glasses, which prompted the sisters to chatter even more. They continued to question the boys about their affiliation to the Southern cause, as well as their religion, education, and upbringing.

After a few hours, David found himself nodding off. The brandy was definitely taking effect, but now it was only making him drowsy. He raised his glass to his lips and swigged down the remainder.

"Ladies," he said, "if it's all right, I'd like to be retirin' now."

"Oh, of course." Mattie glanced up at the mantle clock. "It is nearly midnight, after all. What time do y'all have to be to the station tomorrow?"

"Six o'clock," answered Jake.

"Oh, hell, we'll be up at four, so y'all will have plenty of time," Martha said. She tried to stand, but seemed to have a difficult time pulling herself from the loveseat.

Feeling the urge to be a gentleman, David rose to his feet and held her by the arm so she could balance herself. She smiled up at him, patted his shoulder, and followed Mattie down another hallway. The boys trailed behind. The two elderly sisters went into a dark room while Jake and David stood in the doorway. They watched the old women light a kerosene lamp and pull down the quilt on the bed.

"Y'all will have to share this bed," said Martha, walking past them.

"It'll be fine, Miss Martha," David responded, rubbing his eyes. "We're jist grateful for the hospitality."

"Sleep well," Mattie said. She left the room, pulling the door closed behind her.

Jake turned the lock as quietly as he could. Falling onto the bed, David barely noticed his friend lie down beside him. Jake was saying something about how funny David's face looked when he had to sit next to Miss Martha, but his voice faded away.

What if we don't wake up in time and miss our train? We'll have to stay here. The terrible thought made David frown. He rolled onto his side, and within seconds, fell into a deep sleep.

"Wake up!" Jake jostled him like a bale of hay.

"What?" he asked, too groggy to comprehend.

"We overslept. Come on!"

Someone pounded on the door.

"We'll be right there!" Jake hollered.

David sat up and slowly pulled himself from the warm bed. He didn't remember sleeping at all. Following Jake down the hall, he rubbed the sleep from his eyes and ran his fingers through his hair.

As they entered the dining room, Mattie said," Henry made y'all a big breakfast. Sit down and eat!"

They did what they were told, which wasn't difficult since the smell of fried ham and eggs whetted their appetite.

Josiah entered the room. "Don't stand," he said, as the boys started to rise when they saw him. "Y'all have a train to catch. Keep eatin'."

The troopers shoveled mouthfuls in as quickly as they had the previous evening.

"I'll assist Henry in roundin' up your horses. They'll be waitin' out front."

"Thank you, Mr. Josiah," Jake said.

Martha came in. "Why the hell didn't y'all wake up?" she exclaimed. "I was a-knockin' on the door for half an hour!"

"Sorry, Miss Martha," said David.

She shook her little gray head. "I'll be in the kitchen," she grumbled, and hobbled out.

Jake handed David the silver butter dish, then poured himself a glass of goat's milk from the crystal pitcher. They tried to consume as much as they could, knowing that it might be a while before they would eat again. When they had finished, they followed the voices that led them to the old women.

"Ladies, thank y'all for everything," David said.

They both smiled at him. He noticed how Martha amazingly seemed to have all of her teeth, too.

"We have to go now," said Jake.

He took Mattie's hand, kissed the back of it, and did the same to Martha's. The elderly women giggled. They looked at David. Compelled to imitate the gesture, he kissed each leathery hand.

"I made y'all a lunch with some leftovers." Mattie handed Jake a bundle wrapped in newspaper. "Now be careful, and if y'all are ever in these parts again, make sure to stop by for a visit," she said.

"We will," replied Jake.

The boys walked to the front door and stepped outside into the cool morning air. The sky was just starting to lighten on the horizon. Stella and Renegade still looked asleep as they stood with Josiah and Henry waiting beside them.

"Sorry we didn't have a chance to talk with you last night," Jake said. He took the reins from Henry and mounted.

Josiah handed Renegade's reins to David. "Oh, I'm an old man. Can't stay up that late anymore." He stood back while David climbed up into the saddle. "I reckon those two sisters kept y'all plenty entertained."

"That they did," Jake agreed with a smile. "Thanks again."

"Good luck, young'uns," Josiah said, a slight quiver in his voice. He waved to the two new troopers, who turned their horses and trotted down the street.

Jake and David followed the path they had taken the evening before. Within several minutes, they ended up back at the railway station. They dismounted and tracked down a conductor, who assisted with boarding their horses. Upon completion of the task, Jake pulled out his pocket watch, discovering that they still had half an hour to kill. He suggested they wait inside the depot, but David was reluctant.

"What if they're waitin' for us?" he asked, worried their stalkers were still hunting them.

Jake laughed. "They gave up on us by now, Zeke. Come on."

He went inside, compelling David to follow. Passengers mingled about. Across the room stood four men who looked like soldiers, although they were dressed in civilian clothing. They had haversacks and canteens strapped around them, and appeared to be older than the two troopers.

Relieved Tom's uncle and his two cohorts weren't there, David found his confidence, and walked over to them. "Y'all headed for Knoxville?" he asked.

"Yessiree," one of the soldiers said. He grinned at David through his thick brown beard. "Y'all with the army?"

"Cavalry," replied Jake as he walked up.

The four soldiers looked at each other and chuckled.

"Dandymen, ay?" another one remarked.

David started to think it might have been a bad idea to approach them.

Raising an eyebrow to the point of exaggeration, Jake glared back at the four infantrymen. "Now lookee here..." he started to say, but David intervened.

"Don't want no trouble," he said, tipping his hat. "Nice meetin' y'all." He grabbed hold of Jake's arm, pulling him away. They went back outside while the four soldiers laughed at them.

"What'd you do that for?" Jake asked, yanking his arm away from David's grasp.

"Four against two ain't very good odds. Let's go find our seats."

Jake shrugged. He followed his friend over to the conductor, who directed them to a passenger car toward the front of the train. The boys decided to check on their horses once more before returning to their designated car. They climbed aboard.

"Hey, it's the dandymen!"

At the other end of the car, the four infantrymen jeered at them from their seats. Keeping their distance, the boys took their seats near the back.

"What're y'all sittin' way down there for?" one of the infantrymen asked.

Other passengers gawked. David slumped in his seat.

"Come sit with us! We won't bite!"

"Not much, anyway!" another one hollered.

The four soldiers roared.

Jake and David looked at each other. With a nod, they made their way toward the group and sat across the aisle from them.

The soldier with the brown bushy beard asked, "Y'all from around here?"

"Alabama," Jake said.

David looked at him, worried that too much information would only give them more reason to tease.

"Yellow hammers, eh? Headed for Knoxville?" another soldier inquired. This one had dark brown eyes and a black moustache.

"Richmond." Again Jake was being far too generous with his answers.

"Virginia?" another one of them asked. He had reddish-brown hair, light brown eyes, and wore a goatee. "Let me git this straight. Y'all are from Alabama, fixin' to go to Richmond and fight in the cavalry."

"That's right," Jake said with a grin.

The four soldiers burst out laughing. Jake's grin vanished. He looked at David, who clenched his teeth.

"Y'all some kind of cavaliers or somethin'? Fixin' to go wherever it suits y'all?" the fourth soldier asked. He had dark blond hair down to his chin, which blended in with the beard he wore, all of the same length.

"Well, ain't you?" David retorted.

The four men stopped laughing immediately.

"Reckon so, huh, John," the dark blond said. He grinned, showing brownish-yellow teeth. "Why, we ain't been properly introduced yet. I'm Matthew, this here's John"—he gestured toward the man with the bushy brown beard—"that's Luke"—the man with the goatee nodded—"and this is Mark," he said, pointing at the soldier with the black moustache.

David looked at Jake and snickered

"What's so darn funny?" Luke asked.

"Why, it sounds like y'all came straight out of the Bible," Jake said.

The four soldiers looked around at each other for a moment, contemplated the revelation, and chuckled.

"Reckon we never thought of that before!" Matthew exclaimed, raising his eyebrows.

"I'm Jake, and this is David."

"Why, that sounds right Biblical, too," Matthew remarked with a smile. "Howdy."

The other soldiers exchanged salutations in return and shook the troopers' hands. While they talked, more passengers filed into the car and seated themselves. The train suddenly lurched from the station.

"We're leavin'," Mark noticed out loud.

They'd been so busy talking that no one had realized the train was about to depart. The smell of steam permeated into the passenger car.

"Well, goodbye, dear ole Chattanooga," Luke said. "May we see you again some day."

The four soldiers were solemn for a moment, but soon started talking and joking again.

"You boys new enlistees?" Matthew asked.

Jake nodded in response.

"Did y'all bring horses?" asked John.

"They're in a boxcar toward the back," David replied. "Y'all out on furlough?"

"Yup," Matthew said. "We're returnin' to our regiment in Oak Ridge."

"How long y'all been in?" Jake asked.

"Since the start of the war," said Luke. "If a feller lives close enough to where the army's got winter quarters set up, they'll let him go home for a spell. But I don't reckon that'll happen in y'all's case, because Virginia's too far from Alabama."

Jake looked at David, shrugged, and said, "We realize that, but the war's purt near over."

The four older soldiers nodded in agreement.

"I'm damn tired of fightin' the slave owner's fight, anyhow," Mark said.

A woman sitting behind him glared over her shoulder.

"Oh, beggin' your pardon, ma'am," he apologized. "I mean, I'm tired of fightin' the damn slave owner's fight."

The soldiers snickered.

The woman nervously glanced back at them. She moved farther away to another seat.

"Hell, yeah," Matthew said. "They want us to fight so they can keep their niggers, but they won't fight themselves. It's a rich man's war and a poor man's fight, all right."

The older soldiers concurred.

Jake and David glanced at each other, unsure of what the statement meant.

"Have y'all been in any battles?" asked Jake.

"A few skirmishes here and there. We're assigned to picket duty most of the time," said Luke.

"Why?" David asked with a grin. "Y'all cowards?"

A hush fell upon the men. They glared at him.

"I was only jokin'," he said, his smile fading as they leaned in toward him.

"When you git to the fightin', you'll know what we're talkin' about," said John in a low, threatening voice. "That is, if you see any fightin' at all, dandyman. Until then, you'd best keep your mouth shut."

"Yessir," David meekly replied.

Matthew grinned at him. "We'd gladly kill any Yankee that tries to invade. We'll defend our homeland till the end. Right boys?"

"Right!" they yelled in unison.

David gazed out the window, too embarrassed by the remark he'd made to contribute further, and wished he could take it back. The other five talked on, but his head grew heavy, and soon, he fell asleep. He awoke with a start. Jake was nudging him.

"Want some dinner?" Jake asked. He pulled out the bundle of newspapers from his coat pocket. Inside the wrapping were two sandwiches and two apples. He handed a flattened sandwich to David.

"Mighty nice of Miss Mattie to make these for us," he remarked, and took a bite of his sandwich.

David glanced around at the other soldiers, who were all dozing. He looked back down at his sandwich, then slowly bit into it.

Jake watched him. "Don't fret about what you said earlier," he assured him. "They've forgotten all about it."

"It was stupid," David said, expecting Jake to say that he was being too hard on himself. But instead, Jake snickered.

"Yeah," he said. "I thought they were fixin' to whip you!"

"I thought they were fixin' to kill me," David added with a smirk.

Jake took another bite, shaking his head. "They're too busy killin' Yankees to waste their time on you, dandyman."

David grinned at him, knowing that Jake used the term because it was new to him and he liked the way it sounded.

One of the soldiers stirred, but he immediately fell back to sleep. His comrades snored undisturbed. David and Jake ate the rest of their meager meal in silence, listening to the hum of passengers' voices and the chug of the locomotive.

As the hours dragged on, so did the train, at times chugging uphill so slowly that David thought he could run faster. He stared blankly out the window while Jake dozed, watching the Appalachian Mountains yield to the Great Smoky Mountains, which lived up to their name. A grayish-brown haze enveloped and swirled around them like a ghostly fog.

The conductor entered the car and walked down the aisle, speaking softly to the other passengers. When he reached David, he said, "Ten minutes to Knoxville."

"Thank you, sir."

David nudged his friend, informing him that their destination was near. They awoke the other soldiers, who swung their heads and asked how long they'd been sleeping.

"A few hours, I reckon," he replied.

"Well, thanks for holdin' down the fort whilst we made a visit to slumberland," John said, scratching his bushy beard.

David realized that what Jake said was true; they had forgotten about his stupid remark. "My pleasure," he said.

The soldiers rode quietly, trying to wake up. Within a few minutes, the train pulled into the Knoxville depot.

"Here we are," said John, rising to his feet. "You boys tell ole Bobby Lee I said hello."

He started down the aisle toward the door. The other three followed.

"Sure will," said Jake.

They waited until everyone else was gone, then stepped off and walked back to get their horses. The conductor had told them where to find some oats and hay, so they rode a short distance to a livery.

"We'll be back in the mornin'," Jake said, and handed the stable owner a one-dollar scrip of Confederate currency.

The man nodded. He turned to remove the saddle from Renegade, who was happily chomping on a mouthful of hay.

"Let's go fetch somethin' to eat," Jake said. "I'm starvin'."

"Me too," said David.

They walked down the street, peering in windows until they found a small eatery, and went inside. After glancing down the list of menu items written on a chalkboard near the front counter, they reasoned that they could only afford soup, so they ordered, paid, and sat down at a table with their warm bowls.

"Sure could go for a cup of coffee with this," David remarked.

Jake nodded in agreement. "This soup's a little thin," he observed quietly. "I only count three oysters."

"You boys can have a refill if y'all want," the man behind the counter said. "It's nearly closin' time, and the rest'll jist git thrown out."

Jake quickly put his bowl to his mouth and slurped down the rest. He went back for a refill, then another and another. David was satisfied with just two more bowls full. Once they had finished, they thanked the man, and walked back to the depot, lost in a strange city with no idea of what to do or where to go. They reclined in the grass near the dark depot that would remain lifeless until morning, watching the full moon rise up over the horizon.

"Tennessee's mighty purty," Jake remarked.

"Reckon it is," David said.

They listened to an owl hoot somewhere off in the distance. As moonbeams shone down on the two young soldiers, they fell asleep. Early the next morning, they woke up and sauntered over to the depot, which remained dark.

"Where is everybody?" Jake asked. Looking around, he scratched his head. No one was in sight.

"Let's go over to the livery and find out," David suggested. They walked a few blocks and entered the building.

Upon being asked, the stable owner laughed. "You boys don't know what day this is?"

They responded by shaking their heads.

"It's Easter! No trains are runnin' today." He looked at one, then the other.

They looked at each other, and then back at him.

"Do y'all have anywhere else to go?"

The troopers shook their heads again.

"Well, feel free to bed down in here if y'all want, but I reckon it'll be a long day, since nothin's open." He quickly walked out of the barn toward a little house across the yard.

"I knew today was Easter. I jist forgot is all," Jake said.

"Me too," David said. "I'm hungry." He surprised himself with the comment, for he usually didn't feel empty until midmorning.

Jake looked at him. "Well, there are some oats. That's all we're likely to find, since everything's closed up."

They sat on a bale of hay, but came to no resolution, so they decided to take a walk around. It was a futile effort, however, because they only saw a few people on the street, who disappeared into doorways once they approached. With no other recourse, they decided to return to the livery.

Suddenly, David stopped. "I know!" he exclaimed.

A small white chapel across the street stood like a beacon, its tall ivory steeple pointing up to the heavens.

"Let's go inside," David said, walking quickly and leaving Jake to catch up.

They entered the little church. Some members of the congregation turned to see who the late arrivals were. Removing their hats, the boys slid into a back pew.

The pastor was telling the story of Jesus' resurrection, the same story they all told on Easter, but this time it seemed more poignant. David equated it to the plight of the grand old Southland for which they were fighting, and for which his father gave his life. The Southerners had been persecuted and exiled, but now they would gain the freedom to rejoice in the reincarnation of their own country, even though some would die for the sins of others.

A pianist cued the congregation, so they stood to sing "Rock of Ages." After the hymn ended, the pastor dismissed everyone with a "Happy Easter." He walked from the pulpit to the front doors and greeted each person as they exited. David and Jake waited, smiling politely while the older people, women, and children filed out, and then they took their turn greeting the pastor.

"What do we have here?" the godly man asked. He wore a fine, graying beard and a long black robe. "I'm so glad y'all could come to our service. Happy Easter!"

"Happy Easter," the boys responded.

"Sir, we're only here for today," said Jake. "Our train's been delayed due to the holiday, and we were wonderin'..."

The pastor interrupted. "Are y'all in need of lodgin'?" he asked, his dark blue eyes filling with concern.

"No," Jake said. "We were wonderin' if you might know where we could git somethin' to eat. We didn't bring enough money, and we forgot about allowin' ourselves an extra day's worth of vittles."

"Of course." The pastor smiled. "Jist give me a minute." He went to the back of the church but soon reappeared, dressed in a dark suit. "Come with me," he said.

They followed him down the street to a little white house surrounded by a whitewashed picket fence and went inside. The smell of baked ham encouraged them. They looked at each other and grinned.

"Wait here, boys," the pastor said kindly.

He walked into another room. David and Jake could hear him talking to someone. Pots clanked and plates chinked. Moments later, the pastor emerged with two heaping plates of food.

"Come on in here," he said.

The soldiers followed him to a small wooden table and stood behind their chairs.

"We shall praise the Lord for this blessed day," the holy man said happily. He set their plates on the table and delved into prayer.

David's stomach growled, but he did his best to contain his hunger. Finally, the pastor finished and told them to eat.

"I don't mean to be rude, but my wife and I won't be jinin' y'all. We've been invited to her cousin's house, and we're fixin' to bring the food along with us," he explained.

Gesturing for the boys to take a seat, he walked out of the room, leaving David and Jake alone to consume their dinner of ham, sweet potatoes, creamed corn, and okra. Once they finished, the kind pastor returned, giving them each some morsels to save for supper. They thanked him, bid him a happy Easter, and returned to the livery, where they promptly fell asleep. When they awoke, the barn was dark. Rain clattered down on the tin roof. Jake arose, went outside, and returned a few minutes later.

"I instructed the livery man to wake us at five-thirty," he said, shaking moisture from his hat. He looked down at the grease-stained, brown paper-wrapped package the pastor had given him. "I'm savin' mine for tomorrow."

"Me too," said David. He rolled over and soon fell back to sleep.

When morning came, the livery man fulfilled his promise. The boys acquired their horses, purchased extra grain to take along, and got back to the depot just as the sun rose. This time, passengers were waiting to board. When the train pulled in, David and Jake loaded their animals into a cattle car and found their seats in a passenger car, where they waited quietly.

Finally, the conductor yelled, "All aboard!"

The locomotive jolted and spewed steam in its effort to pull away from the station. Their long train ride was growing even longer.

Intermittently they dozed, and as the day progressed, the train chugged on into Virginia. Their destination, Richmond, seemed like a very far-off place. All along the way, at every stop, they asked for food, not only for themselves, but also for their horses. Everyone obliged with what they could afford in support of their beloved soldiers so far from home. At every station, people came and went, their dialects changing with each location.

After three more long days of riding, the train stopped in Petersburg. An hour later, it arrived in Richmond. Jake and David retrieved their horses. They stood looking up at the enormous station with its arched doorways, and awnings that hung over the upper windows like drooping eyelids. Its domed clock tower read 10:20.

Confused as to which direction they should take next, they decided to start by finding someone who knew where they could locate the Army of Northern Virginia's cavalry division.

They made their way through Richmond's streets, astonished by all the commotion going on around them. Horses neighed, people shouted, and wagons clanked and groaned. The city resembled Huntsville, but to a much larger degree. Citizens of what seemed to be every color and nationality were represented.

The streets were so muddy that horses slid with every step, leaving indentations behind them. The main street, covered with water-filled trenches the width of wagon wheels, allowed vehicles of every sort to pass within inches of each other. Covered wagons, open buckboards, surreys, buggies, cabriolets, and fine black carriages with lanterns attached to the sides and accessorized with footmen made their way through the muck. The smell of people, manure, mud, and cooking food all blended together into a sickening melee.

Richmond's buildings were of a much grander scale: bigger, taller, and more ornate than any the boys had ever seen before. A huge cathedral dominated one corner, and on another, a large white building with tall pillars aligned across the front of it loomed over them, reminding David of an old Roman temple. A great statue of the nation's founding father, George Washington, poised atop a spirited steed, stood high upon a pedestal in the center of an intersection. The street was lined with brick buildings of every sort: hotels, apartments, wainwrights, millineries, cooperages, a post office, and several livery stables. It seemed like everything imaginable was right here.

A piano plunked out a hymn-like tune, and David recognized the melody as "God Save the South." There were soldiers everywhere, some with uniforms, and some without. Men were dressed in worn-out suits, topcoats, and top hats, and women were attired in tattered finery.

As they rode by, a group of wantonly-dressed women noticed them and called them over. Jake threw a grin at David, who grinned back, amused, before turning his gaze to the other side of the street. Signs advertising assorted wares hung from brackets attached to the sides of buildings. The troopers gazed into shop windows, enthralled by all the activity. A banner draped across the main street read "Long Live King Cotton."

"Wonder where ole Jeff Davis lives?" Jake loudly asked his friend, making sure he could be heard above the din.

"I dunno," David replied. "Let's ask somebody for directions."

They spotted a group of Confederate soldiers standing on a nearby corner, so they led their horses over to them.

"Pardon us, but we're new to Richmond. Who do we talk to about findin' our regiment?" Jake inquired.

The Rebels in weathered gray uniforms looked over at Jake.

One of them pointed, and said, "Go down this-a-way till y'all see a three-story building on the left. There'll be a signage on the front that says C.S.A. Provost Office."

"Thank you kindly," said Jake.

They rode in the direction indicated for a few blocks until they found the office. Once they had dismounted and tied their horses, David tilted his head back, gazing up at the tall brick building. The Stainless Banner hung from a post near the door, rippling boldly in the chilly breeze. The boys entered. A sign with an arrow designating the office location pointed to the narrow wooden stairs. They climbed up the creaky staircase until they reached the landing. A long hallway lined with doorways stretched out before them. Their destination, indicated by another sign, was behind the first door, so they went inside.

A gentleman in a Confederate uniform with bayonet insignia turned to see who had entered. "What can I do for you boys?" he asked. He was dressed in gray from head to foot.

"Sir, we're here to jine up with the cavalry, and we're hopin' you can direct us," David politely explained.

"Let's see your papers," the provost marshal requested.

They withdrew their documents from their pockets and surrendered them.

The marshal looked over their enlistment papers. "Alabama, eh?" he remarked.

"Yessir," they both replied in unison.

"Well, I hear the army's camped up near Fredericksburg. Do y'all know where that is?"

Jake threw a quick glance in David's direction.

Reigning in his emotions, David concealed his sorrow, although Fredericksburg was the place where his father had died.

"No sir," he said.

The provost marshal turned to the wall. He pointed at a large map, so Jake and David moved in closer to see.

"Y'all are here, in Richmond, and need to go up yonder." He slid his index finger a few inches along the map. "It's about a two-day ride."

"Any trains runnin' that way?" asked Jake.

"Yes, but it would be quicker to ride. The Confederate army's got most of the railroads tied up at present." He cleared his throat. "And the sooner y'all head out of Richmond, the better. The city's jist recoverin' from a smallpox epidemic."

Jake's eyes widened. "Well, reckon we'll be on our way, then."

He saluted, reminding David, who mimicked the gesture. They bumped elbows once again.

The provost marshal snickered. "Y'all *are* new!" Looking at David, he said, "Salute with your right hand, soldier."

"Yessir."

David switched hands. The provost marshal quickly saluted and put his hand down, which signaled the two troopers to relax. They turned to leave.

"Y'all been gittin' a lot of rain around here?" David asked.

"Purt near every day," the old gentleman said. "And we got five inches of snow on Easter mornin'."

"Is that a fact," said David. "Well, good day, sir."

"Good day," he heard the man say as he closed the door behind him.

He followed Jake down the long, narrow, dark flight of stairs and back outside. They untied their horses.

"I don't know about you, but if we have two days of ridin' ahead of us, I reckon we oughta find us some vittles," said Jake.

"Good idea." David stepped up into the stirrup and seated himself in the saddle.

Excited by the presence of other horses, Renegade nickered and pranced sideways. David turned him, and the boys rode back to the main street, looking around for someplace to eat. With very little money left, they hoped to receive some food from a kindly vendor. Every time they tried, however, they were turned away.

"Could be it's because there are so many other soldiers here," Jake said with a shrug.

They had enough money to buy one meal at a hotel to split between them, but decided against it, since it would leave them without any currency whatsoever. They tried begging for specie, but the attempt to obtain coinage was also uneventful. People were nice enough, so Jake and David assumed they were just stingy. Finally, one young woman in a frayed bonnet and filthy yellow calico dress stopped, dug around in her green velvet handbag, and pulled out a few silver coins.

"Here y'all go," she proffered, and smiled sweetly at the two of them.

"Miss, beggin' your pardon, but, well, everyone here in Richmond seems to be holdin' out," David said to her.

"And for good reason," she said. "We're all starvin' 'round here. Didn't y'all hear of the riot last week?"

"Riot?" Jake repeated.

"Why, yes. A large number of the womenfolk, myself included, decided it would be a good idea to raid the bakeries, since we're starvin', like I said. But President Davis chased us off, so now we're all back to where we started. Starvin', that is."

"You saw President Davis?" Jake asked, astounded.

The young woman was openly friendly and didn't seem to mind sharing all the information she had. David thought she must be a wonderful gossip.

"Uh huh," she nodded. "He ordered us to disperse, which we did. After bein' threatened with our lives, that is."

"When did all this happen?" asked David.

"Last week. Thursday, I reckon it was. April second."

The boys looked at each other. It had happened on David's birthday, and the same day Tom met his untimely demise.

"Thank you kindly, ma'am," said Jake with a flirty grin.

She smiled back. "Good mornin'," she replied, and shuffled down the sidewalk.

The troopers decided they had enough money for a small loaf of bread and two turkey legs, so they visited the baker's and butcher's shops respectively, then ate quickly.

"We'd best be on our way if we want to make the north end of that river by sundown," Jake said, referring to what they'd seen on the provost marshal's map.

"North Anna," David reminded his friend. Oddly enough, when he said it, the name rang in his head like a church bell.

He and Jake rode through Richmond saying very little, for they were still in awe of its gigantic presence. They kept to the roadside so their horses would have better footing. Before long, they reached the city's outer limits, and approached the countryside, greening and peppered with groves of trees.

A farmer in a wagon waved at them as they rode by, and then slapped the reins to prompt his two jennies into tugging harder through the mud. The boys spurred their horses into a canter, covering a mile before they slowed to a trot. David glanced behind him. Richmond was now but a memory. The long train ride was finally over. Their real adventure was just beginning.

How can one forgive such enemies as we are contending against? Despoiling us of our property, driving us from our homes and friends and slaying our best citizens on the field are hard crimes to forgive. — At any rate let me have a chance to retaliate and then I can forgive with a better grace.

Confederate soldier, diary, near Richmond
July 10, 1862

Chapter Five

Jake and David rode throughout the afternoon and into the evening, stopping once at a farmhouse to ask for food. They offered the farmer Confederate currency, but the elderly gentleman refused, sending them on their way with potatoes and beef ribs. As the sky darkened, the troopers decided they could ride no further, so they found an adequate location to sleep, removed their horses' saddles, and picket-tied them. The air was strangely still, except for an occasional chilly breeze that blew through the trees, making the leaves shake like they were shivering from the cold.

David gathered kindling and started a fire to cook the food they had been given while Jake curried their mounts.

"Sure could go for a cup of coffee with this," he remarked, and took another bite of the underdone beef.

"That would be mighty fine," replied Jake with a sigh.

It wasn't long before they finished eating. They cleaned up and rolled out their horses' blankets to lie upon. David pulled his enlistment paper out of his jacket pocket. He had attempted to read it on the train, but the rollicking motion of the locomotive made him nauseous and dizzy.

"Whatcha doin'?" Jake asked, glancing over.

"Readin' my paper," David answered, squinting at the type.

Jake pulled his own paper out from his coat pocket and followed along as David read aloud, slowing on the handwritten words that had been inserted in the appropriate spaces, for the captain's penmanship left much to be desired.

"State of Alabama, town of Huntsville. I, David E. Summers, born in Morgan County in the state of Alabama, aged eighteen years, and by occupation a...oh, he left mine blank."

"Mine, too," Jake said.

"Do hereby acknowledge to have voluntarily enlisted this third day of April 1863, as a soldier in the Army of the Confederate States of America, for the period of twelve months, unless sooner discharged by proper authority, do also agree to accept such bounty, pay, rations, and clothin', as are, or may be established by law. And I David E. Summers do solemnly swear, that I will bear true faith and allegiance to the Confederate States of America, and that I will serve them honestly and faithfully against all their enemies or opposers whomsoever, and that I will observe and obey the orders of the President of the Confederate States, and the orders of the officers appointed over me, according to the Rules and Articles of War. Sworn and subscribed to at Huntsville, Alabama this third day of April 1863. Before…" He hesitated, squinting harder, but the captain's signature was still unreadable. "The captain's name," he said with a shrug.

"Jist call him Captain Scribble," said Jake, grinning.

David chuckled and went on reading. "I certify, on honor, that I have carefully examined the above-named soldier and that in my opinion he is free from all bodily defects and mental infirmity, which would in any way disqualify him from performin' the duties of a soldier." He stopped. "The captain signed as the examinin' surgeon," he observed.

Jake held his paper up closer to his face. "I didn't realize he was a surgeon, too."

David snorted. "I'd be surprised if he is." He continued reading. "I certify, on honor, that I have minutely inspected the soldier David E. Summers previously to his enlistment, and that he was entirely sober when enlisted."

The two boys laughed.

David continued reading. "That to the best of my judgment and belief, he is of lawful age, and that in acceptin' him as duly qualified to perform the duties of an able-bodied soldier, I have strictly observed the regulations which govern the recruitin' service. The soldier has hazel eyes, brown hair, fair complexion, is six feet zero inches high. Received of Captain Scribble, Recruitin' Officer of the Confederate States Army, this third day of April 1863, fifty dollars, bein' by way of bounty, for enlistin' in the Army of the Confederate States for twelve months." He glanced at Jake. "Reckon we were supposed to have a witness sign."

"He must have figured we were each other's witness," Jake stated wryly.

David glared at the bottom of the page. "Signed triplicates, it says. Did he make three copies?"

"Only two that I noticed," said Jake. "One for the office and one for us."

"Oh." David folded the paper and stuffed it into his shirt pocket. He stretched out on the blanket, wishing for a pillow. A chill wind raised goosebumps on his arms. He got up to retrieve his homespun woolen shirt from his saddlebag, and pulled it on over the one he was wearing. The sky began to spit drizzle. Their tiny campfire hissed before sputtering out. The soldiers gathered their gum blankets and shelter tents and set them up quickly, but the canvas tents didn't provide much shelter.

Jake pulled on his jacket. "Reckon it's a hasty bivouac," he remarked, and crawled in under the shelter.

The drizzle became light rain, then steady rainfall.

"I'm f...f...freezin'!" David forced out. He wrapped his arms around himself, shivering.

"Why didn't you bring a coat?" Jake asked.

"I thought it would be warmer than this up here."

Jake blew like a horse. "Well, serves you right, then. Here, wrap up in this." He pulled Stella's blanket out from under him, but David stopped him.

"No, that's all right," he said through chattering teeth. "If this is what soldierin' is like, I'd best git used to it."

Jake snickered. He rolled back onto his blanket and drew a sigh. "I'm fixin' to grow a big ole beard, jist like the one J. E. B. Stuart has," he proclaimed in the dark while the rain thumped down upon the canvas.

David laughed. "Now that would be a sight, bein's you can't hardly grow three whiskers!" Suddenly, Jake punched his arm. "Ow!" he reacted, and gave his friend a retaliatory shove.

"That's because I'm part Cherokee. You know that," Jake growled.

"Yeah," David sighed, "reckon I've heard that once or twice." The rain persisted, but the chill started to dissipate, and he soon dozed off.

Dawn was cool and cloudy. The two troopers collected their belongings, saddled their mounts, and rode north, taking the route that the provost marshal in Richmond had directed. Within a short time, they reached the river that had appeared on the provost marshal's map. While they rode, David began to sing. Renegade pricked his ears back to listen and broke into a trot. David's voice bounced with the motion of the horse.

"As I was a lumberin' down the street, down the street, down the street, a handsome gal I chanced to meet, and she was fair to view. C'mon, Jake, sing along!" he invited.

"You know I can't sing," Jake said with a smile.

"Sing anyways," David persuaded, convincing him to join in.

They sang happily at the top of their lungs, knowing that no one was nearby to hear them. "'Alabama gals, won't you come out tonight, come out tonight, come out tonight? Alabama gals won't you come out tonight, and dance by the light of the moon!'"

When night fell, they were forced to retire, since the sky was black and virtually starless. At least it didn't rain, although the wet wood they found to make a fire cast more smoke than heat into the shelter.

In the morning, they rode again, stopping once to consume what was left of their meager rations. By early afternoon , they reached the town of Fredericksburg. The troopers inquired as to the location of the cavalry and were directed several miles west.

Once they had ridden out of town, David said, "I'd like to see where my pa's buried."

"Reckon we'll git the chance," said Jake.

They cantered up onto the crest of a hill and were suddenly overwhelmed by the spectacle before them. Nestled in the valley below, the immense Army of Northern Virginia spanned the entire countryside, astounding and magnificent in its grandeur. Smoke curled up into the sky from numerous fires. The Southern Cross rippled gently in the breeze above rows of white canvas tents that stood lined up across the fields. They reminded David of a million tufts of cotton tucked into the darkening hills. The boys sat atop their horses, staring down in awe of the sight. Hearing a rider approach from behind, they turned in their saddles.

"Who goes there?" the horseman called out as he rode toward them. Dressed in a gray uniform with a forage cap on his head, he held a long shotgun in one hand and his reins in the other.

"We're here to jine up," Jake told him. "We've been assigned to the cavalry." He offered his enlistment paper, but the soldier brushed it away.

"Follow me. I'll take y'all to where you need to go." He turned his horse.

Jake and David followed the uniformed Confederate down the hillside. Upon entering the camp, David marveled at the sensations that came with it: laughter and singing, the smell of frying meat, the clanking of metal, and a boy drummer pounding out commands in rehearsal. Some of the soldiers noticed their arrival, but most didn't pay any attention. They were busy darning, cooking, writing, and dozing.

"Wait here," the picket said.

He rode toward a large tent, dismounted, and went inside. In a moment, he emerged and pointed out the new recruits to the two officers who had followed him. One of the officers came over to the boys. He had apparently forgotten his hat in the tent.

Jake saluted. David, who was reminded once again, did the same.

The officer returned the gesture. He requested their enlistment papers, scanned over them, and handed them back. "You boys lookin' for the cavalry?" he inquired.

"Yessir," Jake said.

"Go back through camp, ride out a fer piece, and there y'all will find them," he directed.

The two troopers saluted again. The officer threw a salute at them before walking back toward his tent. Reaching the edge of the camp, David and Jake spurred their horses into a canter, and were hardly noticed by any of the infantrymen. They pulled back, prompting their horses to trot.

"Was that a general?" Jake asked.

David looked over at his friend and shrugged. "I don't know how to tell one from the other," he admitted earnestly.

The two recruits rode on for several miles until they found another camp. This time they knew they were in the right place due to all the horses and mules standing around. They rode in, dismounted, and led their horses over to a trickle of a stream, indulging their mounts and themselves in a cool drink. A gray-garbed trooper with spectacles and a dark moustache came toward them. His face was covered with a wide grin, like he had come across long lost friends.

"Hey! I ain't seen you fellers around in camp? Are y'all new?"

He pointed an index finger at them. David wondered if he intended to poke them with it.

Looking the man over, David decided he wasn't an officer, so there was no reason to waste the effort to salute. "We jist got in. Could you direct us to the officer in charge?"

"Reckon y'all need to be talkin' with the general, so follow me," he said. "Oh, and leave your horses here."

David glanced over his shoulder to see Renegade drinking from the clear stream with his eyes closed, so he left him to relish his refreshment.

The cavalryman introduced himself. "I'm Corporal Williams. Pleased to make your acquaintance," he said, and shook their hands.

"Private Kimball. This here's Private Summers," said Jake. He looked at David with a grin.

David recalled the tease Jake had thrown at him a few hours earlier. "Private Summers and public winters," he'd joked. He thought Jake's comparison was ridiculous, and once again, could not compete by using Jake's name, so he had just smiled wearily in return before calling him an ignoramus.

"Y'all from Virginia?" Corporal Williams asked.

"No, we're from Alabama," said David.

"Well, I know of some boys from Alabama who signed on early in the war, but no new recruits. Hey, did y'all know Major Pelham?"

Jake glanced at David. Apparently, the corporal assumed that since they were from Alabama, they would know every other soldier from their home state as well.

"No," Jake responded. "But we certainly know of him. It's a real shame for our country and our state to lose him."

David remembered reading about the gallant John Pelham, who had died at Kelly's Ford just last month.

"Reckon he was a hero at Fredericksburg," Corporal Williams said.

"So was David's pa," Jake proclaimed, throwing a glance at his friend. "He died there."

The corporal stopped and turned toward David. "Sorry for your loss."

David nodded in appreciation.

Corporal Williams started walking again, so the new troopers followed alongside. "I heard about a feller at Fredericksburg. I believe his name was Kirkland. Anyway, he went out on the battlefield after the fightin' to give fallen Feds a drink. The boys nicknamed him, 'Angel of Maryes Heights.' Would've made that Yankee gal, Clara Barton, right proud, I s'pect." The corporal chuckled. "Oh, and they had a big snowball fight in Fredericksburg last winter," he said. "Before the battle, that is. Some fellers ended up with broken bones and black eyes. From what I hear, a few of them died!"

David wondered if his father had contributed to that fight. Bud never mentioned what kind of wound he had sustained to lead to his demise. He decided death by snowball wasn't dignified enough, so he cast the thought from his mind.

They continued through camp, this one similar to the army's except for the presence of equines, and came to an officer's tent. The flap was pulled open; they could see several men sitting at a table inside.

"General," the corporal said, standing in the entrance. "These two boys are here to enlist."

One of the men stood up. He walked around the table to the entrance. Jake and David saluted him, and he did the same. He wore a moustache and neatly-trimmed beard, and was dressed in an elaborate, brass-buttoned Confederate uniform. "I'll need to see your documents." He took the papers David and Jake held out to him. After examining them, he returned them to their owners. "Did y'all bring horses?" he asked.

"Yessir," David replied. "They're down at the stream gettin' a drink."

"We jist got in from Richmond," said Jake.

The general looked at him skeptically for a moment, but then his expression softened. "Go ahead and make yourselves comfortable, boys. Y'all will be here for a spell. Roll call is at five o'clock, and then we'll commence to drillin'. Y'all will be assigned to Colonel Beale's regiment. I believe they're camped over yonder." He pointed outside the tent toward the opposite direction they had come. "Corporal Williams here will provide y'all with any further assistance." He waited for the boys to salute, quickly returned it, and went inside.

The boys followed Corporal Williams back toward the little stream.

"That didn't look like General Stuart from the pictures I've seen," said David.

The corporal chuckled. "That was General Rooney Lee. Robert E. Lee's son," he said.

"Well, how do you tell who's who?" Jake asked.

"Oh, y'all will know who the generals are right off. Can't miss them. Especially General Stuart. Know much about him?"

Jake said, "Only that he whipped McClellan a couple of times."

Yeah," said Corporal Williams. "He's a character, he is. On that last ride around, he sent a telegram to the Yankees in Washin'ton City, and complained that their mules were so poor, they couldn't pull the wagons he stole." He snickered. "He has a habit of expandin' orders."

"What does that mean?" asked David.

"Means he'll go against orders if he gits an inklin' to. And he's right clever. At Second Manassas, he had us drag brush along the roads to stir up dust so the Yankees would think we were larger in numbers."

David recalled a story Mrs. Samuels had told him at his birthday party, which Bud had relayed to her. It was about how the Confederate artillery painted logs to look like cannons, thus tricking the Yankees into thinking their numbers were larger than they actually were, and how Major Pelham had skillfully deceived the Federals in a similar fashion at Fredericksburg by shooting off his only remaining cannon from different locations to give the illusion that he had more cannons to fire.

The boys followed the corporal until they came upon the stream. Renegade and Stella stood side by side, their eyelids drooping.

"Whose horse is that funny lookin' one?" Corporal Williams asked with a chuckle.

"He's mine," replied David, taking hold of Renegade's reins. He brushed his hand along the colt's sleek neck.

"What kind of horse is he?" the corporal inquired further.

"He's a cross between an Injun pony and a thoroughbred," David explained.

Corporal Williams removed his forage hat and scratched his head. "Now, how do you git a combination like that?"

Jake chuckled.

"My pa was in Texas before the war, and he purchased a stallion from the Injuns and brought him back to Alabama," David said. "One day, the stallion got out and found our neighbor's thoroughbred mare, who jist happened to be in heat. And this here's the result." David grinned as he patted his colt. "Our neighbor was so riled up about it that he made my pa buy him!"

The three troopers laughed.

"How old is he?" the corporal asked.

"Three," replied David.

"You like racin' him? Because we have races around here to keep ourselves occupied," Corporal Williams said.

David glanced at Jake, who had an amused smirk on his face. "Why, I'd be willin' to give him a run," he said, cocking an eyebrow.

"Good," said the corporal. "I'll let you boys know when the next race will be held." He paused for a moment. "Reckon y'all will be in need of rations. When you fellers git over to Colonel Beale's camp, find the commissary's tent. They'll set y'all up."

"Thanks," Jake said.

Corporal Williams flashed an easy smile and waved them off.

The boys led their horses back through camp. David noticed things he hadn't before: a banjo plunked, men talked and laughed, others smoked, a few read newspapers and pocket Testaments, and some cooked. Several black men intermingled with the soldiers. David assumed they must be the officers' servants. He turned toward a commotion to see several men taunting a comrade who was astride a hanging log.

"Wonder what that's all about?" Jake asked, pointing at the unfortunate soldier.

David shrugged in response.

He and Jake walked for what seemed like miles before they finally reached their destination. They were directed to Colonel Beale, a stern-looking man with a penetrating stare and a long, bushy moustache. He examined their enlistment papers, provided each new trooper with a saber, and quickly inspected their horses. Commenting on how Renegade's appearance did not conform to standard army regulation, he then directed them to the commissary for rations.

Jake and David saluted their new commander before walking through the campsite. They found the commissary tent, and the soldier inside doled out crackers, bacon, cornbread, and dried peas. He welcomed them to the army and sent them away, wishing them a pleasant evening.

At a loss for what to do next, they looked around, decided on an open area, made their mounts comfortable, and commenced to building a fire.

David sat down on a log by their tiny, makeshift campsite. He opened one of the wrappers the quartermaster clerk had given him. Inside were small square crackers two inches wide with tiny holes punched through them. He pulled one out and bit into it, but immediately winced, and put it back in its wrapper.

"Oh!" he moaned, holding his hand up to his jaw. "I nearly broke a tooth on this thing!"

"That's why they call it hardtack," a strange voice behind them said.

The boys turned to see two soldiers in Confederate uniforms.

"How do," said one of them. "I'm Phillip Warner. Pleased to make your acquaintance." He held out his hand.

"Jake Kimball," Jake replied, shaking the man's hand.

"David Summers," David said, also taking the man's hand.

"This is Sergeant Williams," Phillip said.

The sergeant exchanged greetings with them. "Mind if we jine y'all?"

Jake responded to Phillip's question by inviting them in.

Sergeant Williams rolled a log up next to the fire, and the two men sat upon it. "I found the best way to eat those worm castles," he said, referring to the hardtack, "is to crumble the ole teeth-dullers up in bacon grease and fry them with cornbread and peas. We call it cush."

"Is this all there is to eat?" asked Jake.

"Yup," the sergeant said. "Lucky to git that much right now."

Jake and David looked at each other. They had been excited about reaching the army and camping out, but not if they had to starve.

"Which regiment are we with?" David inquired.

"This is the 9th Virginia," Phillip said. "Did anyone assign y'all to a company?"

"Not yet," David replied.

"Mind if I take a look at y'all's papers?" he asked. The boys presented their documents. After glancing over them, Phillip said, "Reckon I'll put y'all in with Company A, the Stafford Rangers."

"Who are you, sir?" David asked, unsure as to why this soldier displayed so much authority.

"Oh, didn't I mention that? I'm y'all's commandin' officer, Major Phillip Warner."

The new troopers gaped at each other, jumped to their feet, and stood at attention.

The major laughed. "We're not all that formal around here unless it's required of us."

Jake and David put their hands down. The major motioned toward the log they were sitting on, so they slowly sat back down.

"I do demand y'all's respect," he continued, "but I've found that the best way to acquire it is to let my boys know I'm jist one of them. We're all in this fight together."

"Yessir," replied Jake.

The major stood. "Now I'll be retirin'. Sergeant Williams here has been instructed to see to it that y'all get acclimated, so I'll be leavin' him here for the time bein'." He turned and walked away.

The sergeant sat for a moment in awkward silence. "Why don't y'all have supper, and I'll be back in a while," he said, rising to his feet.

The boys agreed and watched him walk off into camp. They managed to fry up the meal as instructed, but it tasted like burnt crackers and grease. Neither one had cooking experience, so their creativity was lacking, along with their provisions. They cleaned up and brushed their horses before the sun set. While they rolled out their blankets, they exchanged questions neither one had the answers to, until they ran out and lay staring blankly at the dying embers of their fire. The camp had grown quiet as the cavalrymen settled in, conversing with each other in low, muffled voices. Someone started playing a melancholy tune, "Lorena," on a fiddle. Once again, David felt the cold. He moved closer to the fire, but it didn't provide much warmth.

"How y'all doin'?"

They looked up to see Sergeant Williams hovering over them, so they sat up.

"We're fine," replied Jake. "A little tired, bein's we had a long ride today."

The sergeant smiled. "Y'all will git used to that," he said.

Jake's face contorted into a quizzical expression. "When we arrived earlier, we met a Corporal Williams. Any relation?" he asked.

"What'd he look like?" inquired the sergeant.

Jake explained.

The sergeant nodded. "That's my brother. He's Willard Williams, and I'm William Williams, and if that ain't enough to confuse y'all, reckon nothin' will!"

The three soldiers chuckled.

David asked about a soldier he'd noticed upon their arrival to camp. "Why was that feller tied to that hangin' rail with a sign around his neck that said 'thief'?"

"Oh." William chuckled again. "We call it ridin' the wooden horse. That's what happens to soldiers who git caught stealin' or startin' a fracas. I'd strongly recommend y'all don't git tempted into committin' any wrong doin's, because if that happens, they'll buck and gag y'all, or put y'all on extra picket duty. The worst I heard of was bein' shot for desertion, but General Stuart doesn't enforce that at all." He looked at David, who had his arms wrapped around himself. "You didn't bring a coat, did you, Summers?" he asked, as though he'd seen neglectful soldiers before.

David shook his head, which wasn't too much of an effort since the rest of his body was already shivering.

"I'll be right back."

William left them to contemplate the disciplinary actions they'd just been exposed to. He returned a few minutes later with a dark shell jacket.

"I got this off a dead Yankee, but I haven't had a use for it, so you can have it." He handed it to David, who thanked him and put it on. "Fits you right nice," William observed. "The arms are too long for me."

David grinned. The sleeves were nearly too short for him. They barely reached down to his wrist bones, but he didn't mind. Wearing the dark blue coat somehow made him feel superior to the dead Yankee, whoever he was.

"We'll dye it so you won't be confused for a Federal once we're out on the field," William said. "I'll show you how to do that tomorrow." He glanced at Jake, who smiled. "Well, if y'all are set for the night, I'll be off. Five o'clock comes mighty early." He flashed a smile before walking off into the dark camp.

A bugler played "Taps." Jake soon fell asleep, but David tossed and turned, thinking about home, Tom's death, the Yankee who had previously worn his jacket, and how excited he was to finally make it to Virginia. Everything astounded him: the sights, smells, soldiers, and surroundings were fascinating. Finally, after almost an hour, his busy mind gave way to sleep.

Reveille blasted through the cold morning air. David sat up. He roused his friend, who gazed over at him with sleepy eyes. They noticed the commotion within the camp as other troopers began to stir, pulling on their boots and assorted clothing they had discarded during the night.

"Come on, Jake. Let's go see what all the fuss is about."

David stood, and Jake did the same. Following everyone else, they took their place at the end of a row. Major Warner paced along the front row while reading from the list he held, and hollered out names. Troopers in the group immediately responded. He called out David's name, who replied "Here," and Jake's, who responded the same way. After roll, the men were allowed to obtain a meal from one of the wagons.

"This is the same thing we had last night," Jake complained.

"Sure could go for a cup of coffee with this," David remarked.

After breakfast, they were instructed to prepare their mounts and ride to a nearby field. The major gave a command, so the company reacted. It was instantly apparent to everyone who the new recruits were. The other members of the Stafford Rangers chuckled and poked fun.

One bushy-bearded soldier said, "We were all new once. Y'all will git the hang of it!"

They were instructed to pull sabers and charge, to mount, dismount, and mount again, and then to gather in assigned groups of four. Once in their groups, the men all dismounted. One took the reins while the other three pretended to fire at the enemy on foot.

Ordered to practice charging again, David held his saber in his left hand with his Colt .44 in his right. The pistol felt especially heavy since he was used to shooting with his left hand, but he eventually got used to firing with his right.

The men were released for their midday meal, consisting of the same viands they'd had for breakfast. They returned to the field two hours later to resume where they'd left off. The drilling continued on into the afternoon until, after more than seven hours, they were finally released.

Jake and David led their horses to the edge of the field to graze, and fell down upon the damp grass in sheer exhaustion. Two other members of their company approached and lay down on the grass next to them. They welcomed each other with a weary, "Hey."

"We heared y'all were from Alabama, so we thought we'd come over and make y'all's acquaintance. You boys jist git in last night?" one asked.

"Yeah," David replied.

He introduced himself and Jake. The two veterans did the same, stating that their names were John Chase and Michael Tailor.

"Do we drill tomorrow, too, or do we git a day of rest, bein's it's the Sabbath?" asked David.

"There'll be no drillin' tomorrow. Ole Beauty's a stickler for lettin' us off on Sundays," John said, referring to Stuart by a nickname the general had acquired at West Point.

"Where y'all from?" asked Jake.

"Why, we're from Georgia!" John exclaimed.

"How come y'all are in with the Virginians?" Jake asked.

"Well, we were over here with my cousin," explained Michael. "Us and some other fellers from our company. Kerr, Smith, Crawford, and Campbell. Anyway, we were supposed to leave to go down south with our brigade, but when we got back, they were already gone!"

"What brigade is that?" asked David.

"Hampton's," John responded. "We're with the Jeff Davis Legion. Reckon we'll have hell to pay when they git back up here!" He and Michael chuckled. "So y'all will jist have to tolerate a few of us Georgians around the place," he went on. "Least till our fellers git back."

"Reckon we can overlook it if y'all can," Jake said with a grin.

John snickered, raising an eyebrow. "I'm inclined to think that us Rebels are all in this together, so I'll forgive y'all for bein' from Alabama."

David and Jake looked at each other and shrugged.

"I have cousins in Alabama," Michael told them. "Y'all know the Ryan's?"

Jake and David gaped at each other in astonishment.

"There are a lot of Ryan's around our parts," Jake replied.

"How about that!" Michael laughed. He seemed happy to hear of any news from home, however obscure it might be. They talked about their families for a while until he stood and said, "All this nostalgic talk is makin' me well up."

John pulled himself to his feet. "Let's meet up tonight, and we'll shoot the bull," he suggested.

Jake and David agreed before following the Georgians back into camp.

"Hey," John said over his shoulder. "Do either one of you boys know how to write, because I've been longin' to send a letter home to my wife, but I jist can't figure out how to put it in words."

"We can write a letter for you," said David, happy to oblige.

John smiled and trudged back toward camp.

Hesitating until the Georgians were out of earshot, Jake gave David a shove, which caused him to stumble.

"What was that for?" he angrily fired back.

"I ain't volunteerin' to write a letter for every soldier out here," Jake stated.

David gave him a crooked grin, knowing that his friend wasn't very good at writing. "Well, I'll jist do it, then," he said.

They returned to camp and scrounged around for something to eat, but could only manage to find the same staples they'd consumed earlier. After they tied their horses out to graze, Sergeant Williams came by and invited them to his fire. Jake and David followed him to discover a large iron kettle hanging over a flame.

"Put that Yankee coat in here, and the dye will turn it butternut," the sergeant instructed.

David removed the coat he'd been wearing since the previous evening. He let it fall into the boiling concoction. "What do you use for dye?" he asked.

"Walnut hulls, acorns, and lye," William replied.

They chuckled at the rhyme. Standing over the kettle, they watched the boiling water roll over the garment as it gradually washed the dark blue coat to brownish-yellow.

When he was satisfied with the result, William retrieved the coat with a stick and hung it on a bush to dry. "You'll have to leave this here till tomorrow," he told David, "but you can borrow my saddle blanket if you want."

"Thanks," David said. "I reckon I'll be all right."

The two troopers exchanged smiles. After bidding goodnight to the sergeant, Jake and David returned to their site, but were surprised by what awaited them. Six men were standing there, waiting for their return.

"There they are!" exclaimed John, a wide grin parting the thick fur on his face. "These boys will write home for us!"

Jake looked at David, scoffed, and shook his head. "I'm illiterate all of a sudden," he muttered.

One of the Georgians they hadn't yet met held out a pen and a piece of wallpaper. David wondered whose wall he'd peeled it from.

"How do," the Georgian said, "I'm Custis Kerr." He held out his other hand and grasped onto David's. "John and Michael here said y'all can write a letter for us." He had a scraggly beard that reminded David of a wire-haired dog he'd seen once. Pausing momentarily, Custis added, "I'd be willin' to give y'all somethin' for it."

"Do you have anything to eat?" Jake inquired.

"Well, I have a cornpone and some honey," said Custis.

David smiled, took the pen and paper from him, and seated himself on the log next to their fire. Custis sat beside him, grinning from ear to ear. Positioning the wallpaper on his thigh, David poised the pen erect and glanced over at him.

"Ain't you holdin' it in the wrong hand?" Custis asked.

"I'm left handed," David explained.

The Georgians howled.

"We ain't never seen a lefty afore!" one of them exclaimed.

David felt a little awkward, but had grown up enduring such teases, so he shrugged it off. "Whatcha want me to write?"

"Dear Mother," Custis dictated, "I am feelin' well and believe the weather is becomin' more mild."

David raised an eyebrow as he scribbled down the words, wondering if this soldier had anything more important to say.

"I am doin' fine and look forward to seein' you a'gin." Custis spoke like he was reading, slow and deliberate, so that David would catch every word. "I am writin' to M. S. B. and C. L. S."

Throwing a glance at him, David wondered how many letters he was expected to write for each and every soldier. He started to regret his hasty offers.

"If you don't have anything more to say, I'll close for you," he said, hoping Custis would take him up on his offer.

"Hold on a minute." The Georgian raised his hand. He nodded and pointed to the wallpaper, coaxing his transcriber to continue. "Received the parcels you sent from home. Many of the boys enjoyed them also." He stopped to rub his beard in thought. "Reckon that's all. Jist put down your lovin' son, Custis."

David finished writing and handed the piece of wallpaper to him. Custis clutched onto it like it was a gold nugget.

"Oh, what's your name?" he asked.

"David Summers."

"Thanks kindly, Summers," Custis said, and walked off.

Another Georgian, Peter Smith, had David write home to his wife and two daughters in exchange for dehydrated vegetables. Alfred Crawford dictated a letter to his sweetheart, gave David a sewn bag of pennyroyal leaves for his effort, and instructed him to place it at the foot of his bed to repel fleas. A newlywed, Robert Campbell, sought assistance in addressing a letter to his wife. He rewarded his comrade with saddle soup and graybacks amounting to three dollars. David also wrote one letter each for John and Michael. In the time it took for him to write the soldiers' letters, he learned more about each cavalryman than most of them would ever know about each other. Graciously, he accepted their offerings in return.

When he had finished, he realized it was getting dark. Thankfully, Jake had taken the initiative to fry some salt pork, so he and David devoured it, along with the newly-acquired cornpone and crusted honey. They cleaned up and relaxed by lying on their backs and gazing up at the stars. David's writer's cramp left him too disabled to pen a letter to his own family, but he reasoned he could do it tomorrow, since it would be a day of rest. He started dozing off, but heard voices growing louder.

"Mind if'n we join y'all?" Michael asked.

David opened his eyes and glanced at Jake, who shook his head, grinning as he sat up.

John chuckled. "You look sleepy. Did we wear y'all out today?" He chuckled again. "We wanted to come over and shoot the bull with you fellers."

David pried himself up. The two veterans seated themselves on logs. John pulled a meerschaum from his pocket and lit it. The pungent odor of rich tobacco intermingled with the smell of burning firewood.

"By the way, Summers," Michael said, his dark eyes twinkling in the firelight. "I'd recommend you get rid of that can of desecrated vegetables Smith gave you."

"Why?" asked David.

"I've heard tell that if'n you eat those critters, they'll expand in your stomach and make you explode!"

David's eyes grew large. He retrieved the can of dehydrated vegetables from his saddlebag, threw it into the fire, and watched along with the others. The can sizzled, popped open, and was quickly consumed by flames. Inexplicably, the recollection of Tom's terrible death back home in the barn entered his mind. He looked away.

"I heard that last month they caught ole Abe Lincoln in a drunken stupor," John remarked nonchalantly. "Heard from a source in Washin'ton

City that he was on a binge for thirty-six hours and was still drunk when he left the drinkin' establishment!" He laughed heartily.

David winked at Jake. It was obvious their guests were extravagant liars, but amusing, nevertheless.

"I heard tell that General Burnside passed on in his sleep," Michael said, "and that General Beauregard was accompanied on a march by concubines and wagonloads of champagne."

Jake and David chuckled.

"I heard from a couple of Louisiana Zouaves that the good people of New Orleans printed a picture of General Butler on the bottoms of their chamber pots!" exclaimed John. He guffawed loudly. "That's one way to git even with that damned Yankee general!" he exclaimed, referring to the dreadful officer who had taken over the city nearly a year ago. The four soldiers laughed loudly at this.

"Is it truthful that General Stuart's a teetotaler?" asked Jake.

John nodded, enjoying his pipe. "That he is, and a ladies' man, but a devoted husband and father over all."

"Where in Georgia are y'all from?" David inquired.

"Savannah," said Michael.

"I heard it's right purty over there," said Jake. "Y'all have any land?" he asked.

"I have about a hundred acres," John replied, "and a few niggers to help run the place, but Michael ain't got any, 'cept what his kinfolk live on. We've got plenty of big plantations 'round our parts."

"When we were ridin' in," Jake said, "we heard some fellers talkin' 'bout a rich man's war and a poor man's fight, but we didn't know what they meant by it."

"Oh." John took a puff from his clay pipe. "The plantation owners and their overseers are exempt from fightin' if'n they have twenty slaves."

"That don't seem right," said David.

"Nothin' in war is right, Summers," Michael said, "and you'll find that out soon enough. But General Hampton's supposed to be the largest slave owner in the South, and he's fightin'. Say, you ain't a conscript, are you?"

"No sir," David responded proudly. "We're both enlistees."

John nodded and smiled, clenching the pipe in his teeth. He puffed again. "That's good. We ain't real fond of conscripts 'round here.

Anyone forced to jine up ain't worthy of the fight, and those fellers will run off first chance they git. Jist like those cowards from our home state who refuse to fight. We call them Georgia crackers. It's downright unpatriotic."

Jake leaned in toward his friend. "You should ask him about your pa," he reminded.

The other soldiers looked at David, waiting for him to speak. He took a deep sigh, and said, "My pa is buried here somewhere, and I was wonderin' if y'all might know where I could find him."

The Georgians exchanged glances.

"Can't rightly direct you," Michael said. "The burial site's mighty large, and not every grave is marked. It could take days, or even weeks, and you still might not find him."

David bit his lower lip and gazed into the fire, disappointed with the answer he'd received.

Jake quickly changed the subject, and they were soon engaged in telling one chilling horror story after another, most of which the other soldiers made up. David enthralled them with "The Tell Tale Heart," a story by Edgar Allen Poe, which none of the others had heard before. To his amusement, they actually shivered at his telling of the story. The four soldiers talked on into the night until they realized it was late and decided to retire. As the Georgians departed, Jake leaned back, mumbling something unintelligible. David fell asleep but was soon startled awake by the bugler's invasion.

"I thought we got today off," he muttered to Jake while they pulled on their boots.

"Reckon they have roll every day," Jake said with a yawn.

He and David sauntered to the field where they again went through military procedures. Their company was informed that General Fitzhugh Lee, who was the nephew of Robert E. Lee, had taken his cavalry brigade northward. After being released, the boys stood in line for rations, disappointed with the lack of variety once more, but they ate it anyway, grateful for the meager nourishment. Afterward, they gave their mounts some seed corn and oats.

Finally finding free time, David settled in to read from his Testament. He opened the leather flap. Inside was the miniature Southern Cross Josie had sewn for him. His heart grew heavy at the thought of her,

Rena, and their mother. He had hardly been gone a week, yet it seemed like years.

Flipping through the sacred pages, he found a scripture that caught his eye: *So we are ambassadors for Christ, God making his appeal through us. We beseech you on behalf of Christ, be reconciled to God. For our sake he made him to be sin who knew no sin, so that in him we might become the righteousness of God.*

Jake sat down beside him, holding a newspaper he had found.

"Where'd you git that?" David asked.

"Down at the sink," Jake replied, opening the paper. "It's a few weeks old, but it's somethin' to read."

"Couldn't find better use for it?" David snickered.

Jake glared at him. "You wouldn't think it was so funny if you had this ailment," he grumbled.

David shrugged. "Seems to me some of that salt pork should've worked its way out by now." Unable to help himself, he snickered again.

Jake threw the newspaper down on the ground and stood. "Reckon I'll see what's goin' on around camp," he announced, and stomped off.

Deciding it would be a good time to write a letter home, David found his pencil and paper and began writing.

Dear Ma and sisters,
I take pencil in hand to inform you that Jake and I arived yesterday evening and are being aclimated to our suroundings. We have plenty to eat and are feeling fine and our horses are fine. We have yet to see General Stuart. To-day is Sunday and you will be glad to know that I am studying scripture and find it very reasuring. Please tell Callie I wish her well if you see her. I would like very much if you could rite to me every particular of what is going on back home. I am thinking of you fondly and will rite again in the near future.
Your son and brother until deth,
David

Intentionally excluding any reference to Tom Caldwell, he placed the folded letter into an envelope.

They must have heard by now, he thought. *They must know I killed him.*

Deciding to hunt for Jake and deliver his letter to the post, he walked around camp, taking notice of the activities around him. He was stunned to see men gambling, pitching horseshoes, cursing, drinking, betting, and slapping papers while they played their poker hands, not only because it was the Sabbath, but also because it was only one week after Easter. One soldier asked David to join him for a sip of "Pine Top," but he refused. Drinking, especially on a Sunday, appalled him. Curious as to why there were no services, he asked another trooper.

"In the beginnin'," the soldier said, "we held services, faithfully, every week." He cocked his head at David. "But the war keeps draggin' on, and I reckon now we've all lost interest."

David found Jake standing in a throng surrounding two Rebels who were seated at a table. In front of them, a Federal canteen lay on its side. The men yelled and squinted at it.

"Come on, Howitzer!" one hollered.

"Go, Minié Ball!" another exclaimed.

The spectators shouted excitedly.

"What's goin' on?" David asked his friend.

"They're havin' lice races," Jake replied. He grinned at David before looking back at the table.

The crowd cheered. One of the contenders sprang from the table and threw his arms up in victory.

"Better luck next time!" he bellowed, shaking his opponent's hand.

The loser presented a Confederate note to his rival, and men within the crowd exchanged currency as well.

David observed the spectacle with amazement, glad that no man of the cloth was there to witness it. He felt a twinge of humiliation for the soldiers in attendance, and wondered why they didn't display any moral responsibility. Deciding he'd seen enough, he walked back over to his campsite. Jake followed, talking all the while about the carefree life of a soldier.

"Do you reckon I'll be able to find Pa's grave?" David asked him.

Jake's joviality quickly changed to solemn reserve. He shrugged in response. "Sounds like the gravesite's mighty large. It could take us days to find him, and besides, the major might notice us missin'."

"Well, maybe I'll ask him tomorrow if he knows where Pa might be."

"Why don't you ask him now?" Jake grinned, motioning for him to follow.

They walked through camp to a white canvas tent and timidly entered.

"Sir," Jake said quietly to catch the major's attention.

Major Warner looked up from the map he was studying. David followed Jake inside the tent, and the two saluted.

"At ease," the major softly commanded. "What can I do for you boys?"

"My friend was wonderin' if you might know where his pa's buried," Jake explained. "He was killed here last December."

"Do you know which regiment he was with?" asked Major Warner.

David nodded. "Yessir. He was with the 4th Alabama. Uh, the North Alabamians infantry division."

The major scratched his head. "What was your father's name, Private?"

"Hiram Summers, sir."

"Well, let me look into it, and I'll git back to you in a day or two."

"Yessir."

The boys saluted and exited the tent. Once again, David was disappointed with the response he'd received, but decided he had no choice but to wait.

When morning came, the cavalry was instructed to prepare several days' rations, so the troopers fried salt pork and cornbread, which they wrapped in cloth and stuffed into saddlebags. Once David was finished, he watched the others dismantle their tents and pack their belongings. Finally, the order was given to mount up. W. H. F. "Rooney" Lee's brigade started out down the road. They rode toward a new destination, past torn up fields of oats, clover, wheat, or corn. Many of the starving Confederates helped themselves, but Jake and David resisted. Green corn only resulted in bowel misery later on, a fact they had learned as children.

As they rode, David and his comrades saw partially burned, zigzagging worm-and-post fences enclosing the fields, and knew the infantry ahead of them had used the fences for firewood.

The cavalry reached a flooded-out area of the road, but the infantry's pioneers had bridged it by constructing a corduroy road of fallen trees across the gap. The riders dismounted and led their horses slowly over the uneven surface. They could not afford to lose a single animal to a broken leg.

During the night of Monday, April 13, the troopers learned that Yankee cavalry was at Morrisville, so officers sent sharpshooters from David's regiment to support pickets stationed at Kelly's Ford. The following day, Federal cavalry attempted to cross the Rappahannock River at the Ford, so Rooney Lee positioned his men by spreading them along the river to Brandy Station. He placed the 13th Virginia out in front to skirmish with the advancing enemy. He ordered the 9th Virginia to move in to attack, but the Federals fled back to the north bank of the river, and for the rest of the day, the artillery and sharpshooters exchanged rounds.

The next morning, Rooney Lee moved his troops to threatened points along the Rappahannock, guarding against any further invasion. Seeing the Yankee cavalry had partially crossed the river, he ordered the Virginians to charge and drive the Union soldiers into the swift waters. Some of the Yankees drowned, but the Virginians captured twenty-five of them.

Two days of uneasy quiet ensued. On Saturday, David awoke with a tremendously sore throat. He sat up as the bugler blasted reveille, but suddenly felt weak and had to lie back down.

"What's wrong?" Jake asked.

David found it difficult to speak. Alarmed by his condition, he put his hand to his throat.

"Whoa," Jake said, looking closer. "Your neck's swelled up like a bullfrog!"

"Hurts like hell, too," David croaked.

"I'll go fetch the doc."

Jake scurried away. In a short while, he returned with the army physician, who examined his new patient and came to the conclusion that David had the mumps.

"You'll have to be quarantined to the hospital," the doctor said.

David stood but staggered dizzily, so Jake helped to steady him. They followed the doctor to a tent filled with suffering soldiers. Wearily, David sank down onto an empty cot and lay back on the striped down pillow.

"Reckon we won't be hearin' that golden voice of yours for a while," Jake remarked, smiling down at him.

"How long will I be out, Doc?" David asked through his misery.

"A week or two at best," replied the gray-bearded man.

David moaned. He wondered if his throat would swell shut and suffocate him. "Why ain't you sick?" he asked Jake.

"I had the mumps when I was a young'un, remember?"

David shook his head.

"When I was seven or eight, due to the miasmic air. Your ma kept you away for two weeks till I recovered," Jake said. "Reckon the air must be causin' sickness here, too."

David's head throbbed. The doctor gave him a cup of salt water and instructed him to gargle every ten minutes, and then he departed to check on his other patients.

Jake pulled a chair up to his friend's bedside. Extracting his pocket watch, he glanced down at it. He looked around, taking notice of a cabinet filled with tinctures, and of the other soldiers lying in the tent. Some men moaned softly, others coughed, and one reacted to his stomach cramps by curling up and groaning.

"Poor feller," Jake muttered, gazing at the man.

"I'll be all right," David said. "Has it been ten minutes?"

Jake stifled a snicker. "Close enough." Rising to his feet, he handed his friend the cup.

David took it and gargled as instructed, only to spit it out, groaning in pain.

"The salt makes it hurt more!" he agonized, falling back against the cot.

"Sorry, Zeke," Jake sympathized. "Reckon I better git to roll, or I'll miss my ration. I'll be back to check on you later." Unable to provide further assistance, he departed from the tent.

David scowled, feeling sorry for himself. This wasn't how it was supposed to be. He wasn't supposed to fall ill, especially so soon after arriving. Looking over at the young man lying next to him who coughed uncontrollably, David realized the last thing he wanted was to die without attaining battlefield glory. He reckoned it was God's way of punishing him. The excruciating pain in his swollen throat became so profound it overcame him, and he closed his eyes.

If I ever lose my patriotism, and the "secesh" spirit dies out, then you may know the "commissary" is at fault. Corn meal mixed with water and tough beef three times a day will knock the "Brave Volunteer" under quicker than Yankee bullets.

Confederate soldier Robert W. Banks
Letter home, October 22, 1862

Chapter Six

Several days went by. David periodically awoke between bouts of restless slumber to hear rain pelting down on the canvas tent he and several dozen other troopers shared. He found out more about a soldier's ailments in those few days than he would have cared to know in his entire lifetime. Men suffered from flux, consumption, camp fever, numerous invisible invaders called no-see-ums, which he assumed to be horrible and unimaginable, and the Tennessee two-step, or what the army doctor referred to as dysentery. The doc doled out the same remedies for each soldier who came and went from the hospital: a pint of whiskey, blue mass, or laudanum. He prescribed lard and iodide of potassium for the camp itch many of the cavalrymen suffered from, instructing them to rub the slippery concoction on three times a week. David hoped he wouldn't contract that mysterious ailment, for rubbing lard on himself seemed repulsive. He was instructed to gargle with dreadful saltwater, but he waited until Jake arrived every day to persuade him.

After less than a week, he decided he'd suffered long enough, so he rejoined his company, even though his throat was still sore and he could barely speak. He lined up at roll call alongside Jake, who gave him a pat on the back before standing at attention.

Major Warner listed off names in alphabetical order. He called out "Summers, David E."

David tried to respond, but his voice was still too hoarse, so Jake said, "Here. Here he is, Major."

The members of Company A glanced at David with sleepy eyes.

Their commanding officer looked up from his document and said, "Good to have you back, Private." He then proceeded down the list. After roll, he released them, requesting they report back in one hour.

John, Michael, and Custis walked over to their recuperated comrade.

"Feelin' a damn sight better, I hope," Michael said to him.

"You weren't playin' old soldier, were you?" asked Custis.

David shook his head in response.

"No, I don't reckon you were pretendin'." Flashing an amused grin, Custis said, "Oh, by the way, your colt has been a holy terror since you fell ill." He chuckled and walked away.

David frowned at Jake. "What's he been doin'?" he croaked.

Jake shrugged. "Well, I didn't really want to say anything while you was ailin'. I reckon he jist got bored without you." He paused, but David held his gaze, compelling Jake to continue. "He tore up some of the campsite and ran all over lookin' for you."

John chortled. "Damned horse nearly got hisself shot!" he exclaimed.

"You missed all the excitement," Michael said with a laugh.

David's mouth gaped open. He couldn't believe what he was hearing. "Pshaw," he finally said. "Where is he?"

"Over yonder, in that makeshift barn." Michael pointed at a deteriorating wooden structure.

"We're off to fetch us some victuals," announced John. "See you fellers later." He and Michael chuckled and walked away.

Jake followed his friend across the campsite, and David pulled the door open. To his dismay, there stood Renegade in the dark.

"Renie, what have you done?" he moaned.

His horse immediately recognized him, pricked up his ears, and nickered. Taking hold of Renegade's halter, David brushed his hand along the horse's smooth cheekbone.

"Tell me what all happened, Jake," he requested, gazing at his colt with concern.

"Renie got to missin' you a day or two after you took sick, and he was fine for a while. But the longer you were gone, the more agitated he got. I tried ridin' him a few times, but he wouldn't have anything to do with me, and he wouldn't respond to any of my commands."

David entered the stall. He led Renegade toward the barn door, pausing long enough to take his bridle from a nail before coaxing the horse outside into the fresh spring air. "I can't believe he would misbehave so badly," he growled.

"He jist got restless or somethin'," Jake said. "He got everyone's attention, all right. One feller threatened to shoot him if he got into his supplies again, but I convinced him and everyone else that Renie would simmer down once you recovered. Word even got back to General Stuart. He came over yesterday to git a gander for himself."

David's large eyes grew larger. His jaw dropped. "What?" he gasped. "J. E. B. Stuart was here? Why didn't you fetch me?"

Jake grinned. "I thought you were still too sick, so I let you rest."

David groaned. "What did he say?"

"He said he'd never seen anything like Renegade. I told him he could outrun any horse in the cavalry, and he said he'd like to see that. So you're racin' this Saturday."

"Saturday? That's two days away!" David scowled, and put his hand to his scratchy throat. "I heard tell the Yankees are close by. Why are they fixin' to have a horserace now?"

"Well, because we all need somethin' to relieve the tension. And a race will only last a few minutes. You'll feel better by Saturday, won't you?" Jake chuckled with evident amusement.

David could see that his friend was getting some sort of perverted pleasure out of torturing him. "Do I have a choice?" he grumbled, placing the bit in Renegade's mouth.

"Reckon not." Jake shrugged again. "Let's go eat." He sauntered off, glancing back with a grin.

Taking hold of the reins, David led Renegade away from the dilapidated shanty. "Renie, you ought to be ashamed of yourself," he said in a low, gravelly voice.

The horse responded by shaking his head.

"Next time I have to leave, I expect you to behave yourself, savvy?" He looked into the horse's big greenish-brown eyes. "You're lucky you didn't git yourself shot."

Renegade snorted. David led him over to the field where Stella was grazing, picket-tied him, gave him a pat on the rump, and added, "Don't you ever do that again, you hear?"

The colt nodded, his flaxen mane swirling up into the air. He slowly meandered off to nibble grass.

David caught up to his comrades and took the rations the quartermaster distributed: salt horse, which was actually beef, cornbread, and more hardtack. He stared disapprovingly at it as he walked over to the campsite he and Jake had constructed. Taking a seat on a log, he bit into the tough strip of meat.

"This ain't no better than shoe leather," he complained, glancing over at Jake, who was frying bacon in a cast iron pan while swirling his cornbread in the grease.

"This here's what they call sloosh," Jake explained. He rolled the bacon and fried cornbread onto a stick and took a bite.

"Where'd you git the pork?" David asked.

"Had it left over from last night," said Jake. "I'm glad to see you're feelin' better."

"I jist couldn't linger in that hospital any longer," said David. "All that sickness and sufferin' made me feel more unhealthy."

They finished their meal, retrieved their mounts, and led them to the field for another long day of drilling. David became a bit weak and worn out at times, but he pushed through it. By the end of the day, he was almost feeling like himself again. He hadn't realized until he was on Renegade how much he'd missed riding him, and apparently, Renegade felt the same way. David was lost without the horse, for they had been together nearly every day since Renegade was a foal. From Renie's behavior, the horse wasn't too happy without David, either.

After being released from drill, Jake and David sat down in the sweet-smelling, pungent grass, watching the other cavalrymen depart from the field.

Jake said, "Remember how we used to do ridin' tricks?"

"Yeah."

They grinned devilishly at each other. Both boys sprang to their feet and jumped up on their horses. Stella protested with a shrill whinny, but Jake spurred her into a gallop.

"H'ya!" David hollered.

Renegade bolted into a run. David quickly caught up to Stella and passed the old mare. Laughing, he looked back at Jake, who flapped his arms and legs and hollered 'git up now!' to encourage Stella to catch up, but to no avail. They rode around the field. David passed his friend two more times before finally deciding to rein in his horse.

"You don't need to be showin' off!" Jake called.

He led Stella over to where Renegade was standing, giving her a chance to catch her breath while the young stallion pawed at the ground and blew.

"Let's do back flips!" David exclaimed, his eyes twinkling.

"Sure you're up to it?" Jake asked with a wry grin.

David nodded. "I feel fine now," he declared, even though his voice was still scratchy.

117

Jake agreed. They rode side by side, starting at a trot and accelerating to a canter. Each one took turns with the most elaborate stunts and acrobatics they could dream up. Jake swung his leg over so that he was standing in the stirrup on Stella's left side, then hoisted himself back over onto her back. David lowered himself down near Renegade's belly, holding onto the girth for dear life as the horse's hooves thundered dangerously close to his head. He pulled himself back up into the saddle. Jake got his feet up under him and squatted on the back of his mare. He lifted himself into a handstand, holding the position for a few seconds before easing himself down. David spurred Renegade to go faster. He threw himself backwards off Renegade's rump, springing with his arms before pushing himself up and away from the colt's rear hooves with his feet. He catapulted himself into the air, somersaulted, and landed standing on the ground. Riderless, Renegade galloped around in a wide circle.

"Bet you can't top that!" David yelled.

"Oh, yeah? Watch this!"

Jake slapped Stella's shoulder with the reins. As she picked up her speed, he brought himself up into a handstand on the back of the saddle, turned so he was facing forward, and rotated himself again so that he was facing behind. He pushed off, landed with his feet on Stella's rump, propelled himself over, and attempted to flip in the air like David had done, but ended up landing on his rear end instead. He lay there writhing and groaning.

David ran over to him. "Jake! Are you okay?"

"Oh," Jake moaned. "I broke my coccyx!"

"Your what?"

"My tailbone!" Jake held out his hand. "Help me up!"

David pulled Jake to his feet, but couldn't help laughing while Jake hobbled around, bent over like an old man and holding onto his buttocks.

"Should I take you to the doc?" David asked between guffaws.

"Naw, I'll just walk it off." Waddling around until he could finally straighten, Jake looked over at David, who was still chuckling. "Go fetch the horses, okay?"

David obliged, snickering. Handing Stella's reins to Jake, he asked, "Can you ride?"

Jake grinned, rubbing his backside. "Reckon there's only one way to find out." He hoisted himself into the saddle, letting out a big groan upon seating himself.

David snickered again and shook his head. "A good night's rest will make you all right," he said.

They rode into camp. Jake moaned and groaned with each step.

Morning reveille came too soon. The boys dragged themselves over for roll, Jake still hobbling from the fall he'd taken. When they returned to their campsite with breakfast, he looked over at the field where they had tied their horses the previous evening.

"Where's Stella?" he asked.

He hurried over to the edge of the open pasture. Renegade stood guard over the still form of Jake's black Morgan mare.

"Stella!" Jake hollered.

He sprinted across the field, the bruise on his backside not slowing him much. David reached Stella first.

"Reckon she's dead, Jake," he observed sympathetically.

Stella lay on her side, her eyes mere glazed -over slits. Her tongue hung from her slack mouth. Jake bent down and gently patted his precious mare. For several minutes, their surroundings grew quiet except for a few chirping birds. At last, he slowly stood, and wiped his eyes with his shirt sleeve.

"She was a good horse." He sniffed. "But she was old. I knew she might not make it. I was jist hopin' she'd last a little longer."

"She got you this far," David said, "and that's somethin' in itself." He walked over to Renegade and led him away from the dead mare.

Jake walked back to camp. He picked up a branch, lit it from the fire, brought it over to the deceased mare, and set Stella's corpse on fire. Some of the men noticed, so they approached out of curiosity.

"Your horse give out on you?" Robert Campbell inquired.

Jake nodded in response to the obvious.

Alfred Crawford said, "Reckon someone should go tell the major."

"I'll do it," offered another cavalier, who ambled off in the direction of the major's tent. Within a few moments, he returned with Sergeant Williams.

"Jake's horse died," David told the sergeant.

Jake stared at the dead mare, his eyes mirroring his disbelief.

"That's a shame," the sergeant responded kindheartedly.

David asked, "What'll happen now?"

"Well, Kimball has ninety days to git himself a new horse. Otherwise, he'll be reassigned to the infantry," William explained.

"Ninety days? That ain't till the middle of July!" Jake exclaimed. "I can't wait till then to fight!" He looked at David and snorted. "Besides, where will I git another mount?" He gazed over at burning Stella, forlornly shaking his head. "Damn!" he spat.

The wind changed direction, forcing the small group of men to move away from the smoke and dreadful smell. They stood hypnotized, watching the flames die down to glowing embers, slowly envelope the deceased mare, and convert her carcass into smoldering ashes. Some of the men drifted back into camp until only Jake, David, and William remained.

"Reckon I'll jine the infantry then," Jake stated matter-of-factly. He winked at David, who was taken aback by his nonchalant reaction to the preceding event. "That's what I'll do," he said to William. "Tell Major Warner I'm fixin' to fight with Stonewall Jackson!"

"I'll have him make the arrangements right away." William gave him a reassuring smile before walking off.

"You sure you want to do that?" David asked.

"Hell, yeah, Zeke!" Jake exclaimed. "I didn't come all this way to miss out on the fightin', jist because my old horse up and died. She was bound to die sometime, right?"

"Reckon so," David responded with a shrug. He wished in a way he wasn't so attached to Renegade, just in case something should happen to him. The thought of his beloved colt's lifeless corpse made him cringe.

"But I'm stayin' till Saturday," Jake said. "So I can watch you win that race!"

On the morning of April 25, following roll call and breakfast, David saddled Renegade. He and Jake walked over to the wide, emerald field designated as the race course. No one else had arrived, so they said a quick prayer for the safety of horse and rider and for the chance to show the other cavalrymen in Rooney Lee's brigade just how fast a little horse from the back hills of Alabama could run. Talk of the race had spread from company to company until the entire brigade caught wind of the event, and several other riders expressed interest in racing as well. This didn't worry David in the least, since he'd been racing Renegade for months at every opportunity that presented itself in Morgan County. They had always won.

He checked Renegade's legs for heat or swelling. "Tell me again which regiment you'll be with," he said to Jake.

"The 26th Alabama, under Colonel O'Neal," Jake replied. "Reckon when I git over there, they'll issue me a haversack."

"You'll be needin' somethin' better to walk in," David observed, glancing down at Jake's dusty riding boots.

"These'll git me by for a while." Jake kicked a stone. "At least until I can locate me a pair of brogans."

He looked across the field, and David followed his gaze. Men on horseback approached, along with a crowd of soldiers on foot. Two troopers fashioned a finish line constructed of a thin rope at the other end of the field. The crowd grew louder. David and Jake walked toward the commotion.

"Are you in the race?" a young soldier in gray asked.

David nodded.

The soldier pointed at the starting line, which was also to serve as the finish line. David stepped into the stirrup and mounted.

"Good luck, Zeke!" Jake yelled. Removing his slouch hat from his head, he waved it in the air.

David grinned. He directed Renegade over to the starting line, took his place on the end, and glanced over at the other six horses. They were all taller and more muscular than his little colt. Their riders turned to sneer and chuckle at him. David touched the brim of his hat in response. Two fiddlers commenced to play "Camptown Races" in harmony.

"Gentlemen," an officer announced, a pistol in his hand. "When I fire, y'all are to ride around the edge of this field, counterclockwise, which is a quarter of a mile in length, until returnin' to this spot. Anyone cuttin' across will be disqualified. Good luck, and may the best man win!"

The crowd cheered. At the outburst, some of the horses grew frantic and reared. The officer raised his pistol into the air and fired. Renegade sprang, easily pulling ahead in great stretches, his hooves thundering against the ground in rapid rhythm.

David lowered himself close to the horse's neck. Out of the corner of his eye, he saw two other riders closing in on him. He held Renegade back until he thought they were about three quarters of the way around the track. One of the other riders jeered at him, yelling about how that homely spotted pony couldn't outrun *his* steed. David let him pull ahead by a length.

The horses grunted with each stride, their hoof beats drumming down upon the turf in quick cadence. The riders whooped and hollered to make their mounts go faster. A couple of the contestants thrashed at their steed's flanks with sticks.

David glanced back over his shoulder. The other five horses were close at his heels. He looked ahead and spoke into Renegade's ear, using every ounce of love and trust between them to coax the stallion into giving his all.

"Okay, Renie! Let 'em have it!"

He slapped Renegade with the ends of the reins. The little horse surged forward, ever faster, easily passing the rider in front of him. He pulled far into the lead and galloped toward the crowd of people. David's heart thumped in his ears with exhilaration as the wind whipped his face. Horse and rider burst through the finish line. The spectators cheered. The six other contestants came in five lengths behind. David eased back on the reins, letting his horse slow to a trot. He walked Renegade back to the finish line where a mass of soldiers swarmed around.

"That was some race!" one exclaimed.

"I never expected this funny-lookin' one to win!" said another.

"Summers, I don't reckon I ever saw a horse run that fast!" John yelled. "And you jist won me five dollars!"

David grinned, removed his hat, and brushed his damp hair back from his forehead. He looked around for Jake, who was standing near the back of the crowd with his arms folded in front of him, smiling and shaking his head.

"Private Summers." Colonel Beale rode up to him on his horse. "Congratulations! That was remarkable!"

"Thank you, sir," David replied.

"General Stuart would like to have a word with you." He pointed to a knoll at the other end of the field. David looked over to see four officers on horseback.

"With me?" he asked, awestruck.

The colonel smiled and turned his horse. David rode alongside toward the other end of the field. As he neared, he recognized two of the officers immediately. One was General Rooney Lee, whom he had met upon his arrival, and the other was General Stuart, the commanding officer of the Confederate cavalry. David had eagerly anticipated catching a glimpse of the legendary general, but had never considered meeting him in person. Riding up onto the knoll, he saluted modestly. The officers returned the gesture.

"This is Private David Summers, who jist recently jined us from Alabama," General Rooney Lee explained, his eyes twinkling. "He's with the 9th Virginia."

"Private Summers," said General Stuart. "I am very impressed with the way you ride."

David was astounded by the man before him. General Stuart wore a gray jacket with gold braiding in the configuration of the Austrian knot on his collar and sleeves, a wide yellow sash around his waist, elbow-length gauntlets, dark blue trousers with gold stripes, a red-lined cape, and golden spurs attached to his high riding boots. On his head of curly brown hair perched a wide-brimmed gray felt hat, turned up on one side and clasped with a gilded palmetto star. A black ostrich plume feathered out from behind it. His tanned face was covered with a light brown moustache flowing into a cinnamon-colored beard that reached down to his chest. His bright blue eyes sparkled from beneath the brim of his hat as though laughing at the world and amused with everything in it.

"Thank you, sir," David said.

"This is Colonel Von Borcke." General Stuart motioned toward a large man on his left with a long, blond, curly moustache and short beard. "And this is Major R. C. Price," he introduced, nodding toward the young man on his right, who didn't look much older than David.

"I would like to have the opportunity to race your little stallion in the near future," Colonel Von Borcke said with a heavy Prussian accent. "I'm certain my horse will win!"

The officers chuckled.

David grinned. "I'd be honored, sir," he replied.

"Private, I would like to take the opportunity to use you as need be for special assignments," said General Stuart. "That is, for errands where speed will be of the utmost importance."

"Yessir," David said.

"I assume your horse is sound," said the general.

"Yessir."

"And you are willin' to take certain risks for the good of your country."

"Yessir."

"Very good, Private. It is my opinion that a good man and a good horse can never be caught, and you have displayed admirable qualities."

David grinned with delight. "Thank you, sir."

"You are dismissed," the general said.

David saluted. General Stuart put his gloved hand to his hat and smiled slightly. He released the salute. David turned Renegade toward the base of the knoll.

"Congratulations on your victory," General Stuart called after him.

"Thank you, sir!" David called over his shoulder.

He spurred Renegade into a trot across the field. All the while, his heart was rapidly thumping. He couldn't wait to tell Jake about what just happened. Now he truly was one of Stuart's "invincibles."

The crowd had thinned, but Jake waited beside the officer who had fired the starting gun.

"Zeke!" he yelled. "Git over here and collect your winnin's!"

David looked at Jake quizzically and coaxed Renegade toward his friend.

"Here you are, son," the officer said. He handed David a one hundred dollar Confederate note. "Congratulations! I hope we git to see that little horse run again soon!"

David's eyes grew wide in astonishment. "Thank you, sir!"

He stared in exhilarated awe at the note that read, "Confederate States of America, one hundred dollars." Pictures of two soldiers, a woman's face in profile, and a man he assumed to be a politician were displayed on the front of the scrip. He hadn't expected to win anything, especially not this much money. His only desire had been to race for the recognition and to rectify Renegade's bad behavior in front of his company.

Glancing back at the knoll, David saw that the officers had gone, and with them, his moment of glory. He sighed, dismounted, and walked alongside Jake back to camp.

Once they returned, David helped his friend pack. He tried to convince Jake to take the money he had won, so Jake could use it to buy a new horse. But Jake stubbornly refused, saying that he was looking forward to fighting in the infantry under Stonewall Jackson and Bobbie Lee.

"Besides, you're the one who earned it," he said.

"There'll be other races," said David.

Jake grinned. "You keep it," he insisted, and pushed the paper back into David's hand. "This'll be the start of your college fund."

Reluctantly, David shoved the note into his trouser pocket. "Well, maybe they'll pay you for Stella, like you thought."

With a snort, Jake said, "They told me they'd pay me five hundred dollars for her."

David gawked at him. "That much?" he asked.

"Yup. That's how much they thought she was worth." Hesitating, Jake shrugged. "But then I found out I'd only git paid if she was killed or injured in battle. If they pay me a cent, it'll be downright amazin'," he quipped.

David scowled. "I'm fixin' to go over yonder and talk to Major Warner," he said, tromping off against his best friend's wishes.

Arriving at the officer's tent, David thought better about bringing up compensation for Stella, so he asked for permission to accompany Jake to his new brigade instead. Major Warner kindly obliged.

By mid-afternoon, the two young soldiers were on their way to the Army of Northern Virginia's infantry division. Upon their arrival, they asked for directions to O'Neal's command, and as they neared the officer's quarters, noticed how many of the lean soldiers were barefoot. Like the cavalry, the infantrymen were dressed in various garments: some in uniforms, some in plain clothes. Jake slid down off of Renegade's back and grinned up at David, who waited outside with his horse while Jake entered the tent.

A toothy soldier wandered over. "Hey, fellers, we got us a fop in camp!" he announced.

"Whatcha doin' here, dandyman?" another mustachioed soldier asked. They walked around the newcomer and his horse like they were oddities in the circus.

"My friend's here to jine up with you boys," David replied with a grin. He was still feeling cocky and self-assured from his win earlier in the day. "His horse gave out, so he's here to assist y'all in the fightin'."

"Is that a fact?" the mustached soldier remarked. "Well, I reckon he got here jist in time, because we're headin' out tomorrow."

David's grin faded. "What do you mean?" he inquired.

The soldier laughed, exposing several missing teeth. "Talk is that the Yankees are headed in our direction. We're breakin' camp at daylight."

"Oh," David said, suddenly at a loss for words, not sure if he should be excited or apprehensive.

"We'll be whippin' ole fightin' Joe Hooker soon as he's brave enough to take us on!" the mustachioed soldier exclaimed.

"Is your friend from Alabamie? Because that's where we're all from," the toothy soldier said. "We're Yellow Hammers and proud of it!"

"We're both from Alabama," David replied. "Morgan County."

"Well, I'm from Tallapoosa County," the mustachioed solder said, and the toothy soldier nodded in approval before shuffling off into camp. "Pleased to make your acquaintance." He held out his hand. "The name's Robert Hall."

David gripped Robert's hand firmly in brotherly kinsmanship. "David Summers."

Jake came toward them. "We're headin' out tomorrow," he said. "Could be another big thing awaitin' us."

"Reckon I jist heard," said David. "This here's Robert Hall from Tallapoosa County, in our grand state of Alabama."

"How do," Robert greeted, shaking Jake's hand.

"Jake Kimball," Jake introduced himself. He looked over at David. "You know what this means, don't you?"

David hesitated for a moment. He realized what Jake was getting at. "I won't be able to look for Pa," he said sadly.

"Your pa is here?" asked Robert.

"He's buried here somewhere. Died in the battle last December," Jake explained.

"Oh," was all Robert had to say. "Well, I'll show you around, Kimball, soon as you're ready."

"Thanks kindly, Hall," Jake replied with a gracious smile and then turned toward David. "Sorry, David. I know how disappointed you must be that we can't look for your pa."

"Maybe we'll be back here before the war's over, and I can look for him then. Or maybe one of these gentlemen will know where Pa might be."

Jake said, "I'll see what I can find out." He paused. "Well, reckon this is it." He grasped David's hand. David was suddenly awestruck by their impending separation, as well as the confusion and uncertainty of their future.

"I'll come find you in a few days after we've relocated," he assured Jake.

He hugged his friend, his brother, and climbed up onto his horse. Jake grinned up at him. Giving Renegade a gentle nudge, David directed the colt out of camp. He glanced over his shoulder to see Jake and Robert wander off. Turning back around, he spurred Renegade to a trot.

The troopers began to stir early the following morning. Excitement spread throughout the camp: a large body of Yankee infantry was preparing to cross the Rappahannock. David tried brushing his emotions aside, but he couldn't help feeling at a loss, even though the situation was intensifying. He couldn't deny he was all too lonesome without Jake there beside him. It was like no other Sabbath he'd ever experienced. He stood near Renegade while the horse grazed. The other soldiers scurried around camp in disarray. John and Michael sauntered over to him.

"Did you git your friend, Kimball, off to the infantry all right?" John asked.

David nodded with somber regret.

Michael glanced over at John and said, "We was wonderin' if'n you wouldn't want to be messmates with us."

"Y'all don't need to be concerned with my welfare," David said.

"T'ain't that," said John. "We need someone close to us who can write a good letter." He and Michael chuckled.

David gave them a crooked grin. "In that case, I'd be honored," he said.

"I don't know if'n anyone's told you this yet," said John, "but you ought to pin a name tag to the inside of your jacket, jist in case we see some fightin'."

David looked at him quizzically.

John continued. "Then you'll be assured that, in case the good Lord comes to claim you, folks'll be able to put a proper marker on your grave."

"That could be why Major Warner ain't got back to you yet," said Michael. "Could be your pa was buried without a name."

David scowled. The thought of his father being forgotten in an unmarked grave made his heart ache.

"Wouldn't want that to happen to you," John said. "Here's a piece of cloth to write your credentials on."

"Much obliged," David said quietly.

John presented him with an ink pen and a small piece of canvas. The young trooper recorded on it his name, county, and home state. As he sat near the campfire with his housewife in hand, struggling to sew the small piece of canvas onto the inside of his Yankee jacket, he learned from passersby that the Confederate infantry had headed off in another direction, increasing the distance between himself and his best friend even more.

Michael and John were a comfort, even though David didn't want to admit it. He knew he was their new charity case, but he was grateful, nonetheless. He still felt lost, however. All he could think about was meeting up again with Jake and doing what it was he'd come all this way to do: kill as many damned Yankees as he possibly could.

On Wednesday morning, April 29, the 13th Virginia engaged in skirmishing, and David heard pops from nearby gunfire. Once Rooney Lee's brigade, now consisting of only the 9th and 13th Virginia cavalry regiments, chased the Yankees off, they proceeded to the Rapidan River, where they safeguarded the town of Gordonsville and the Central Railroad. Later, a courier informed them that Fitz Lee had brought his cavalry brigade back from Salem.

A thick fog engulfed the regiments the following morning. Later in the day, David learned that Jake's infantry unit was camped near the Rappahannock, so he decided to ride off in search of him. He informed his new messmates he would return early the next morning, and they agreed to keep his movements a secret, unless he was discovered missing.

David rode for over an hour. He reached the infantry and wandered from campsite to campsite, tolerating stares and verbal insults until he discovered the whereabouts of O'Neal's brigade. He finally located his friend. Jumping down off of Renegade, he gave Jake a hearty handshake. Jake returned the fond gesture and hugged him.

"How've ya been, Zeke?" he asked with a wide smile.

"Jist fine," David replied with an even wider smile.

"Where's the cavalry?" Jake asked.

"They're several miles west of here," David enthusiastically replied.

"Have you heard anything about the invaders comin' our way?" Jake asked.

David nodded. "I heard they crossed over the river yesterday at Kelly's Ford."

One of the foot soldiers he had met earlier, Robert Hall, sauntered up. "Hey, it's the fop!" he exclaimed, sticking out his hand for David to accept. He smiled, showing his missing teeth. "What brings you over here with us?"

"I was jist missin' the company of you boys from home," David replied with a wry grin.

"Well, you've come to the right place then! Come on, and we'll scrounge you up some vittles!"

Jake raised his eyebrows. He grinned at David, who chuckled. The boys followed the lanky, mustached man in tattered gray. They walked over to a campsite that David assumed belonged to his friend and their new acquaintance, and approached a partially constructed tent.

"Moore, we have company!" Robert hollered.

A soldier rolled out from under the tent. David recognized him as the toothy one he had first come in contact with upon Jake's arrival.

"Well," said Moore, "if it ain't the dandy!" He grinned his huge, toothy grin and strode toward them, nodding his head in exaggeration. "I reckon you got tired of the easy life, so you decided to come over here and see some real fightin'."

Jake laughed. "This here's my best friend, David Summers. He's from back home. We both jined up together. Zeke, this here's Wiley Moore. And Robert Hall, you already know. They jined up together, same as us."

"Moore, how do," David said, and shook the toothy soldier's hand.

"I don't know what all they feed you dandies over yonder, but here we have the finest dinin' elements any infantry soldier could ask for," proclaimed Robert. "We have cornbread, fried pork, not to be confused with chitlins, and of course, water. If you want somethin' green to chew on, then you'll have to take up grazin' with your horse!"

The soldiers broke into laughter. David could see why Jake had fallen in with this character. He was entertainment in himself.

Dusk eventually faded into darkness. Sprinkles lightly fell around the campsite. A chill blew in from the river, but the soldiers were so busy talking they barely noticed. Renegade was a wonderment to all of the infantrymen. They constantly walked by to gawk at him and ask David questions. After darkness settled in, a few soldiers came up to them, excited about the proximity of the Yankees to their bivouac.

"They're jist across the river," one of them said, half-whispering, as though the Federals could overhear. "We can see their fires and hear them a-talkin'."

"Let's go have us a look!" exclaimed Robert.

David, Jake, and Jake's two messmates followed the other soldiers to the river's bank, which was about a quarter of a mile from the camp. Across the river, the Yankees stood in groups or moved about, the sparks of their bonfires reflected in the river's slow-moving water. David felt his heart leap, but he wasn't quite sure if it was from hatred, admiration, or just plain exhilaration for finally encountering the enemy.

One of the Bluebellies hollered from the opposite bank. "How's old Jeff Davis getting along?"

Some of the other Union soldiers laughed, and then it seemed as if they all held their breath, waiting for a response.

"Why don't y'all come on down to Richmond and find out!" a Confederate a few feet away from David retorted.

Robert guffawed. "They ain't been able to come close to the capital yet!" he exclaimed.

"Are you Johnnies starving to death by now? The sooner the better, so we can end this damned thing!" another Federal yelled.

"Are all you Billies married off to nigger wives yet?" a Rebel hollered back.

"And has it improved the Yankee breed any?" another added.

The Confederates howled at this.

"Won't be long before you Rebs will be surrendering and begging for mercy, since your money ain't worth scratch!" a National retaliated.

"We'll see about that in the next few days!" someone close to David yelled.

Both sides mumbled and chuckled for a moment. Someone on the opposite bank of the river from where Jake and David were standing began to bow a fiddle. The melody was so calming that both sides stopped to listen. It wasn't a tune David recognized, so he assumed it must be an alien Northern song.

"Hey, play 'Yankee Doodle'!" one of the Bluecoats yelled.

The fiddler began to perform the request, and a banjo, fife, and drum joined in. When the song ended, the Union soldiers cheered, and the Confederates jeered. A band down the riverbank from where David and Jake stood burst into "Dixie." All of the soldiers around them sang along.

"This is somethin', ain't it?" Jake remarked to David, who nodded with a smile.

The Federals retorted by playing "The Battle Hymn of the Republic," then the Rebels played "The Bonnie Blue Flag." The bantering of ballads continued until the Union musicians began to play "Home, Sweet, Home," and the Confederate band joined in. Both sides sang the lyrics in unison. When the song ended, a long, solemn silence followed.

David bit his lower lip and looked at Jake, who had his eyes down-turned. Everywhere around him, he could hear men sobbing. Several minutes went by until the soldiers on both sides of the river dispersed and returned to camp without speaking.

Not long after, a few camp musicians broke the somber atmosphere with "Rose of Alabama" before an officer commanded them to cease.

Jake and David talked all night about home, Callie, and whether or not Tom's uncle was still hunting for them. They discussed how exciting it was that there must be a battle looming. They exchanged views about the new soldiers they'd met, about poor Stella, and how David could make a fortune racing his little stallion. With the money he won, Jake reasoned, he could pay for his own way through college. David agreed with the idea, and thought if he let Renegade run in a number of races, he could win enough for the both of them to go.

The horizon began to brighten. Some of the foot soldiers stirred.

David and Jake watched the sky light up in pastels. Suddenly, a strange contraption floated by.

"Look at that!" Jake gasped. "What is it?"

"A hot air balloon," David said. "I've read about them, but I ain't never seen one before. It's an amazin' sight."

"That it is," Jake agreed.

They watched as the balloon floated farther upstream.

"They're up there a-spyin' on us!" one of the infantrymen yelled.

Several of them grabbed their muskets and ran toward the mysterious orb, taking pot shots at it. Soon, the large, manned balloon floated to safety on the other side of the river.

"Reckon I'd better be gittin' back," David said. "John and Michael will only be able to afford me an alibi for so long."

"When the fightin's done, ride back over," Jake instructed.

David nodded with a grin. He mounted Renegade. "See you in a day or two!"

Jake gave an exaggerated salute. David laughed. He spurred his horse to a trot and rode several miles until he came upon Hampton's brigade.

Arriving back with his company, he discovered many of the men sharpening their sabers on a grindstone: a battle now seemed imminent. John and Michael had managed to find an excuse for his absence from roll call, which fortunately enabled him to escape any disciplinary repercussions.

During the course of the day, the cavalrymen occasionally heard the boom of cannon fire, but they were too far away for it to cause any alarm. Talk of their present condition made its way through the ranks. David was informed by an officer that some cavalry brigades were to guard the roads south of the infantry while his brigade remained east. The Yankees had been traveling with several days' rations and herding cattle for fresh beef. He also learned the Bluecoats had plundered the homes and fields of citizens in the area. This enraged him and his fellow soldiers, who witnessed the report from Thomas Jefferson Little, another soldier in Company A. He was a cousin of David's messmate, Michael Tailor, and was a long-time resident of Stafford County, thus making him keenly familiar with the local countryside.

While the men bedded down around their campfires, a bright moon rose overhead, illuminating the stillness. Somewhere in the darkness of the surrounding woods, whippoorwills chanted their eerie calls.

The next morning, reports came in that a battle had begun west of them near the Chancellor House. As the day progressed, David and his fellow cavalrymen experienced little action and could only talk of how they wished they could be a part of it.

On the next day of battle, May 2, David and his comrades learned that General Stuart's assistant adjutant-general, Major R. Channing Price, had been killed. Their commanding officer, Major Barnett, asked that a moment of silent prayer be given in honor of their fallen officer. David tried his best to contain his dismay, for he was deeply affected, since he had personally met young Major Price only a week before.

A thick, creeping mist rolled in off the Rappahannock, and obscured the following dawn. While the day wore on, the entire cavalry learned their beloved general, Stonewall Jackson, had been wounded, causing the troopers to groan in desperate unison. General Stuart left to take over Jackson's command.

Because of the increasing carnage, it seemed to David the country west of him had burst open with the flames of hell, like Dante's *Inferno*. Smoke and flash could be seen from his stance, and sporadically, when the wind changed direction, he could hear shelling. He prayed hourly for Jake's safety.

At the end of the third day of fighting, a full moon rose in the night sky. David took it to mean the end of the battle had finally arrived. He didn't understand what had happened. The only explanation he received came from an officer who said the cavalry was to remain south and east of Chancellorsville, barring the Yankees' advancement in those directions. His fellow cavalrymen expressed disappointment that they hadn't been allowed to participate in the battle proper.

Word arrived the next afternoon. The battle had indeed ended. A shell hit the Chancellor House, which had been used as a Union hospital, and it burned to the ground. All of the victims inside perished in the fire. The Rebel army won the fight, and the Yankees retreated back across the river.

Upon receiving the news, everyone cheered, celebrating with songs and shots of "Woe-Be-Gone." Many expressed concern for their fallen commanders and comrades. David wondered about Jake's safety, since the infantry had taken the brunt of the fighting. Without telling a soul, he stole away from the cavalry before dawn the following morning.

It is well war is so terrible, or we should get too fond of it.

—General Pendleton
Personal Recollections of General Lee

Chapter Seven

David rode Renegade at a walk for a few miles, unsure which direction to follow. The early morning sky and surrounding forest were so dark he could barely make out the road, let alone anyone foolhardy enough to be out in the unfamiliar countryside...like him. He hoped he wouldn't encounter any Yankees. The possibility of being apprehended and thrown into a Northern prison was all too real, but his desire to find Jake outweighed his fear. After riding for nearly an hour, he encountered a Rebel soldier on picket duty, who directed him to where he thought O'Neal's brigade was camped.

"You're on the Orange Plank Road now," the picket said, gazing out from under his forage cap. Even though it was still night, David could make out dark circles under the picket's eyes. "Go up a ways until you reach Brook Road, and keep goin' till you git to the Orange Turnpike. You'll see the Hawkins farmstead and the Wilderness Church in front of you. Turn right and keep travelin' on the turnpike until you see their camp. You should run into them before you reach Chancellorsville."

"Thank you kindly," David responded.

The picket turned, walked back to a fence post, and lit a pipe. The glow from his burning tobacco faded into the darkness behind David as he proceeded in the direction the picket had indicated. Reaching the intersection, he could barely make out the Hawkins farmhouse, which sat back from the road. The chapel, a small, whitewashed frame building, stood closer to the road, giving him a sense of reassurance as he rode by. A zigzagged wooden-post fence lined the turnpike, and behind it in the fields, David thought he could distinguish objects on the ground. He assumed they were bodies of dead Yankees. The smell of burnt timber hung in the air, making the darkness feel even thicker.

He rode another mile or two. At long last, he saw rows of white tents off to the side of the road. The soldiers within them were just beginning to stir, rising with the dawn. He asked one man for directions to O'Neal's brigade. The soldier pointed without saying a word. Nudging Renegade, David headed off on the route the silent soldier had specified. He saw another foot soldier, asked for the location of O'Neal's command, and was directed to a different area. Over and over he was misled, until almost an hour and a half later, he finally found O'Neal's brigade. He didn't recognize anyone, so he asked one of the soldiers if he knew where Private Jacob Kimball might be. The infantryman shook his head.

"Don't reckon I know a Kimball," he stated.

"He's a new enlistee," said David.

The soldier stood shaking his head and scratching his dark beard. "We'll be havin' roll call in a few minutes. You can find out if he's here then."

David swung down from the saddle and tied Renegade. He followed the infantryman to a clearing where several other members of the brigade congregated. A bugler signaled reveille, prompting more tattered soldiers to wander over to the gathering. David looked closely for Jake or one of his friends but didn't recognize a soul.

The sun peeked out from the horizon, casting long shadows around camp. An eerie, stifling stillness hung in the cold morning air, and a sharp breeze pierced the soldiers bedraggled and soiled clothing. They stood shivering in irregular rows, their breath casting misty puffs into the chilly air.

An officer approached. He glanced over at David before calling out names. "Albright," he hollered.

"Here," came a reply.

"Allen."

"Here."

"Andrews."

The officer hesitated, looking around at his soldiers before speaking the name again, but still no one answered. He continued to callout names on the list. Some received responses, some did not.

"Kimball."

David's heart leaped. His eyes darted around the group of soldiers. There was no answer.

"Kimball!"

Silence. Then the officer continued on to the next name.

"Reckon you ought to check the hospital," the soldier with the dark beard whispered loudly to David. He heard his name called, and bellowed, "Here!"

David looked down at the trampled ground and drew a heavy sigh. He returned to Renegade and mounted, starting his search again. His heart hurt, but he was determined to find his best friend. As the sun appeared above the horizon, he sent up the same prayer request he'd repeated since the start of the battle.

Please, dear Lord, protect Jake and keep him safe from harm's way. Amen.

He asked for directions to the army hospital. A short, stocky soldier directed him back to the turnpike toward Chancellorsville. He rode for a few miles, asking several infantrymen if he was headed in the right direction. All of them knew the exact location of the hospital.

By midmorning, he reached the hospital tents marked with bold red flags. He dismounted, tied Renegade out to graze, and after inhaling a breath of courage, went inside one of the tents. Immediately, the smell of death assaulted him. He quickly backed out, nauseated, struggling not to gag, and took in huge gulps of fresh air before attempting to reenter. More cautiously this time, he pulled open the tent flap and stepped inside.

Dozens of men lay on cots and on the ground, moaning and crying in agony. Flies swarmed in the stagnant air and clustered on the canvas walls. Several people milled around, offering aid and comfort to the wounded and dying. Some carried pitchers of warm water to administer to the soldiers, while others transported them back and forth on stretchers. Blood oozed through white sheets of the many who had suffered through amputations, their stumps still bleeding and raw. The stench of blood and rotting flesh was so overwhelming it made David's eyes burn.

"May I help you, sir?" a nurse asked, touching his forearm to get his attention.

David's voice caught in his throat. He had never seen so much misery in his young life. "I...I..."

"Yes?" the nurse asked softly, her large, kind eyes as soothing as her voice.

"I'm lookin' for my friend, Jacob Kimball. Have you seen him?" He could tell by her expression that she felt sorry for him.

"I don't know every man by name," she said, "so I recommend you take a look around for yourself." The smile she gave him faltered. He saw the sympathy in her eyes. With a gentle pat on his arm, she turned away and returned to her duties.

Uncertain where to start, David mustered enough courage to begin his search one row at a time. He moved slowly down the aisles, looking into the battered faces. Some reached out to him in despair, begging for help. Others, he hoped, merely slept, their eyes closed and their mouths drawn tight. He stopped to assist one of the wounded, giving him a drink from a tin cup, but soon realized the enormity of his task, for every alert soldier made the same request, so he gave up his crusade.

Crimson covered everything, from droplets sprinkled about to massive puddles and stains on the bedding. The blood-covered ground, compounded with the agonizing moans of the wounded, was almost too much for him to bear. He trudged through the aisles but didn't find Jake, so he rushed outside, gasping for air.

A noise scraped at his nerves, making his teeth clench. Not far from where he stood, a surgeon wearing a blood-splattered rubber apron drove a saw back and forth across a soldier's arm. David watched in horror while the doctor separated the soldier's arm from his body and cast it on top of a heaping pile of appendages. A row of soldiers on stretchers, attended to by other infantrymen, waited in line for their turns at dismemberment.

David squeezed his eyes shut and looked the other way, trying not to let his nausea overpower him. He had only eaten Renegade's feed corn for the past day and a half and knew he had to keep it down, since he wasn't sure when he would eat again. Trying to collect himself, he gazed in the other direction. A row of hospital tents, over half a dozen more, stretched out into the adjacent field, their red flags billowing in the cold wind. He shuddered. This was more than he had anticipated, but he had to find Jake.

Taking several deep breaths, he forced himself to enter another tent and gaze into the mangled faces disfigured by inexplicable horrors. White sheets completely covered some of the bodies, their faces hidden from view, their souls gone. One boy whom he assumed to be a drummer had a deep gash in his leg. David hoped the same fate with the saw didn't await the child, who couldn't have been more then twelve. He passed men with horrendous wounds, hastily stitched together or bandaged until time allowed for a better effort, but for many, that time might never come.

Brushing away flies, he walked through the tent, but he still didn't locate Jake. With each step he took, and with every tent he entered and exited, his heart sank further. After walking through the last hospital tent, he stood outside, unable to make his mind function from all the gore he had just witnessed. Jake wasn't in any of the tents. Immediate panic seized him.

One of the orderlies noticed. "Soldier?" he asked.

David glared at him, his eyebrows furrowed, his large hazel eyes now darkened to brown. "I can't find my friend," he explained, his voice riddled with alarm. "I looked through all these tents, and he ain't here!"

The orderly frowned. "Well," he said grimly, "then I reckon you best be checkin' the battlefield." David scowled at the orderly, who said, "They've already started buryin' the dead, though. You might not find him at all." He patted David's shoulder and walked into the tent.

Unable to endure the sounds of moaning agony any longer, David returned to Renegade, mounted, and spurred him into a canter, anxious to leave the gruesome spectacle behind.

Dark clouds threatened the early afternoon horizon. David's heart struggled to beat normally against the weight that threatened to crush it. He found it difficult to breathe, but still held out hope that he might find Jake alive. Once again, he prayed. When he reached O'Neal's brigade, some of the soldiers gave him directions to the fields where they had fought. He traveled west, back toward the Wilderness Church, his remorse replaced with determination.

Now that it was broad daylight, everything appeared much differently. The shadows David had noticed in the ditches alongside the road were indeed corpses, but they were Federals and Confederates combined. He tried not to look too closely at the remains, since he had already witnessed enough death and dying in the army hospital tents, but resolve soon gave way to curiosity. He glanced at the crumpled bodies. Unable to resist, his glances became stares, and he gawked in disgusted disbelief. His stomach roiled, threatening to heave. He gagged, trying hard not to vomit. The smell of death permeated the earth. David covered his nose and mouth with his hand. He held his breath and moved away from the dead. The breeze changed direction, causing the smell to float away. Although the day was bright, a darkness loomed over him.

A number of soldiers milled around the battlefield, some scrounging through dead Northerners' pockets, others walking about aimlessly. Many collected the deceased for burial.

The realization that he might never see his friend again started to sink in. David couldn't bear the thought, but he knew it was becoming a definite possibility. He still held out hope, but a voice in his head insisted on telling him otherwise.

He rode until he found a group of men hunched over, digging a trench to cast the bodies into, the uneven rhythm of their tools clinking and swooshing with the movement of the earth. He dismounted and walked toward them. Their dour faces expressed a mixture of apprehension, fear, and something else he couldn't quite define. Perhaps it was gladness that they wouldn't occupy a space in the mass grave they sweated over. They broke from their digging and straightened as he approached.

"You're lookin' for a friend or relative, ain'tcha?" one of them said.

David nodded. Apparently, he wasn't the first to come looking. "I'm afraid he might be buried unmarked, 'cause I ain't sure if he had his name pinned to his coat," he said, barely recognizing his own voice.

"Any idea where his brigade's fightin' took place?" asked another gravedigger.

"Yessir," David replied. "He was with O'Neal, and I reckon they were somewhere around these parts." He swept his arm northwest toward the Hawkins farm.

Members of the burial party threw glances at each other.

"Well, you might start there," one responded. "But if you can't find him, look over yonder." He pointed in another direction. "I surely hope your friend ain't in that location, though, because a lot of them fellers got burnt up. Shells caught the grass on fire and raged all night through. We could hear them a-screamin', and t'wasn't nothin' we could do."

David grimaced.

"Good luck," one of the men said. They returned to their grisly task.

David led Renegade through the field and gazed into the faces of the dead, becoming more heartsick with each corpse he glanced upon. Federals and Rebels lay side-by-side in mangled heaps, body parts and internal organs strewn everywhere. Dead mules and horses littered the field, and the sickening smell of death rose up from the tainted ground. Some of the soldiers didn't appear dead at all until his mind registered the mortal wounds in their abdomens, necks or backs. Smoke still smoldered up from the field, forming charcoal clouds that cast ominous shadows over the grizzly scene.

He came upon a tremendous oak, and observed what appeared to be a soldier sitting against the opposite side, but when he went around, he saw the poor man's head had been completely blown off. The stump that was left of his neck was covered in a brownish-red stain, which had flowed down onto his chest and saturated his shirt. David's heart leaped into his throat. He gawked in disbelief. Finally coming to his senses, he quickly moved away. He walked under a mahogany tree. Compelled to look up, he noticed a bloody scalp swaying above him in the breeze with the hair intertwined in the branches. Forcing himself to avert his eyes to the ground, he shook his head and turned away, struggling to contain his horror. Abruptly, he faced another soldier, whose dead eyes stared blankly up at him.

David fought to keep his wits. Wincing from the sight, he looked out across the fields, sadly observing all of the bodies he had yet to force himself to gaze at, and wondered if his job would ever be done. Near a grove of trees, hogs were feeding on the dead. He hoped Jake hadn't become part of their meal. He closed his eyes for a moment and took a few deep breaths.

Maybe he missed roll call for some reason, he thought. *Maybe he went somewhere else, anywhere else but here.* His optimism was beginning to wane, but he carried on with his quest.

He stumbled over a dead Yankee still holding a piece of bread in his stiff hand. Flies swarmed around the Federal's face, and over the bite still clenched in his teeth. Impulsively, hunger gnawed at David's belly. His mouth flooded with saliva. He pulled the stale bread from the dead man's hand, brushed the dirt and mold off, and shoved it into his own mouth without allowing himself to think or feel, but to just remain numb. He picked a path between craters, roughly circular and rimmed by bodies missing arms, legs, and faces. Odd bits of cannon shells marked the ground, as did the body parts, blown into soft flesh by the force of the blast.

The wind picked up, and the sky released icy drizzle. No birds chirped, and the only sound were distant murmurs of a few men milling around the field, cutting through the unnatural silence.

One soldier, who was taking the boots off a dead National, looked up at him.

"All a Yankee's worth is his shoes!" he proclaimed with a smile.

David watched in morbid fascination as the young Rebel struggled to remove the dead man's frock coat, too, but the sight repulsed him. A short distance away, the corpse of a Confederate soldier sprawled across the body of a Yankee officer, the Rebel's hand still inside the officer's greatcoat pocket. It took David's overwrought brain several seconds to make sense of the scene. The Rebel must have been plundering the Yank's lifeless body. The canister killed him right in the midst of his thieving act. The Yankee wore no shoes. David couldn't find a corpse within sight who did.

The sky opened up. Droplets fell but David didn't notice. He stumbled through the mass of bodies while pulling his little horse behind him, and stopping occasionally to tell Renegade it was all right, it would all be all right. The reassurance sounded hollow to his ears.

Most of the Union soldiers' belongings had been picked over, but he found an Enfield rifle lying beside one and claimed it for his own. His fingers traced the tiny crown engraved into the stock. He rummaged through the dead Federal's clothing and took the cartridge box he found as well. He stuffed it into his coat pocket and stood, barely aware of the icy rain that trickled down his neck and seeped into his shirt. Dusk tinted the sky to deep purple. It was now too dark to continue his search. He needed somewhere to stay for the night.

David led Renegade over to a cluster of trees and tied him. He pulled several branches together to construct a makeshift shelter. Because he had left his company hastily that morning, thinking he would find Jake with no effort, he'd assumed he would either spend the night in O'Neal's camp or return to the cavalry later in the day. But instead, he was forced to bed down on the cold, wet ground. His belly cramped with hunger. He was tempted to fight Renegade for the few blades of grass the horse found, but instead spoke softly to him and then curled up under the thin branches. He closed his eyes, unable to pray or think, unable to even move. Finally his exhaustion pulled him into restless slumber.

When morning came, David forced himself up from the damp earth. He led Renegade to a puddle for a drink, sifting the mud out between his fingers, sipping in a few swallows that did little to ease his sore throat. The scene before him had hardly changed from the previous day, except more men were on burial duty. They worked with precision, loading the corpses onto wagons and dumping them into mass gravesites. Crows and vultures perched on the fence line, and darted in to pick at the bodies lying in the field. The hogs were still there, too. David wondered why they hadn't eaten their fill by now.

He staggered through the muddy field, taking up his ghastly undertaking where he'd left off the night before. His stomach growled, but he was too numb to care. Faced with his own mortality, his head spun, making him so dizzy that he stumbled at times.

Some of the bodies, stiff with the rigors, had swollen and burst open from the force of gases inside them. The pungent, overpowering smell of death prevailed. At times, the stench forced him to cover his nose and mouth with his handkerchief, thus protecting himself from breathing in the deadly vapors. He noticed two soldiers lying side by side, and knew they were Louisiana Zouaves by the way they were dressed. To him, they still looked noble in death, their red fez hats lying beside them, and their scarlet trousers tied with blood-soaked blue sashes. With their brightly-colored uniforms, they must have been easy targets for the Federals.

Two men a few feet away started insulting him.

"Know why you never see a dead cavalryman, Joseph?" one asked.

"Why's that, Ben?" the other responded.

"Because they never see any fightin', that's why."

Both soldiers sneered at David. He nearly turned away, but the reason he was in the middle of this death-infested field in the first place surged up inside him and his fingers clenched into fists.

"Ain't you had enough fightin'?" he asked. "Ain't all this," he swept his hand wide over the field, "enough? Y'all got to pick a fight with your own side, too?"

The men had the grace to look ashamed, but as David continued his search, guilt flooded over him.

I should have been involved with the fightin', he thought to himself. *I should've been there beside Jake.*

The pale sun peeked out momentarily from the last of the storm clouds. He noticed something sticking out from under a dead Yankee, so he pushed the corpse over with his foot. A huge centipede and several carnivorous beetles scurried off into the grass. There, glistening in the weak sunlight, lay a full bottle of Chesterfield rye whiskey. It appeared as if the Bluecoat had retrieved the bottle from his pocket and prepared to open it when he was hit in the back by grapeshot. David shoved the bottle into his coat pocket.

Three ragged infantrymen drew near enough for David to overhear their conversation as they walked by.

One said, "I know'd enough to head fer the hills when I seed trouble a-comin'. He who fights and runs away will live to fight another day, so they say!"

David stared at them. They glanced in his direction and went on with their discussion.

"Some fellers said they could hear the bombs explodin' a few miles away," another remarked, "but I didn't hear nothin' from where I was at."

"They call that 'acoustic shadows'. Right strange, ain't it?" the third soldier asked, and the other two nodded in response.

David led Renegade closer to the trio. "Would any of you fellers know where O'Neal's brigade might've fought at?" he asked.

The three soldiers observed him. "Have you looked all over this here field?" one asked.

"Yessir, I have," he replied.

"Well then, you'll have to go search over yonder," another instructed. He pointed toward the Hawkins farm.

David tipped his slouch hat and led Renegade through the mud. As he walked away, he heard the three infantrymen continue their conversation.

"I found a pocket knife and a diary on one Yankee bastard," one of them said. "And I hope there'll be somethin' amusin' written on the pages."

"I got some picture trophies that I'll be sendin' back home to my wife," another added.

The third man said, "I reckon I can sell what I got and make a mighty fine profit!"

They all chuckled.

David made his way toward the forsaken battlefield he had been avoiding. From what the gravediggers had told him, nothing but horror waited there. He realized just how right they were.

The dry foliage and groundcover had acted as tinder, fueling the fire. Bodies lay naked, some charred beyond recognition as anything human. Ash covered everything in a thick, sooty layer.

David clutched Renegade's mane; his forehead leaned against the horse's side as he dry-wretched. He couldn't go on, couldn't look at those poor men who no longer resembled human beings.

The horse nickered, a comforting sound that stiffened David's resolve. With somber determination, he tied Renegade to a tree at the edge of the burned area and exhaled a deep, heavy sigh.

The morning sun shone down through wispy clouds, casting dancing shadows across the landscape, but it did nothing to brighten the ominous, dark cloud that hung over David. He couldn't keep his heart from breaking. Mindful of every step, he carefully made his way, looking into burned and blackened faces. Smoke still floated up from the ground in places. Hot spots heated the soles of his boots, remnants of the inferno that had blazed there.

Strangely, some areas had escaped the burn and remained intact. Around some of the corpses, leaves, twigs, and dry grass had been pushed away so the dead lay in cleared spaces. The peculiar phenomenon didn't make sense until David realized the soldiers, who were alive when the fire approached, tried in desperation to push the dry underbrush away, but the flames had engulfed them anyway.

Wondering if he would recognize Jake, if he might actually find him, David's throat tightened. His eyes stung from the smoke, but he wouldn't allow his best friend to be buried in an unmarked grave like his father might have been, so he kept pushing on.

A few feet away, a dead Confederate soldier lay near a charred tree. David drew nearer and immediately recognized him. His gut clenched and heaved, doubling him over, and he stared into the scorched, lifeless face of Robert Hall, the toothless soldier from Tuscaloosa County. Several minutes went by before he came to his senses and straightened up. He muttered a short prayer, asking God to save Hall's soul. Wiping the back of his hand across his forehead, he glanced back at Renegade, who was watching him with his ears pricked.

A wagon lumbered toward him. Five soldiers with spades slung over their shoulders shuffled along beside it. The undertakers had arrived.

David turned his gaze back down at to the blackened ground. An outstretched arm poked out from behind a singed mulberry bush. Curiously, he walked closer. His heart thumped in his chest, reverberating in his head. He knew. He knew who it was before he even looked, and the moment he had hoped would never arrive swooped down on him.

The soldier lay face down. David knew him instinctively, and immediately ran to him. Falling to his knees, he gently rolled him over and brushed leaves and ash off Jake's face. Jake's skin was untouched by the flames, but his mortal wound, a bullet hole, covered the right side of his head with dark, dried blood.

"Jake!" he screamed. "Jake!"

He gasped for air. Reality assaulted him, like a knife plunged into the middle of his heart. He threw his head back.

"Nooooo!" he howled, but his anguish dissolved into sobs. "No, no, no, no," he moaned, while tenderly brushing the leaves from Jake's cold, lifeless face.

The rumbling wagon approached and came to a stop. He looked up at the burial party.

"Reckon you found your friend," one of them said stoically.

David glared at the man he'd had words with earlier, unable to speak or respond now, too overcome with shock and sorrow.

"Your friend's done yielded up the ghost," another added.

Collecting himself, David looked back at Jake, at the dried blood plastered in his dark brown hair. When they were younger, they had cut each other with what they deemed a sacred hunting knife and smeared their blood together, vowing to be blood brothers until the end. With a deep, forlorn sigh, he wiped his face with the back of his sleeve. He laid Jake on the ground and, moving like a very old man, stood.

"We'll be needin' to load him on," another soldier said, pointing toward the wagon.

David saw that there were corpses already heaped up in the back of the bed.

"I want to help y'all bury him," he said, his voice filled with distress. He drew several more heavy sighs, attempting to contain his sorrow.

"Why don't you collect any valuables he might have afore we take him," the first man said.

Dumbfounded for a moment, he stared at the ground, but finally knelt down beside his deceased friend.

"It's okay, Jake," he muttered. "You're gonna be okay."

While the other men looked on, David fumbled through Jake's pockets and discovered the buckeye Jake had kept for good luck. The chestnut didn't bring luck to his best friend after all, and he gently replaced it. He found the bag of tobacco Jake had brought along for

146

barter and the pocket watch with Callie's picture inside the lid. He stuffed them into his own pockets. Checking Jake's holster, he discovered a Colt Army still strapped inside. The sight of it infuriated him. The despicable Yankee had shot Jake in cold blood without even giving him a chance to draw. Pulling the gun and holster out from under Jake's body, David handed them to the wagon driver.

"I'll make sure these get turned in," the driver said.

David's shock was all consuming. Gazing down at Jake, his heart ached so badly that he wanted to cry. Taking several deep breaths, he sadly looked up at the waiting burial party and nodded. One man took hold of Jake's feet while another took his arms. They lifted him onto the pile of carcasses in the wagon.

"I need to fetch my horse," David said.

The others waited until he retrieved Renegade. Slapping the reins, the driver prompted his two mules. The wagon lurched forward, hauling its load of morbid contents through the ash and muck. David walked beside the wagon past the burned-out area and into the grassy field, where a freshly dug trench awaited. The undertakers lifted Jake's lifeless body from the heap of dead soldiers and lay him beside the trench. They repeated the process with each body until all the corpses were lined up next to their allotted graves.

David didn't feel heat, cold, or physical pain, but only grief, bewilderment, and disbelief, like he was trapped in a terrible nightmare and couldn't awaken. The undertakers lowered each dead soldier into the shallow trench. When they had gone down the line, they mounded dirt and mud over the gravesite. David forced himself to watch as they covered Jake's face, turning away while the men continued throwing dirt on the bodies. His eyes welled up, blurring his vision, but he wouldn't let the tears fall in front of the other soldiers. He walked over to a nearby tree and tied Renegade to it, allowing the horse to graze. He needed distance, something between him and that long, shallow trench behind him. Wandering through a thicket of trees until they blocked the sight of the mass grave, David gave in to the sobs he could no longer contain. Hot tears trickled down his cheeks, half-blinding him. Where it penetrated the trees, fading sunlight cast long shadows, adding to his diminished vision.

He tripped over a branch and nearly went down, then snatched up the branch and carried it out of the thicket.

Pulling his knife from his pocket, he broke off several brittle nodes, and peeled off the bark, shaving it away until the branch was fairly flattened. While he sat in the damp grass, he carved carefully, his left hand trembling as he completed his task. He carried his creation back over to the trench. The other soldiers had finished covering the makeshift mass grave over with dirt, and had departed on their morbid mission to gather more bodies.

David looked down at what he had just carved, a headboard for his lost friend, which read:.

RIP
Jacob Arthur Kimball
Born 8-20-1845
Died 5-3-1863

Not sure of Jake's actual death date, David decided on the third. He blinked several times to hold back tears. Compelling himself to proceed, he clawed a hole into the ground above where he approximated Jake's head to be. He stood the piece of wood in it, pushing the wet earth down around its base to keep it in place.

"You're on your way to paradise now, Jake," David muttered. "And I'll be jinin' you soon."

He straightened, staring blankly at the carved board. His head throbbed and his throat hurt, but he mumbled a short prayer, asking that Jake's soul be accepted into Heaven.

Renegade whinnied behind him. He wheeled around. A group of soldiers surrounded Renegade, so he ran over. The men turned to look at him as he approached.

"This here your horse?" one asked.

"Yessir," said David.

"Why, you must be a cavalryman," another said, raising an eyebrow. "Whatcha doin' over here?"

David glanced back over his shoulder at the long grave.

"Oh," responded the soldier. "Come to bury the dead."

David nodded, his heart clenching within his chest.

"Why don't you come with us?" another soldier offered. He had a short, thick beard and a long mustache. "We heard the Yankees left their campsite in a hurry, and we found out where it is!"

David frowned. He wasn't certain if he was ready to leave just yet.

As though he could read David's mind, the bearded soldier said in a gentle voice, "T'ain't nothin' you can do for him now, son."

"Come with us!" the first soldier yelled, and ran off.

"We gotta hurry! It's nearly dark out!" another shouted, following the first soldier across the field.

David hesitated, glancing back at the gravesite, but the bearded soldier was right. There was nothing David could do for Jake anymore. Jake was gone, and no amount of sitting and wishing would bring him back.

He mounted Renegade and followed the other Confederates. They traveled for nearly half a mile until they reached the rumored camp. The other four soldiers scurried around the abandoned site, collecting discarded booty.

"Coffee!" one squealed, jumping up and down while holding up a cloth bag. "I found coffee!"

"There's cans of food over here!" another one exclaimed. "Lobster, peaches, and 'maters!" He lifted a demijohn, uncorked it, and took a whiff. "And beer!"

"Hey!" the bearded soldier called out. "I found a bottle of wine and some cigars! From Havana, no doubt!" He noticed David still atop his mount. "Git down off'n that critter, dandyman, and claim your prize!"

Reluctantly, David dismounted, and walked over to the bearded soldier, who handed him the spoils before turning to hunt for more treasure. Other Rebel soldiers appeared on the scene, proving the rumor had spread.

David walked around the campsite, discovering a tin of coffee and another bottle of whiskey for trade.

Suddenly, an entire hoard of Confederate soldiers invaded the campsite. He'd lost his opportunity. The camp would be stripped clean in moments. He returned the bearded soldier's plunder to him, walked back through the group of scrounging Confederates, and retrieved Renegade, leading him toward the turnpike.

Unsure whether or not he should attempt finding his way back to the Stafford Rangers in the now complete darkness, David opted to wait until morning. He returned to Jake's grave and set up a makeshift camp similar to the one he had constructed the previous night. His heart ached and his head throbbed from lack of food, water, and sleep. He laid back in the damp foliage, closing his eyes, trying not to think, but his mind couldn't deny the harsh reality. Tears oozed from his eyes, scouring his cheeks raw. Finally, in desperate exhaustion, he fell asleep.

He awoke several times during the night, shivering, and listening to the wind blow through the canopy of leaves above. When dawn finally arrived, he stood and stretched the stiffness from his body. His newly-acquired belongings bulged within his pockets. He pulled out the buckeye Jake had given him, wondering if it still held any good luck, since the luck in Jake's buckeye had obviously given out. He put it back in his pocket anyway and withdrew the pocket watch. The front was dirty and dented, but the eagle was still embossed. David ran his thumb over the creased cover and then pushed the button on the top. The watch clicked but didn't open completely. With his fingernail, he pried it the rest of the way. The face was cracked; the timepiece had stopped working at two-thirty. Was that when Jake had actually met his maker?

Inside the lid, Callie still shown in all her glorious wonder and confidence. David's heart beat fast in his chest. Thank God her picture hadn't been destroyed. He snapped the watch shut and slid it back into his pocket, his safe-hold.

He stashed the whiskey bottles, coffee and tobacco pouch in his saddlebag. His fingers encountered his Testament inside and pulled it out.

"Reckon I don't need this anymore, do I, Renie?" he asked his horse.

Renegade looked up at the sound of his name, but immediately went back to grazing, tugging enormous mouthfuls from the ground as if he knew he wouldn't get a chance to eat again for quite a while.

David frowned at the little Bible he held in his hand, which Josie had given to him for his birthday. He'd believed in it and the God whose words it contained. He'd prayed to that God, pleading with the good Lord to keep Jake safe. But God had decided not to acknowledge him, that he wasn't worth listening to.

"How could you forsake me?" David yelled up at the sky, his voice riddled with pain. "Lord!" he cried, "How could you forsake the both of us?"

Through his sobs, his anger seethed. In a fit of rage, he grasped the Testament and tried to tear it in half, but was unable to, so he threw it on the ground and stomped on it a few times. He turned away to gaze off down the turnpike for several minutes. Forcing himself to calm down, he took in several gulps of air. He looked back down at the small Bible, its black cover nearly concealed with dirt, and pushed it around with his foot. Guilt consumed him, not because of God's wrath, but because he knew if Josie ever found out what he'd done to the Bible she had given him, she would never forgive him. He knelt down, picked it up, brushed it off, and stuffed it back into his saddlebag.

"Maybe someone else will have a use for it," he reasoned to Renegade, who turned his head to look at him. "Because I sure as hell don't anymore."

He mounted his steed, rode over to the gravesite, and sat there in the saddle for several long minutes, gazing down upon the headboard he had carved. Finally, after drawing a last heavy sigh, he turned Renegade toward the turnpike and started the solitary ride back to his company with his head bowed, for he was unable to look behind him.

The recollection of the past two days made his throat constrict. He tried his best to hold back the sobs, but they forced their way out. It was his fault Jake had died. If it hadn't been for him, Jake never would have come all this way to Virginia. If not for him, Stella would still be alive, and Jake never would have joined the infantry.

It's all my doin' that he's dead, David thought. *I'm the one who's responsible for all of this. I might as well have pulled the trigger myself.*

He spurred Renegade into a trot as burning tears of anger and guilt streamed down his dust-covered face. Two deaths, both within weeks of each other. Both unintentional, but both still his own doing. Tom Caldwell's death might have been an accident, but David could never forgive himself for what he had done to Jake. His beloved friend. His brother. He would never be able to live with the shame and the torment. And he would never, ever spare the loathsome Yankee who shot his best friend, whoever he might be.

Because of David, King Arthur was dead.

Let us cross over the river, and rest under the shade of the trees.

Stonewall Jackson, May 10, 1863

Chapter Eight

Oblivious to all time and space, David rode back to the cavalry, allowing his weary mind to wander. Renegade plodded along a narrow road surrounded by thick woods for hours. Finally, horse and rider reached Company A of the 9th Virginia Regiment. David found his messmates' campsite, half expecting Jake to grin up at him from one of the fireside logs. Knowing he would never see Jake's grin again slammed into him so hard that he doubled over Renegade's neck. The horse skidded to a stop and David fell out of the saddle, catching hold of the stirrup before he hit the ground. The knowledge hit him again. Jake was never coming back.

David slid the saddle off Renegade and tied him out with the other horses before making his way to the tents. No one else seemed to be around. He draped his saddle over a log and fell upon the dank earth, draping his arm over his eyes to block out the morning sunshine, but he was too exhausted to sleep. Before long, other troopers returned, their muffled voices growing louder with their approach. He recognized his two messmates talking, so he pulled himself up.

"Hey, Summers is back!" Michael exclaimed as he and John drew nearer.

"Where've you been?" asked John with a smile.

David swallowed hard. His throat hurt so badly it made his eyes water. His messmates looked at each other and sat beside him.

"I went over to where the fightin' was," he mumbled. "I went lookin' for Jake."

"Did you find him?" asked Michael.

David nodded, unable to speak.

"Reckon he's seen the elephant," John said to Michael.

"Reckon he's seen a whole herd," Michael said.

"I...I...found him in a burnt-out field...and helped to bury him... because he's dead."

The finality of his own words jarred him. He clenched his teeth, fighting to hold back his sorrow, and looked up at the other two, who sympathetically gazed back at him. David knew by their expressions that they had both seen more than their share of destruction.

"Right sorry about your friend, son," John said softly.

Michael nodded. " We're a brotherhood of sufferin', all right. Now Kimball's in a better place than we are." He glanced at John, who nodded.

Heaving a heavy sigh, David shrugged, not sure anymore if the Heaven he'd been brought up to believe in really existed. His messmates unexpectedly sprang to attention, so he followed their gaze to an approaching officer, rose to his feet, and came to attention as well.

"Private Summers," Major Barnett said, his voice stern.

He put his hand to his hat before releasing it. The three soldiers stood at ease.

"I need to have a word with you. Come with me."

"Yessir," David replied.

He followed his commander to the officer's tent, entered behind the major, and stood in silence, his mind and body numb.

"You missed roll call for three days in a row, and you were unaccounted for in camp. As far as your superior officers are concerned, you are guilty of desertion. Are you aware of the punishment for such a crime?" the major asked, his voice booming.

"No, sir," David responded.

"You could be court-martialed, Private. And if found guilty, you could serve jail time, or even be hanged." The major looked at David with piercing eyes, his anger apparent.

"I didn't desert, sir," David explained. "I went to find my friend."

"Your leavin' without permission is desertion, Private, and certainly no way for a soldier of the Confederate cavalry to behave." Major Barnett's voice softened slightly. "However, since this is your first offense, and since you have returned to duty, I am reprimandin' you to picket duty for the next three nights, and you will be assigned to root detail for the next three days." The major glared at him. "Dismissed," he growled. He threw a salute and stomped out.

Slumping over in submission, David exited the tent, enduring inquisitive stares from the other cavalrymen. He returned to his messmates, who squatted near their small campfire. They stood when they saw him coming.

"What happened?" asked John, his blue eyes sparkling.

"I have to do picket duty and root detail for three days," David replied with a frown. "I don't even know what root detail is."

Michael chuckled.

John shook his head in disgust. "I'll be back in a while," he said. "Michael, see if'n you can find somethin' for this feller to eat." John flopped his slouch hat onto his head and shuffled off.

"There ain't much around, but I might have some blue beef, if'n you want it," Michael said.

David accepted and forced himself to eat the pickled beef Michael offered him. It was the most revolting thing he'd ever tasted. He took the chunk of day-old cornbread his comrade handed to him and devoured it, his mind in a fog as he washed the grainy crumbs down with creek water he'd stored in his canteen.

"Thank you," he said, swallowing the last bit.

John returned from his errand. "I jist had a word with Major Barnett," he said, "and he's agreed to givin' you two nights of picket duty and one day of detail."

"How's that?" Michael asked.

"I explained to him what happened, and he decided to go easy." John's smile faded as he looked directly at David. "But if'n you go off a'gin, you'll be facin' the stockade. Or worse. He wanted me to tell you that."

"Thanks, Chase," David said.

John sat down and lit his pipe, but they were soon called back to duty by one of the buglers. The troopers saddled and mounted their horses, and spent the afternoon drilling. This time, they drilled with rifle fire and artillery, and many of the equines reacted hysterically. Renegade was no exception, for he had never been exposed to the loud boom of cannonade before. The noise continued to roll across the fields, and eventually he calmed down.

The air was filled with billowing puffs of smoke that smelled like rotten eggs. David did his best to ride out of them in an effort to avoid the stench. Exhaustion made him careless. He accidentally pricked several horses with his saber, nearly causing a stampede, which aggravated his superior officers.

After several hours of drill, the cavalrymen were released for supper. David led Renegade out to the field, removed his saddle, and carried it over to his campsite. He dropped it on the ground and dropped himself down beside it. He didn't care about the dust covering him. He'd find a bath in the morning. His head throbbed from lack of sleep. All of his strength had been drained away. He stretched out his long frame and pulled his hat down over his face, but sleep evaded him again. Finally, toward dusk, he dozed off, falling into a deep, fitful slumber.

He stood in the middle of a spacious field, surrounded on all sides by mountains. Two horsemen materialized, riding toward him over the ridge, but they resembled shadows. He couldn't make out who they were until they drew nearer. The first rider was an Indian with eagle feathers tied into his long black locks. The warrior stopped a few feet in front of David and stared down at him from atop his black and white spotted steed, but David was unafraid. The Indian turned his pinto and rode away. David watched until the Indian faded away and then turned to the second rider. After a moment, he recognized the face.

"Zeke, I'm all right," Jake said, smiling.

David awoke with a start.

"Time to put in the roots," Michael said, giving him a nudge.

With much effort, David pulled himself up, ran his hand over his face, and placed his slouch hat on his head. He saddled and mounted Renegade in a fog, trying to shake the grogginess from his mind. The dream he'd just envisioned seemed so peaceful, but reality bore down on him, making his heart wrench.

Overcome with melancholy, he rode over to the officer's tent, received directions to his post, and prompted his colt to the designated location northeast of the cavalry's camp. Finding a group of pickets, he exchanged acknowledgments. Gradually, he led his mount away from them, and chose a spot near a stream where he thought a despicable Yankee might attempt to cross. Perched atop Renegade, he watched the sun set behind thick woods. Nightfall approached. The woods quieted down, until the only thing audible was the distant chirp of crickets.

His eyes drifted shut, but he caught himself before dozing off. He dismounted. Withdrawing his boiler from a saddlebag, he poured some water from his canteen into it, and pried open the coffee tin he'd discovered at the Yankee campsite, but to his dismay, the container was empty. Holding the tin up to his nose, he took in several deep whiffs of the delectable aroma.

"Sure could go for a cup of coffee, Renie," he sighed.

Renegade merely blinked his long eyelashes, half dozing.

As darkness settled in, strange sounds presented themselves, sounds he didn't recognize. Reasoning that they must be coming from native animals, he wondered what kind of unusual beasts thrived in the Virginia woods.

Renegade nickered softly at the sound of rustling nearby. David spoke to him in a low, calm voice and climbed into the saddle. If something was out there, his chances were better on horseback. He sat listening, his head bobbing as he fought off sleep. Renegade shifted his weight from side to side.

The minutes dragged by. Too tired to fight sleep any longer. David's chin fell onto his chest while he dozed. Suddenly, Renegade jolted under him, whinnying loudly. Startled into alertness, David heard a rustle in the foliage off to his left.

"Who goes there?" he hollered.

There was no answer. He pulled his Colt .44 from its holster and cocked the trigger, patting Renegade on the side of his neck to reassure him. Several minutes passed. Renegade relaxed beneath him, his heavy breathing becoming more rhythmic. David found himself being lulled to sleep again. He heard another rustle.

"Who goes there?" he yelled again, hearing the alarm in his own voice. His imagination ran rampant. What if it was some strange beast he'd never encountered before? Or worse yet, a witch? His heart thumped wildly in his chest.

"Don't shoot. I'm a friend," a voice called out.

Terrified, David sat staring into the dark abyss, his breath coming in tiny shallow gasps. He heard the trees rustle again. Suddenly, a dark figure emerged. It slowly approached, and he could make out that it was a horse and rider.

"Don't shoot, Johnny," the man said. "I come in peace."

David squinted to get a better look. He was tempted to pull the trigger, but the rider had a wide grin on his face, so he decided against it for the time being.

"Whatcha doin' in these parts alone?" he asked.

The man rode up beside him and stopped his horse next to Renegade. With a chuckle, he replied, "I'm scouting the area. But I ain't a Jessie scout, if that's your concern."

The two horses rubbed noses. David was able to distinguish that the intruder was about the same age as he was. He didn't recognize the man's accent. It sounded strangely foreign, although the soldier was wearing Confederate clothing, and even wore a shirt similar to his. The man stepped down off of his horse, but David remained in the saddle with his pistol poised.

"You can put that away, Johnny. I don't aim on giving you a reason to use it." He pointed at the pistol.

David released the trigger, but kept the gun in his hand. Something about this man didn't sit right with him.

"Where abouts you from?" he asked the stranger. The fact that he kept calling him "Johnny" made him uneasy.

"Fine looking animal you have here," the scout observed. "What breed?"

"He's a cross." David glanced around, wondering if he was surrounded by Northerners, ready to pounce on him at any moment and take him into custody. "But you didn't answer my question. Where…"

"Virginia," the young man interrupted. "Say, you wouldn't happen to have any tobacco, would you?"

David hesitated for a moment before he remembered the tobacco he'd taken from Jake's lifeless body. For some reason, the scout's casual demeanor eased him. "I do, sir," he said.

"I'd be willing to trade you some coffee for a taste of that delightful weed," said the scout, flashing another smile David's way.

"I'm willin' to take you up on that offer."

"But first, you'll have to put that pistol away."

David obliged and returned the gun to its holster.

The scout turned toward his horse, rummaged through a saddlebag, and withdrew a tin. He pulled the handkerchief from around his neck. Laying it flat upon the ground, he poured a mound of coffee beans into it, collected the cotton cloth, and presented it to David, who smiled in response as he received the offering.

"Thanks kindly." He stuffed the handkerchief into his saddlebag and took out the packet of tobacco. Pinching off a good portion of it, he handed it over to the man, who held his hand out to accept it. The scout smiled again. Holding his palm to his nose, he deeply inhaled.

"Ah!" He laughed, and the reassuring tone made David chuckle along with him.

"Much obliged, Johnny!" the scout said.

They hesitated for a moment, looking at each other.

The man held out his hand. "My name's Edward Logan. Sorry we have to meet under these circumstances."

He grasped hold of the soldier's hand. "David Summers," he said. "What is it you're scoutin' for?"

The soldier smiled. "If I told you that, I'd surely be dead!"

David gawked at him. "You're a Yankee?!"

"I'll be off now," the soldier said, "and leave you to your sentry duty." He saluted.

David pulled his pistol and aimed, but the man had vanished into the darkness. He heard him call out in the distance, and the scout's steed responded by trotting off into the woods.

It was too dark to see, and he had been too slow to react.

"Damn!" he spat, knowing the opportunity to kill a loathsome Yankee had escaped him.

Renegade nickered. Calming himself, David stroked the horse's neck as he sat in the saddle and allowed his anger to wane. He wondered if he had possibly been dreaming, whether the moment had actually occurred, and what time it was. The only timepiece he had was Jake's broken pocket watch. Alarmed by what had just transpired, he knew there wasn't anything he could do about it now. He bent down to check his saddlebag, rediscovering the coffee that had been given to him. Throughout the night, he repeated the motion, and warily waited for Edward Logan to return with a hoard of Federals.

At long last, dawn presented itself, so he returned to his company. Arriving barely in time for roll, he fell out with the other soldiers, dead on his feet, and drowsily responded when he heard his name. Following roll, he managed to eat a few morsels of food the cavalry provided for breakfast before he returned to his site and reclined back against his rolled gum blanket. His eyes quickly drifted shut, but he was soon awakened and requested to go to the officer's tent.

He dragged himself over to where a small group of soldiers congregated. The sergeant handed him a knapsack and directed the group of offenders to a field east of camp. Wearily following the others, David tried his best to stay awake while ignoring their conversation, for he knew if he confessed his offense, desertion, he would be scorned by all those around him.

It didn't take long before he found out what root detail was. With the others, he spent the entire morning searching the countryside for wild onions, poke sprouts, lamb's quarter, dandelions, garlic, mustard, and artichokes. He didn't mind it so much, except his head was ready to burst from lack of sleep.

Near midday, the penalized troopers walked back to camp. Thinking he would finally get a chance to rest, he flopped down on the ground to sleep. Minutes later, the bugler summoned them to drill. David groaned. His head throbbed, and his pulse echoed in his ears. Dragging himself to where he had tied Renegade, he slowly mounted and rode to the field. To his dismay, the cavalrymen were called to drill all afternoon. The hours seemed like days, and David made many mistakes, including charging the wrong way several times. Enduring scolding from the officers, as well as laughter and teasing from his comrades, he was finally released and allowed to sleep for a few hours before he was summoned again for picket duty.

He obediently mounted Renegade, but was still too tired to think clearly. The throbbing in his head had subsided to a mild ache. Softly coaxing and praising his horse, David returned to the same spot he had occupied the previous night. He soon found himself distanced from the other pickets, but was comforted with the knowledge that this time, he actually had some coffee, as Michael had boiled a few beans for him. David poured the lukewarm fluid into a tin cup, smelled the robust aroma with relish. Closing his eyes, he sipped the dark fluid slowly, savoring the familiar flavor he hadn't enjoyed in almost a year. He gnawed on a piece of hardtack, thinking tree bark probably tasted better. The night drifted by. A few field mice occasionally scurried in the grass, but thankfully, no strangers appeared. He had too much time to think about Jake's premature demise, but it didn't lessen his own self-blame and loathing. Because he was so exhausted, his mind easily wandered. He wished with all his heart Jake was there, and missed him tremendously. Attempting to rein in his feelings, he failed. Tears streamed down his face. He wiped them away with the back of his hand and sniffed. The burn in his throat returned. He wished he was still in Alabama, and there had never been a war. The long night seemed to never end.

When dawn finally came, he made his way back to his company for roll call. Once he had freed Renegade of his saddle and tied him out, he fell down upon the ground. Unconcerned that he was missing drill, he slept the entire day away.

He awoke to John's gruff voice asking him if he wanted some supper, which suddenly made him aware of his intense hunger. The three messmates pooled their resources. They came up with a concoction of dried beef, onions, garlic, and peas, which they combined in a fry pan. Michael topped it with a layer of cornbread. Pretending to relish their creation, they ate, but David knew it was only a variation of the same thing they had eaten every day for nearly every meal. He sighed and ate it anyway, appreciative of the other two soldiers' efforts.

"You feelin' better now?" Michael asked. "I mean, about the state of things."

David looked at him curiously, but then understood he was talking about Jake. "Reckon it'll take me a long time to feel anything, let alone better," he replied, mustering a slight smile.

"We was wonderin' if'n you wouldn't mind writin' for us a'gin. That is, after you've sent your letters," John said before inserting a last forkful into his mouth. He evidently noticed David's confused expression, because he continued, "You'll be needin' to inform your loved ones of the loss."

"Me?" Such a responsibility was too monumental for David's torn soul. "I thought one of the officers did that."

"If you was Kimball's ma, would you rather hear the news from his friend, or from an officer of no relation?" John pointed out. He lit his pipe, blowing a puff of smoke up into the darkening sky.

David frowned. He knew John was right. It was his obligation to write home. "Reckon I'd best do it tomorrow, then, 'cause it's been nearly a week since Jake..." His voice trailed off.

"I'll clean up," Michael said. He collected the dishes and carried them away.

David rested his head on his blanket, trying to decide what he would write and how he would say it.

As though reading his thoughts, John said, "If'n you want, I'll help you come up with the right words to say."

"Thank you." David closed his eyes and soon fell back to sleep.

The following morning was Saturday, May 9. After roll, breakfast, and a short period of drilling, the men were allowed the afternoon to themselves. David had to force himself to write home, so after avoiding it by wandering around camp for an hour, he returned to his site, found his paper, borrowed a pen and ink bottle from John, and sat down to contemplate the situation. A nearby fiddler played "Old Folks at Home." David thought it ironic. Finally, he wet the nib and proceeded to write.

Dear Mr. and Mrs. Kimball,

I take pen in hand to sadly inform you with much pain and grief of the untimely deth of your son and my friend Jacob. He was killed at the great battle of Chancellorsvile on Sunday, the 3rd of May. It was unfortunate that Stella fell dead of old age nearly a week prior, and so he bravely took it upon him self to fight with honor along side the grand Confederate infantry. I my self found him and helped to put him in the ground after he had sustained a fatal shot in the head which took his life imediately and left him not to suffer. I put his name on a board at his head so you can locate him. I deeply sympathise with you for the loss of so noble a person as Jake was. You should be proud that he died in honor and glory, for there never was and shal never be again a more galant friend and soldier.

Your friend,

David Summers

David stared down at what he had written. Jake's mother would take to her bed with the terrible news. His father would never forgive him. They'd blame him forever for Jake's death. The stunt riding competition might have caused Stella's collapse, but David had gone along with it. He thought maybe he should change his signature, cross out 'your friend,' and write something else. But without a better idea, he left it.

When John returned from his game of horseshoes, David read the letter aloud to him. John replied that it sounded right nice and soon walked off, leaving David to write a similar letter to Callie. He took care to leave out any mention of the terrible night when Tom Caldwell was burned alive. He then wrote a letter to his mother and sisters, this time replacing the flowery words with instructions as to how they could send him some food, followed by a short apology for his hasty departure. Once he'd finished, he sealed all of the papers in envelopes, addressed them, and took them to the post.

As he walked back, he heard a mourning dove call from somewhere above in the trees. The sad sound made him feel very alone. Never again would he be able to share his thoughts, fears, joys, or sorrows with his best friend. Inevitably, his battle to fight back tears ended in vain, and they seeped forth.

In an effort to hide his weepy eyes from the other troopers, he collected a piece of lye soap and a towel, walked down to a nearby stream, stripped, and waded waist deep into the chilly water. He noticed his skin had turned a yellowish hue, since the butternut dye from his coat had bled through. After plunging his head under several times, he scrubbed his body with soap. The lye stung and scratched his skin. Careful not to get lather in his eyes, he rubbed it through his hair, dunked himself a few more times, and waded back onto the bank. While he dressed, he saw the yellowish hue to his skin had faded.

Upon returning to camp, one of his comrades approached him.

"Summers, would you mind writin' another letter to my wife?" he asked.

"Of course."

"I ain't got nothin' to give you, since we ain't got paid in months, but I can give you somethin' when we do."

David forced a smile. "That's fine. You don't have to give me nothin'."

He was happy to oblige, to keep his mind occupied. When nightfall came, he managed to sleep again.

The next day was Sunday, so the cavalrymen were allowed a full day of rest. He normally would have spent a portion of the day reading from his Bible, but not now. Instead, he stole into the woods and took nips from the Chesterfield rye whiskey he had found at the battlefield under the dead Yankee. He despised the vermin, except for the scout he'd met, and this curiosity made him hate himself even more. He mourned Jake's death more than ever. Even the warm sensation of liquor flowing down his throat failed to ease his horrendous pain and block out the memory. He spoke to no one, but sat alone, suffering in silence, pitying, despising, and reprimanding himself for allowing Jake to die. Ashamed, he avoided his messmates. They didn't understand, anyway. No one cared.

Stuart's entire cavalry congregated in fields near the town of Culpeper. David learned they had moved due to lack of forage at their previous camp, and he saw for himself how much healthier the pastures were. Releasing Renegade to graze, he watched as the horse lifted his head, snorted, and pricked his ears before trotting out as far as his lead rope would allow and burying his muzzle into the fragrant, emerald grass.

Not long after they made camp, General Hampton's brigade arrived. David's messmates requested that he be reassigned with them to the Jeff Davis Legion, or the "Little Jeff," as they affectionately referred to it, and to their surprise, Colonel Beale consented.

John and Michael presented David to General Hampton, an imposing man with a thick, bushy moustache and equally thick beard. The general assigned him to the same company as his messmates: Company F, otherwise known as the Dixie Cavaliers. He was then introduced to his commanding officers: Lieutenant Colonel Waring, a young man with dark, deep-set eyes and a dark goatee and moustache to match, Major Conner, and Major Ivey Lewis.

David was also introduced to some of his new comrades, including Champion Knapp, the quartermaster clerk, Timothy B. Chisholm, who, like Michael, was from Savannah, and Jefferson Hyatt, a Virginian.

Once he had settled in, he wrote a letter to his mother, notifying her of his new assignment, and requesting that she inform the local newspaper, as well as the recruiting office in Huntsville. He didn't care if Tom's uncle saw the notice and came after him. It was what he deserved. He considered turning himself in for Tom's murder, and mulled the idea around while he walked to the crest of a hill. The cavalry's horses below quietly indulged in the lush green grass, giving him a sense of peace. It was a drastic change from what he'd witnessed only a few days previously.

Suddenly, a loud cry went up behind him. He hurried to camp, where chaos was everywhere. The men looked distraught, their faces wrought with anguish. He found Alfred Crawford, one of the soldiers he wrote letters for, and asked him what had happened.

"We jist received word," Alfred said woefully. "Stonewall Jackson died yesterday." He wandered away.

David stood dumbfounded for a moment. Returning to his campsite, he found John sitting under a tree, puffing on his pipe, and staring off. Michael was weeping. The death toll continued to climb, and there was no end in sight. Now the Confederacy's beloved general, "Old Jack," was dead, too.

In the morning, General Lee issued *General Order #61*, which Lieutenant Colonel Waring read to the men during roll.

"With deep regret, the commandin' general announces the death of Lieutenant General T. J. Jackson," Lieutenant Colonel Waring orated. "Let his officers and soldiers emulate his invincible determination to do everything in the defense of our loved country."

One of the buglers, Charles W. Peters, played "Taps." The men stood in solemn mourning with their heads bowed and their hats held in their hands.

Overwhelmed by the tragedy, David felt completely powerless and alone. His heart ached, and with each day, he grew more despondent and depressed. He didn't have anyone to express his sorrow to except his horse, and Renegade could only communicate so much. One by one, he was losing everyone he loved. The romantic dream he had shared with Jake only a few weeks ago was now crumbling down around him, smothering him. It was like a smoldering fog surrounding them all and suffocating them. He longed for his family to write. The memory of their dear faces was the only thing that gave him hope. Painful, heartbreaking loss was all around, but somehow, it gave him more resolve. He knew he had to defend his homeland and family by repelling the Northern tyranny, at any expense.

The next few days were spent with endless drilling. On May 15, President Davis ordered a day of fasting to honor their fallen general, since it was the day of Stonewall Jackson's funeral. The cavalrymen wondered how an official fasting day was any different, because they were all starving.

David vaguely noticed how loose his clothing had become, but he remained in a haze, wrought with sorrow. He spent as much time as he could with his colt, riding him for hours around the countryside while trying to sort his thoughts, but to no avail. After days of solitude, his messmates cornered him.

"We know you're in mournin', David, but you have to put it behind you," John said, scratching his shaggy beard.

"Reckon I can never do that," he softly replied.

"J. E. B. Stuart lost a daughter not too long ago, but he's still carryin' on," John told him. "You should let him be an inspiration to you."

Michael said, "I spoke with my cousin yesterday, and he's fixin' to come over here around suppertime. You remember him, don't you, Summers?"

David couldn't recall, since everything seemed blurry. He shrugged.

"You'll know him when you see him," Michael said.

Just as he had predicted, David did recognize the trooper when he arrived.

"Heard tell you've been sufferin' from the melancholy," Thomas Jefferson Little said, greeting him with a smile. "We'll take care of that!" He pulled several cards from his breast pocket.

"Whatcha got there?" asked Michael.

"*Carte de visites*," Thomas replied. He handed them to his cousin, who gazed upon them and giggled. "They're imports from Europe," Thomas said, allowing the photographs to be passed around.

David took the cards from John and glanced through them. Blushing at the pornographic images, he quickly returned them to their owner.

Thomas chuckled at his reaction. "Reckon you're green, all right."

Uncertain as to what he meant by the remark, David scowled at him.

"Tom and I decided that what you need is some company with the fairer sex!" Michael proclaimed. "And since Tom's familiar with the surroundin' countryside, he's willin' to assist."

"Y'all have been talkin' about me?" David's self-consciousness grew.

John patted his shoulder. "We're concerned about you is all." A grin spread from under his shaggy beard. "Tonight after dark, we'll help you git your mind off'n your troubles. But for now, let's do some celebratin'!" He pulled a bottle from his pocket, exclaiming, "Tanglefoot!" as he opened it.

The troopers stood around in a small circle, holding out their tin cups and inviting him to pour a swallow into each one.

"To the cavalry," John said. "Twenty Yankee horsemen ain't no match for one of us!"

"Here! Here!" Michael and Tom toasted in unison.

The troopers partook. David wondered what they had to celebrate. He took a swallow and winced when the raw alcohol ran down his throat. Before the burn diminished, John filled his cup again.

Tom produced another bottle. "Try this," he told his cousin, who took the puncheon, grimacing as he swallowed.

"What is it?" he asked.

"Homemade treacle liquor," replied Tom.

Michael handed the flask to David, who took a sip of the strong molasses concoction. He coughed and passed it on to Custis Kerr, who had joined the party. For some reason, the thought of General Stuart popped into David's head, and he was glad the general, who was a teetotaler, wasn't around to witness their shameful indulgence. Besides that, their discovery could result in court martial for all of them.

He noticed several of the other men around camp were drinking as well, this being Saturday night. Custis shared his bottle of wine with everyone, and David decided he could spare one of his bottles, so he produced the partially consumed bottle of Chesterfield rye whiskey from his saddlebag. He told the story of how he'd found it, intriguing the other men, who seemed impressed, like he had actually killed the Yankee himself to obtain it.

After nightfall, the men saddled their steeds and stole out of camp. None of them had a pass, and all were aware of the penalty should they be caught. The Virginian directed them down a road while they laughed, sang, and exchanged ridiculous jokes. It was the first time David had smiled in days. Momentarily, he forgot his sorrow.

The five cavaliers approached a two-story clapboard house set back from the roadside and surrounded by clusters of trees and outbuildings. They dismounted, noisily laughing and singing as the liquor took effect. The troopers walked up the steps onto the front veranda, and the Virginian rapped on the door. A middle-aged woman answered.

"Well, hello, kind sirs. How may I be of service?" she asked.

David stood at the back of the group, too timid to step into the light. He thought she looked stunning in her red silk gown, her graying hair tied up in a black snood. From inside the house, someone plunked out "Jeanie with the Light Brown Hair" on the piano.

"Evenin', Miss Adalia," said Tom. "We would like to meet some fine young *nymphs de monde*." He pulled his hat from his head, sweeping it across himself as he bowed.

"Oh, please do come in," the woman invited with a smile.

The men walked past her into the parlor, and she closed the front door behind them.

"I don't recall seein' this tall one before," she said, standing so close to David that he backed away, shyly grinning with embarrassment.

"This here's David, and he needs some special attention, Miss Adalia," Tom explained. "He's sufferin' from the melancholy awful bad."

"Is that a fact?" Adalia said, a sympathetic smile on her handsome face. "Wait right here, boys."

She walked into an adjoining room. The soldiers removed their hats and stood awkwardly by the door, snickering as they eagerly glanced around. Adalia returned, followed by several scantily-clad young women. She took one of them by the hand and pulled her close to David.

"This is Miss Charlotte. She'll keep you company for awhile."

Charlotte smiled up at David. He was taken aback by her beauty. Her dark eyes sparkled.

She took hold of his hand, and sweetly asked, "What's your name, honey?"

"David, miss," he responded, his voice wispy with awe.

"Well Mr. David, why don't you come upstairs and show me Goliath." She pulled him toward the steps.

Glancing back over his shoulder, David stumbled on the stairs. The other troopers bellowed with laughter. He followed Charlotte to the landing and down a dark hallway illuminated only by a flickering lamp that sat on a table at the far end of the hall. Charlotte opened one of the wooden doors, pulled him inside, and closed it behind her.

David suddenly felt dizzy, only vaguely aware of what was happening and barely able to distinguish the piano still plunking downstairs.

Gently, Charlotte pushed him down on the bed. The candlelight flickering behind her made her thin white cotton dress nearly transparent. David felt a twinge of uncertainty, and a surge of guilt rushed over him. He tried to sit up but she put her hands on his shoulders, pushing him back down.

"Jist relax now, darlin'," she said softly. "Everything's all right."

She sat beside him on the edge of the bed, her breathing slow and even.

David's muscles unwound. He reached over and pulled her closer to him, drawing her mouth down toward his.

"No, darlin'," she said in a quiet, lilting voice, touching her fingertips to his lips. "You save all your kisses for your one true love." She smiled and stood. "Now don't you go anywhere. I'll be right back." She opened the squeaky door and slinked out.

The plunking piano music began to dull and fade. David's eyelids grew heavy. Jarring himself back into reality, he wondered how long he had dozed off. He stood, staggered out, and went downstairs to find his fellow cavalrymen sitting around the piano, some with girls on their laps. Miss Charlotte wasn't among them. They looked up at him as he entered, and broad grins spread across their faces.

"Thank you kindly, Miss Adalia," Tom said, and stood on wobbly legs.

The young women around him drifted off like falling autumn leaves.

"Why, it's our pleasure," she said, escorting them to the door.

The soldiers stepped out. As David passed her, she stopped him.

Patting his cheek, she said, "You're a fine young man and an upstandin' soldier. I'm sure you will do us all proud."

"Yes'm," he replied, bowing his head.

He wondered if Miss Charlotte had told her he'd fallen asleep. Or had he? He couldn't remember anything for certain. Hurrying past her down the steps, he quickly untied Renegade from the hitching rail and mounted while his comrades climbed up on their steeds. They started the ride back to camp, laughing and singing like before.

"Ain't nothin' better than enjoyin' some horizontal refreshment!" Tom exclaimed.

"That gal I was with had the biggest feet," Custis said, "and there ain't nothin' worse than a woman with big feet!"

"Not that you need to fret," Michael remarked. "She's jist a Cyprian." He looked at David. "You feel better now, don'tcha Summers?" He laughed.

Custis chuckled, and added, "Reckon Miss Charlotte found a way to make you forget your woes!"

David snorted. His head was still spinning, and he wondered if he could stay on his horse without sliding off. He also wondered what had actually transpired at Miss Adalia's bordeaux between himself and Miss Charlotte. His mind was in a fog, refusing to allow his memory to kick in.

"That she did," he replied, trying to sound bold, which prompted the men to giggle. "Why, she's absolutely breathtakin'." He looked over at the other riders, their faces nearly obscured by darkness. "Some kind of exotic, she is. From India or Persia, I reckon."

The others laughed hysterically. David looked around at them, humiliated by his remark, although he wasn't sure why.

"From India! That's a hoot!" Custis roared.

"She ain't that exotic," John said. "She's an octoroon."

"What's that?" David asked, his eyelids becoming heavy. He realized his speech was slurred.

"Means she's part darkie," Tom said with a chuckle.

David had heard the term "octoroon" before, but he'd forgotten its definition. Now it took hold. He suddenly felt nauseous. His stomach churned and his head spun as he comprehended what had happened. He had lost his virginity to a Negro. Or at least, he thought he had.

Morning reveille blasted. David awoke with a start, arrested by the excruciating pain in his head. He didn't remember falling asleep, or even reaching camp, for that matter. Attempting to sit up, he swayed for a moment, moaned, and fell back against the ground. Discipline would surely find him for missing roll, but he didn't care. He turned over and tried to go back to sleep

John kicked him gently. "Git up, David. You miss roll and we'll all be in a heap of trouble."

David moaned again, rolled over, and pulled himself up with the assistance of John's extended hand. Standing took great effort. He stumbled, but John caught him and stood him up straight.

"Come on," John said, allowing his young friend to lean on him while they made their way across camp.

David stood next to Michael, weaving slightly as he propped himself, splay-legged, unable to focus. He still felt drunk. He breathed, "Here," when he heard his name called, swaying between John and Michael until roll call at last ended. John assisted him back toward the tents.

"What's ailin' him?" asked Robert Campbell. "He ain't bein' a loafer, or playin' old soldier to git out of workin', is he?"

"Now, Campbell," John replied. "You know this is Sunday, and if'n he was playin' old soldier, don't you suppose he'd save it up for a day of drillin'?"

Campbell shrugged and walked off.

Michael returned with a chunk of pork fat and cornmeal and proceeded to fry the bacon. The smell reached David, who grimaced.

Michael noticed. "You okay, Summers? You're lookin' mighty green around the gills."

David responded by springing to his feet, running into the nearby field, and vomiting convulsively. For the remainder of the day, he fought off bouts of nausea and nursed his headache with a cool, damp cloth on his forehead. John woke him several hours later.

"How're you feelin', young'un?" he asked, concern evident in his voice. "Dealin' with those katzenjammers all right?"

David moaned, holding his stomach.

At one point in the afternoon, several cavalrymen decided to play a practical joke on another by putting gunpowder in his firewood so when it was lit, the campfire exploded, sending nearby troopers running for cover. John was especially amused. David normally would have found humor in it, but the noise was so excruciatingly loud that he thought his head would explode along with the gunpowder.

Custis came by. "You can always tell who's new to drinkin'," he remarked, handing David a mysterious pill. "Here, take this."

"What is it?" David whimpered, putting his hand to his temple. "Will it make my head stop hurtin'?"

"It's blue ball. Take it so you don't come down with an ailment the young professional lady might've given you."

David winced. He still couldn't remember much of what had transpired the previous night, but he didn't want his comrades to catch on to his possible deception, so he swallowed the tablet.

His self-loathing was still acutely prevalent. He should have insisted when Jake refused to buy a new horse. If he had, none of this would have come about. He deserved to suffer.

Days passed, and the men drilled. In the middle of the week, they held a boxing match, but David didn't wager. He wanted to keep his hundred dollar note as a reminder of what had occurred, and possibly save it for tuition, like Jake had suggested. His trousers had become too loose to stay up on their own, so he bartered a C.S.A. belt buckle from one of the men in exchange for writing a letter, and a belt from another who had taken it off a dead Yankee.

Orders came down to polish their sabers and saddles. All five cavalry brigades congregated together, along with six batteries of horse artillery. By mid-May, the entire cavalry consisted of over ten thousand men.

On May 22, the cavalry staged a review for the local townsfolk near the Orange and Alexandria Railroad depot at Brandy Station. It seemed like just another drill to David, but with more pomp, participants, and spectators this time. With much difficulty, he forced himself to concentrate on the present, and managed to get through the drill without stabbing any of the other horses. He saw General Stuart and his staff watching at the edge of the field, and felt confident he hadn't disgraced himself in front of their presence. But the cavalrymen were called back again to re-stage the drill.

David rode up beside his messmates, preparing for another advance.

"I'm gettin' mighty tired of these drills," Michael said as he pushed his slouch hat back on his head and wiped the sweat from his brow.

'Reckon ole Jeb is makin' us go through more drills to git us ready for the Grand Review," said John.

"When's that agin?" asked Michael.

"In two weeks," said John.

David sighed. He didn't know what a Grand Review entailed. He only wished the drilling would end.

On the evening of June 4, Major Ivey Lewis ordered David to deliver a dispatch to General Stuart, which wasn't unusual, since he had been summoned as a courier several times during the past few weeks. Although he was physically tired and emotionally drained from a long week of drilling, he obediently stuck the sealed envelope in his pocket, saddled Renegade, and received directions to the Culpeper Court House.

Once he rode up, he was awestruck by the enchanting scene. Belles in beautiful ball gowns of every color stood out on the lawn with officers attired in dress uniforms. Lively music floated through the air. The song was "Cindy," one of his favorites.

David couldn't help but smile as he dismounted. "What's all this?" he asked a servant, who took hold of Renegade's reins.

"Massa Stuart's havin' a grand ball, suh," the tall, bearded black man said. "He invited ladies from the whole vicinity. Most came by rail, all the way from Richmond."

David raised his eyebrows and grinned at the slave. "Is that a fact?" he asked.

"Sho is." The servant smiled with a nod before tying Renegade to a post.

With eager anticipation, David sauntered toward the courthouse entrance and absorbed the sumptuous sight. The grounds, illuminated with Chinese lanterns, invited him closer. Southern gentry milled around in the warm evening air, the hum of their genteel conversations filling his ears, along with the clink of goblets tapping together. The sky glittered with fireflies, and the lawn was swathed in candlelight. Another song commenced. David recognized that melody as well: "Cumberland Gap."

He climbed the steps and entered the courthouse, immediately enthralled by what he saw. Couples in ballroom attire danced joyfully in the center of the room, swirling in time to the melody like wispy dandelion seeds floating in the breeze. Several musicians congregated together toward the back of the room, and they appeared to be enjoying themselves just as much. Chatter and laughter intermingled with their lively music. Chandeliers of flickering candles hung from the rafters, and the sweet scent of perfume drifted through the air.

David made his way through the crowd, suddenly mindful of how ordinary he looked. Bashfully, he smiled at the ladies, but they haughtily glanced over him before turning away toward their escorts. He noticed a table of wine, punch, and viands off to the side, which sparked his voracious appetite. The thought crossed his mind that perhaps he could sneak a few tidbits into his pockets on his way out. Spotting General Stuart, he made his way over to him.

"Sir," he said with a salute.

The general turned from the belle he was conversing with, noticed David, and saluted back.

"I have orders to deliver this to you personally." David handed him the envelope that had been sealed with wax.

"Very good, Private," Stuart said.

The general didn't seem to recognize him. Disappointed, David saluted again and awkwardly remained at General Stuart's side, waiting for a response. Stuart turned away. Without knowing quite what to do next, David stood there for a few seconds before deciding he had been cold shouldered, so he turned and made his way back toward the door.

He paused to watch the musicians, who were surrounded by admiring ladies. They stopped their performance momentarily, allowing for applause before proceeding to play "Ring, Ring the Banjo." Two fiddlers enthusiastically sawed on their instruments. A dark-haired, mustachioed man plucked away on his banjo, and a mulatto servant smiled widely as he played the bones. David remembered what the other troopers had told him about General Stuart's mulatto footman, Bob, and about the banjo player, Sam Sweeney, who was said to be the brother of the man who had actually invented the banjo. He also heard that General Stuart was a music lover who never missed an opportunity to be entertained by his musicians. If only they had a guitar, he might find the courage to go up there and sing alongside them, but his heart was too heavy for him to feel exuberant enough to sing. He wished Jake was there to see the grandiose scene. It was so dazzling that he felt like he was in a fairy tale.

He glanced around the room, reminded again of how out of place he was. The young ladies looked upon him with disdain, obviously repulsed by his shabby appearance. The musicians began to play "Cavalier's Waltz," prompting dancers to swirl around in synchronized whirlwinds. To his dismay, the food table was too far away for him to attempt thievery without being noticed, so he reluctantly turned and went outside. He met Colonel Von Borcke on the way out, and discovered by standing next to him that the Prussian was enormous. The colonel recognized him immediately.

"I'm looking forward to racing your little horse!" he said, laughing, and walked into the courthouse.

David was left alone on the portico. Once again, he wished he could be a part of the celebration, but instead, he let out a sigh, climbed up on Renegade, and rode off into the darkness.

The following morning, he and his fellow cavalrymen mounted and rode onto a wide, level plain known as the Auburn Estate, which they were told was owned by John Minor Botts, a prominent Unionist. The number of troopers was immense.

One rider behind David said, "I'll wager ole man Botts is havin' a fit with all us Rebels tramplin' down his land."

The men around him chuckled at the thought. Excited cavaliers, some in full dress uniform, surrounded David on all sides. Under the sunny sky, a crowd gathered on a grandstand that had been erected on one side of the field. The audience consisted mostly of ladies from neighboring towns who, they were told, had been transported by train into Brandy Station via the Orange and Alexandria Railroad. Like noble knights, sans mail and armor, the cavaliers sat majestically upon their steeds, their heads held high, and their regimental flags rippling in the breeze.

Trumpeters on fine chargers announced General Stuart's arrival. Damsels floated from the stands out onto the field, strewing flowers before his path. The festooned general, leading a cavalcade of resplendent officers, galloped past the troops. His soldiers cheered thunderously while he rode down the length of the entire cavalry, which stretched for nearly two miles, and returned back to the florally-adorned reviewing stand.

The horsemen followed the commands that had been relentlessly drilled into them. Every squadron walked past the reviewing stand, saluting as they did so. A band began to play "Dixie's Land," and the crowd clapped, cheered, and shouted their approval. David's heart swelled with pride. All of the drilling was now put into perspective. He knew at that moment how appreciated he and his fellow cavalrymen were by the Southerners, and especially, by the ladies.

Lieutenant Colonel Waring rode up and down the line at a canter, inspecting the Jeff Davis Legion while other senior officers scrutinized their own commands. They ordered the troopers to ride the length of the field before circling back and trotting past General Stuart and his officers.

David glanced over at his commanders. Although they wore serious expressions, they also appeared to be pleased with the presentation. He and his comrades reached the opposite end and turned their steeds. Through the rising dust, he could make out the horse artillery drawn up in battery at the far end of the field.

Withdrawing their swords, the officers gave the order. The cavaliers charged, pulling their sabers and yelling wildly in a shrill, high-pitched screech that sounded like ten thousand coyotes yelping at once. Exhilaration raced through David's veins as the troopers galloped full speed toward the twenty-four guns of artillery, which fired upon them in return. Puffs of smoke and loud booms echoed across the field. The rounds were blank, but the spectators seemed to be unaware, because many of the women swooned and fainted into their escorts' arms.

With that, the Grand Review came to a close. The crowd flowed out of the stands, and the cavalrymen sat atop their mounts and congratulated each other on the splendid occasion.

David wished once again Jake had been there to bear witness. Perhaps, in some way, he had.

Later that evening, the men were informed that another Review was to be held, because General Lee had been detained from attending the day's events. The troopers were required to polish their tack and metal two days later for the benefit of the Commander of the Army of Northern Virginia.

On June 8, the Review was held between Culpeper and Brandy like before, but no civilians were present this time. General Hood's infantry came to watch the military exercise. While the cavalrymen rode past to take their positions on the open field of the Auburn Estate, the suntanned foot soldiers jeered at them.

"Come down off'n that horse!" one yelled. "I can see your legs a-danglin'!"

"Come out from under that hat!" another hollered. "I can see your ears a-wigglin'!"

"They're jist jealous of us because we git all the pretty girls' attention!" Michael yelled over at David, and flashed a grin.

The horsemen reached the open field and lined up in columns, their regimental colors rippling above them. Ordered to halt, they sat with all eyes on their commanding officer.

General Lee rode the two-mile line at a brisk trot. He searched out saddle-sore horses and deficient carbines, mandating corrective actions as he carried out his inspection. He came to a halt in front of Renegade.

"Is this the little horse that won the race I heard tell about?" he asked.

Stunned the magnificent general was speaking to him, David's heart leaped. He found it difficult to reply, let alone comprehend General Lee was actually addressing him. The general, dressed in flawless brass and gray, his white beard and entire appearance immaculate, gazed at him intensely. He didn't know if he was required to salute, so he just sat there, stupefied.

"Yessir," was all he could finally manage to say.

General Lee nodded, glanced over Renegade once more, and spurred his gray steed away. The cavaliers surrounding David turned to gawk at him. He looked at John, who winked at him.

"Reckon he's got plans for you!" Michael said, grinning as he raised an eyebrow.

David wondered what those plans were, and couldn't help cracking a smile. Although he'd given up on his fantasy of becoming a Pony Express rider, he hoped now to be chosen for some dangerous, daring mission on behalf of the Confederacy, since the adventure he and Jake had dreamed about seemed to have eluded him thus far. His utmost desire was to receive a perilous assignment, one nobody else was willing to take, because he was prepared to lay down his life for his beloved country. If that happened, there would be no doubt he would acquire exoneration for Tom's death. He wanted to die in honor and glory, just like his father and Jake had done. But he hoped, most of all, he wouldn't be sealed in an unmarked grave and forgotten.

Sitting astride Traveller, General Lee watched from the top of a hillock. General Stuart, with his usual flamboyance, wore a long, black ostrich plume in his hat, and his horse, Virginia, was adorned with a wreath of flowers around her neck. Stuart signaled; the bugles blared. Twenty-two cavalry regiments wheeled into columns of four, and three bands commenced to play "The Bonnie Blue Flag" while General Stuart led the parade of prancing horses. The cavaliers walked their mounts down the length of the field before turning into a trot. An immense cloud of dust billowed up from the ground. There was no mock charge against the guns this time, so following the reviewing maneuvers, the men were congratulated and released.

They led their horses back to camp, and celebrated the splendor of their review. The supply and baggage trains had been loaded, awaiting the cavalry's departure across the Rappahannock with the infantry, which was now encamped on the other side of a hill. Unbeknownst to David and his fellow cavaliers, however, an ominous presence lurked in the shadows. Morning would come much sooner than expected.

My principle is to kill a Yankee wherever I find him. If they don't like that, let them stay at home.

Confederate scout William D. Farley

Chapter Nine

"The Yankees are comin'!" someone shouted in panic.

David startled awake. A bugler blasted "Boots and Saddles" as he sprang to his feet. Heavy fog engulfed the early morning so completely he could barely make out silhouettes passing by. Men around him scurried through camp, pulling on their boots and gathering their horses. Everyone was yelling or giving orders at once. He heard distant explosions and pops coming from the northeast. Negroes leading horses to their masters ran by frantically. Several ambulances raced off in the direction of the gunfire.

"Git the canvas!" Michael hollered at him.

David gathered the makeshift tent, quickly rolled it up, and ran over to Renegade, who whinnied and pranced with excitement. As fast as he could, he saddled his colt, tied the canvas onto the cantle, and mounted. A bugler repetitively blasted the signal "to horse." Michael rode up beside him, directing him to their waiting company assembled on the road between Stevensburg and Brandy Station.

Major Conner galloped past, commanding, "Cavalry Forward! March!"

Bugler Jed W. Boggs blared the order, and the troopers started out at a rapid trot toward Brandy Station. The fog, thick as gravy, made it challenging to see the road.

David wondered where John had gone, but decided he was most likely caught up in the whirlwind of soldiers. "Do you think we'll see battle?" he asked Michael, who chuckled at his naivety.

"If'n there's Yankees," he said, "we'll see battle."

David gulped. This was the moment he'd been waiting for, but it terrified him. Although his mind was still groggy, his excitement grew, and within an hour, the horsemen reached their destination, tying in with Grumble Jones' brigade.

The fog dissipated somewhat, allowing them vague glimpses of a battle already in progress. The artillery line lay between Jones' and Hampton's brigades. Sporadically, the ferocious boom of cannons shook the ground, followed by muffled yells and screams. Officers shouted orders for the cavalry to form a line between a knoll on the side of a road near St. James Church and the edge of the woods. While they took their positions, Union horsemen charged them with sabers drawn. Regiments in gray met their advance, screaming the Rebel yell.

Confederate artillery poured grape and canister into the Yankees, sending some flying with horrible shrieks. The explosions scattered dirt and body parts in all directions. Sharpshooters picked off Federal riders who drew closer, murderously knocking the Bluebellies from their mounts. A line of dismounted Rebel cavalrymen fired upon the Yankees. Shrieks, shouts, gunfire and thunderous booms from the artillery filled the air.

Dred replaced David's earlier exhilaration. Prayers from the men around him punctuated the sounds of battle. He considered bowing his head in ritual, but then recalled how God had forsaken him by allowing his father and Jake to be taken. His anger burned. He'd kill every damned Yankee who dared cross his path.

"Soldiers of the Confederate States of America! The honor and glory of your country relies on you this day!" Lieutenant Colonel Waring bellowed at the top of his lungs while riding up and down the ranks. The troopers cheered in response, their voices filled with jubilation. The Jeff Davis Legion waited for the order.

"Draw saber!" Major Lewis commanded, withdrawing his own sword from its sheath. Holding it up in the air, he pointed the weapon out in front of him. "Charge!"

The cavalrymen burst forward like a forceful wave breaking onto a ship's bow, shrieking like banshees, their sabers held straight out in front of them. They thundered toward the opposing dragoons, coming together in a tremendous crash as their sabers clashed. Horses somersaulted, rolled, and threw their riders. Men, crushed beneath their mounts, cried out in agony. Troopers yelled, screamed, and cursed. The crackle of pistols, rifles, and carbines rang out in every direction. Friend and foe were hurled together in a combined stew of soldiers. The air was thick with smoke, dust, and the gagging, acrid smell of rotten eggs from the Howitzers. Confusion reigned over the field.

Adrenaline raced through David's veins. He met his first foe.

"Die, you bastard Rebel!" The Yankee screamed.

He slashed at David, who ducked, narrowly avoiding the point of the Yankee's saber. Another soldier in blue came at him on his left. David vehemently slashed out and the Bluecoat rode by, screaming in pain.

A sudden memory flashed in his mind. He and Jake jousted like regal knights when they were younger, and he always managed to knock Jake from his horse whenever he attacked on David's left side. Realizing his advantage, David thrust his saber at opponents who came up on his left. He grasped his pistol in his right hand, and fired into attacking Bluebellies before they had a chance to pierce him with their sabers. Bullets whizzed like hornets, but none found their way into David's flesh.

Renegade bolted through the melee, seeming to sense what was required of him. He dodged and maneuvered in and out of crazed Federals who galloped around him, some coming at him to intentionally make him throw his rider.

A Confederate trooper in front of David screamed out as a Union officer's saber found him. He fell from his horse, blood spewing from his neck. Swept along in the tide of charging cavaliers, Renegade jumped over him.

Rebel riders encroached upon enemy lines, trampling over Union cavalrymen and horses that lay piled up in writhing heaps in a ditch. Callous with his desire for revenge, David directed Renegade toward the terrible ditch and fired a shot into the head of a wounded Bluecoat.

The field was filled with turmoil, making visibility nearly nonexistent, except for the lurid flash of ammunition. Riderless horses galloped about screaming frantically. Men threw themselves at each other on the ground in brutal hand-to-hand combat, clubbing each other with the butts of their rifles.

A bullet whizzed by David's head, shocking him. His surprise turned to rage. He rode toward an approaching National. The man drew a bead on him, but he viciously slashed out before the Yankee had a chance to fire.

"You son of a bitch!" he screamed.

He lopped off the Federal's head, which flew off to one side. Glancing back over his shoulder, David watched in stunned disbelief to see the headless rider, still erect in the saddle, disappear into the dust and smoke. He turned back to see another Bluecoat coming at him, so he cut him down as well.

"They're leavin' the field!" he heard a rider behind him exclaim.

The cavaliers galloped after their retreating rivals, capturing as many as possible before they escaped. Those who surrendered were sent to the back with a motion, but whoever opposed was shot or stabbed, and

David didn't hesitate to shoot or capture his share of loathsome Yankees. The Rebels chased the retreating Federals into the woods before they were commanded to halt.

It was now midmorning. A strange, uneasy calm came over the field as the dust settled, and both sides reeled in shock. David looked out across the battleground, watching men from both sides run out, followed by ambulances, to carry away the casualties. Horses littered the ground. A few still clinging to life and screaming in agony were mercifully shot in their heads.

The heat of battle left him soaked with sweat. His damp clothing clung to his lanky body. The heat and humidity combined caused rivulets to run down his cheeks, so he wiped them away. He looked down to see blood on the back of his hand, as well as splatters of blood on his clothing, and wondered if it was from the Federal he had decapitated. Realizing he'd taken another man's life, a twinge of regret swept over him. He struggled with his guilt, reasoning that it was a Yankee he'd slain, the same despicable scum who had murdered his father and his best friend. Even though he felt remorseful, he believed his actions were justified.

The cavaliers dismounted. They checked their horses for injuries, so he did the same. Finding Renegade to be free of wounds, he drew a deep sigh of relief.

"Reckon this is jist a lull."

He turned to see John grinning down at him from atop his steed.

Michael rode up. "We was wonderin' where you went off to," he said.

"Got mixed up in the confusion, but I managed to thrash me a few of them," said John, his blue eyes twinkling.

The men were instructed to mount and prepare to move. After waiting for the road to be cleared of dead and dying Yankees, they set out at a gallop, their regimental flags rippling above them. The midday heat was unbearable, and the sun, a flaming orb overhead, felt like it was hovering only a few feet above them. Down dusty roads the cavaliers rode, past the train depot to a ridge, where they swung to the left flank. Almost simultaneously, Federal cavalry materialized on Fleetwood Hill.

General Stuart appeared in front of them. He drew his sword. "Give them the saber, boys!" he commanded.

The cavalry charged, a Rebel yell once again bursting from them, the earth trembling with the quake of beating hooves. Dozens of Federals went down at the onslaught. Others scattered at a gallop over the hill, but the Union artillery retaliated by firing a torrent of shells into the charging Confederates.

All around, men suddenly fell from their saddles, screeching in agony, but Renegade thundered ahead. Somehow, David and his messmates managed to stay together through the turmoil and ride through the storm of bullets unscathed.

"Fall back!" one of the officers yelled.

Reluctantly, David obeyed the command. He turned his colt, even though he wanted to keep pressing the Yankees.

The two armies engaged in a series of confusing charges and countercharges. Entire regiments rushed toward each other in a whirlwind, colliding in a swirling cyclone of firing, slashing horsemen that covered the hill. The Confederates regrouped and charged again.

David choked on dust. His eyes burned from the smoke as he fired at an oncoming attacker but shot the Yankee's horse instead. The animal shrieked and rolled forward, sending its rider head first into the ground. Rounds of canister exploded in all directions. Renegade managed to elude the Union soldiers and cannon fire. Somehow, he instinctively knew where the next attack would come from, so he avoided each assault.

Shells whizzed by, men screamed in anger and pain, horses shrilly neighed, and Minié balls whistled all around. Oblivious to the ominous peril engulfing him, David gave no thought to his own safety. He was driven with the desire to kill or capture as many Northern aggressors as he possibly could. Suddenly, he realized the Yankees were retreating, so he pulled back on Renegade.

"Git them!" John bellowed. He galloped past, followed by a legion of Rebels.

David spurred his colt in pursuit of the retreating Bluecoats. The cavaliers drove them through the woods like they were in a steeple chase. Into ditches, over fences, and through the underbrush they flew, tearing their hands, faces, and clothes on outstretched limbs as they ran down the cowardly Nationals.

General Hampton, on his steed, Captain, ordered the men to withdraw. Charles W. Peters relayed the command on his bugle.

Pulling Renegade to a halt, David watched the Bluecoats gallop off through the trees into the thick underbrush. He turned his colt, and headed back toward Fleetwood Hill.

John rode up beside him. "Did you ever see such a sight as that?" he said with a laugh. "All those yellow Yankees runnin' for their pitiful lives!"

"That's somethin' I won't soon forget!" exclaimed David. He looked around to see the smoldering earth laden with fallen heroes, both blue and gray, and surprisingly, regretful sadness crept into his heart.

The sun faded, drawing an end to Tuesday, June 9. The entire afternoon had been consumed with fighting. Exhausted, dust-covered, and thirsty, the cavaliers rode back to bivouac on the field where they had camped the night before.

In the morning, the rested troopers excitedly discussed the previous day's events with one another in an attempt to analyze and understand what had actually taken place.

"Seems that, before dawn, the Federal cavalry crossed over the Rappahannock and chased our pickets in," Michael said.

David listened with fascination as his messmate continued.

"Once the fightin' commenced, the Yanks purt near captured our artillery. But we captured three of their guns instead."

John informed that the Nationals were led by Brigadier General Pleasanton, and the Jeff Davis Legion had confronted the brigades of Colonel Benjamin F. "Grimes" Davis, who was killed early on in the battle, and Colonel Judson "Kill-Cavalry" Kilpatrick, who had acquired his nickname by disregarding his own men's safety. "Some of us estimate the battle lasted fifteen hours. Maybe even more."

Fifteen hours. No wonder David felt drained. He learned from another trooper that the Union soldiers he'd seen piled up in ditches were mostly from the 6th Pennsylvania, and recalled how he had fired into the head of one of them. He wondered if the man had perished because of it. But strangely, he didn't feel any remorse.

He and his messmates were told by an officer that the Confederate infantry was moving out, but the cavalry was remaining behind to rest and refit.

"General Lee came to the battlefield last night to assess the damage," he said. "His son, Rooney Lee, was injured in the fight, and General Hampton's brother was mortally wounded in a nearby battle. So was General Stuart's aide-de-camp and key scout, Captain Will Farley."

"That's a damn shame," John said with a slight shake of his head.

During roll, the men discovered some of their comrades were missing. One soldier, Robert Campbell, whom David had written letters home for, failed to answer. Once the men were released, he asked John if he knew what had happened to him.

"Got a deep gash in his head," John replied, "but he'll be all right. Reckon he's fixin' to go home to his new wife soon."

Feeling a twinge of jealousy, David wished in a way the same thing would happen to him. What better reception than to be considered a hero by his loved ones? It might be enough to outweigh the fact that he'd killed Tom Caldwell.

"Sure hope we don't have another *coup de main*," said Michael, referring to how the Rebel cavalry had been taken by surprise.

His ominous words sent a shiver down David's spine.

The next day dawned warm and sunny. After breakfast and roll, General Stuart gathered his cavaliers together to congratulate them.

"Comrades!" he began. "Two divisions of the enemy's cavalry and artillery, escorted by a strong force of infantry, tested your mettle and found it proof-steel. An act of rashness on his part was severely punished by rout and the loss of his artillery. Your saber blows, inflicted on that glorious day, have taught them again the weight of Southern vengeance."

Although many valuable lives had been taken, David felt only pride and superiority over the Yankees, and his comrades amplified the sentiment. But his confidence waned when he read an article in the *Richmond Enquirer* a few days later. It stated that "General Stuart has suffered no little in public estimation by the late enterprises of the enemy."

And the opinion expressed in the *Richmond Examiner* was harsher still, criticizing what it called the "puffed up cavalry."

"The more the circumstances of the late affair at Brandy Station are considered, the less pleasant do they appear...If the war was a tournament, invented and supported for the pleasure of a few vain and weak-headed officers, these disasters might be dismissed with compassion...The surprise of this occasion was the most complete that has occurred. The Confederate cavalry was carelessly strewn over the country."

After they read the berating editorials, David and his fellow troopers questioned whether they were as invincible as they perceived themselves to be. The Union cavalry, once a mockery, had now become a threatening foe; one that had to be reckoned with.

On Tuesday, June 16, General Stuart departed with the brigades of Beverly Robertson and Rooney Lee, now under the command of General John Chambliss. Before he left, the general issued a congratulatory order to his remaining troopers. An officer read it to them during roll call.

"With an abiding faith in the God of battles, and a firm reliance on the saber, your successes will continue. Let the example and heroism of our lamented fallen comrades prompt us to renewed vigilance and inspire us with devotion to duty."

David gulped. Was it his fault all this had happened? He wondered if the Jessie scout he'd met had caused the attack. *I should have chased after him*, he thought to himself.

The commanding officer informed his cavalrymen that they were to serve as a counter -reconnaissance screen, thereby preventing Pleasanton's Union cavalry from discovering General Lee's objective, which was to cross over into Pennsylvania. Within a few days, General Hampton's brigade, after being told to prepare three days rations, broke camp and departed north.

The day grew increasingly hot and humid. The men swatted at flies that bit them and their horses relentlessly. Some removed their hats and wiped trickles of sweat from their brows. Nevertheless, the horsemen did their best to distract themselves from their discomfort. While they rode, the Georgians sang at the top of their lungs.

"Sittin' by the roadside on a summer day,
Chattin' with my messmates, passin' time away,
Lyin' in the shadows underneath the trees,
Goodness, how delicious, eatin' goober peas!

"I wish this war was over, when, free from rags and fleas,
We'd kiss our wives and sweethearts and gobble goober peas.
Peas! Peas! Peas! Eatin' goober peas!
Goodness, how delicious, eatin' goober peas!"

The Georgians sang with such exaggerated conviction that David couldn't help but chuckle. Once he'd learned the lyrics, he happily joined in, and boisterously sang along, too.

Later on in the day, the horsemen learned from a courier that General Stuart and his brigades had engaged in a battle near the small towns of Aldie and Middleburg. Heros Von Borcke, Stuart's Prussian aide-de-camp, had been seriously wounded, and was expected to be incapacitated for quite some time. Upon hearing the news, David became greatly disappointed, since he had been looking forward to the day when he could race the colonel. Now he wondered if the opportunity would ever present itself.

The troopers continued their quest. They encountered a pontoon bridge the Confederate cavalry ahead of them had constructed. David clucked to Renegade, coaxing him to cross the Chickahominy River. He and his comrades rode on until evening.

Shots rang out through the trees. Hampton's brigade confronted a Union regiment. The men dismounted and fired into the fray. Thunder rolled overhead, and grew louder as a storm approached. Within minutes, a heavy downpour broke out. The countryside was swallowed in darkness, and the sky burst open in a thunderous downpour. Unable to see anything, the Rebels were driven into the woods, where they were forced to spend the night wet, cold, and miserable.

"This rain jist won't let up," Michael said through chattering teeth.

"My hands are freezin'" said John. "I'm havin' a hard time holdin' onto my horse's reins."

"Me too," David agreed. He shivered in the darkness.

Rain fell incessantly throughout the night and into the morning, drenching the men to the core. It was replaced by sweltering heat and humidity that afternoon. As night fell, a hailstorm erupted, pummeling the horsemen with stones the size of hens' eggs. Unable to set their tents up in time, some of the men pulled heavy overcoats over their heads, which provided their only shelter.

"Does this happen every night?" David wondered aloud.

"I sure as hell hope not," said Michael.

"At least we got our tent up in time," said David.

With only prepared rations to eat, he shivered in the chilly rain while he waited for morning to finally arrive.

At sunup, the overcast sky constantly released drizzle. The cavaliers mounted up and continued their march, reaching General Stuart's brigades later that afternoon. No fighting had taken place this Saturday, May 20, due to the inclement weather, so they rested and cared for their horses, seeking cover in the woods behind a stone parapet. The cavalry was now over five thousand strong.

One of the officers approached David and his messmates. "I'm officially tellin' y'all that if anyone is captured, y'all are not to release any information about our mission."

"Yessir," the three messmates chanted.

Peter and Custis approached their bivouac.

"On this day," said Peter," the great state of Virginia has split in two."

"I heard it might be happenin'," said Michael.

"The western half of the state is jinin' the Northern cause," said Peter.

"Where's our infantry?" asked John.

"They're makin' their way through the Blue Ridge Mountains," said Custis.

"That means our infantry is now on Yankee soil," John observed.

With a nod, Custis chuckled.

Another trooper overheard their discussion. "Our cavalry triumphed over the Yankees in Aldie and Middleburg," he said.

"How do you know that?" asked David.

"I heard two officers talkin' about it. They also said the infamous John Mosby had made an appearance, too."

David had heard of the "Gray Ghost" and his Partisan Rangers, a small band of guerilla fighters who were notorious for destroying Yankee railway and telegraph systems, stealing their supplies, and sabotaging their tactics. Mosby was a legend in his own time, but even though he was nearby, he remained elusive to David and his comrades.

Damp, chilled to the bone, and hungry once again, the troopers attempted to sleep, but they were awakened early, and alarmed to learn that Yankee cavalry was nearby. At eight o'clock, Federal guns opened fire on them. Artillery on both sides exchanged fire for nearly an hour.

Suddenly, the Bluecoats struck an ammunition chest behind Confederate lines. Shells exploded thunderously for several minutes, sending the cavaliers running for cover. Shrapnel sprayed, showering some of the men. They cried out in pain, and litter-bearers hurried out onto the field to carry the wounded off to the rear. Compelled to abandon their position, the Rebels retreated.

"Charge!" their officers yelled, and the Jeff Davis Legion attacked the Federals' left flank, but the Union soldiers drove them back. The "Little Jeff" re-formed and charged again, racing along stone walls that lined the narrow roads. Flying at their foes, the troopers slashed and jabbed wildly. They were forced to seek shelter in a large stand of trees, so they dismounted and fired into the Yankees, holding the line with the rest of General Hampton's brigade for over three hours.

A regiment of Nationals approached. They crossed a bridge that spanned Goose Creek, and bombarded the Rebels with artillery. As shells flew and burst overhead, the Yankee dragoons charged over a hill.

"Shoot them!" they screamed. "Take them prisoner!"

J. E. B. Stuart's entire cavalry was compelled to retreat back through Upperville. Refusing to give up the town, the cavaliers mounted and got into position.

Galloping along the line, General Stuart grasped his Le Mat revolver, and commanded, "Be steady and never break ranks!"

General Hampton ordered the Jeff Davis Legion to "right about wheel." They met the Union line, and charged while Confederate sharpshooters fired at the Yankees from behind a hill. The Bluecoats attacked, but David and his regiment counterattacked.

A confusion of close clashes jammed the road, and the men fought desperately with carbines, pistols, and sabers amidst great clouds of swirling dust. Artillery from both sides thundered in a constant roar. Pistol pops, shouts, and screams filled the air. Flashes of light from the cannons exploded through the thick dust. Horses ran in a confused frenzy, some with empty saddles, others dragging their dead riders behind them, their backs and saddles covered in blood. Sabers glistened in the sunlight that beamed through the billows of dust and smoke, like thunderbolts from Zeus, sent to strike down the unworthy. The men intertwined in a writhing mass of unfurled fury.

David fought off every attacking Yankee he encountered with brutal force. Regardless of his lack of sleep and food, exhilaration pumped through his veins like venom, making him keenly aware of what he felt driven to do. Beside him, one of his comrades, Champion Knapp, fell wounded from his horse, which had been shot out from under him.

General Hampton's brigade fought off the Yankees until, at last, they were called to retreat. The Confederates chased after them through Upperville, and on toward Middleburg. Along ravines, over ridges, and through woodlots they rode, jumping streams, screeching and whooping in their pursuit, and capturing all that fell. They rode with a vengeance through Middleburg, which was abandoned, with all of its houses and shops either closed or splintered apart. Finally, the Rebels gave up the chase and rode back to Ashby's Gap.

David looked up at the sun sinking behind the Blue Ridge Mountains. He stopped for a moment to take in the sight. The rolling hills rose above him in periwinkle hues, and the fading, amber glow of the sun outlined the upper ridge. He sighed from sheer exhaustion, taken aback by the astounding spectacle that reminded him of the hills back home. Distant artillery-fire jolted him out of his daydream. Fighting still persisted around Upperville. He gave Renegade a slight kick, and followed his comrades back to their makeshift camp.

The men were too tired to do anything but unsaddle their horses and fall upon the ground in dust-covered heaps. It wasn't long before a driving rain swept over them, so David and his messmates sought shelter under their canvas. He lay awake for a short time, listening to the steady drum of rainfall, and John and Michael's snoring, before dozing off himself.

In the morning, the cavaliers understood they had nearly been beaten and forced to retreat, which left a bitter taste in their mouths.

"Seems like the loathsome Union cavalry is rapidly becomin' every bit our equal," said John.

"Damn them all to hell!" cursed Michael.

General Stuart claimed victory, but the troopers knew better, even though their main goal was still intact: to screen the infantry's northern advance.

Two days later, after being instructed to prepare three days rations, J. E. B. Stuart's cavalry congregated in Salem, Virginia. General Stuart chose three brigades to travel with him: Hampton's; Rooney Lee's, now under Chambliss; and Fitzhugh Lee's. Generals Jones and Robertson were to remain behind to guard the gaps in the Confederate army as they traveled through the Shenandoah.

Just after midnight, the troopers moved out, four abreast, riding through the cover of darkness.

"I'm tired as an old work mule," John complained.

"I'm bored out of my gourd," said Michael.

David was too tired to respond, and Renegade plodded wearily beneath him like he was in a trance.

They rode throughout the day and into the night. Just past midnight, word came down the line, passed from rider to rider.

"The Bluecoats are blockin' the road ahead. We have to detour."

The riders turned north toward Glasscock Gap in the Bull Run Mountains.

When morning sunlight finally penetrated the gap, they were traveling single-file down a road no wider than a wagon. On each side, limestone rocks formed precipices of immense height. Trickling fountains sprung out from the crevices, and trees formed a dark canopy above them, so thick that rays of sunlight could only penetrate in a few places. The clatter of thousands of hooves, the creak of leather, and the clank of steel reverberated off the rocky walls. The thought crossed David's mind that the narrow passage they were in could be a mighty tomb for all of them if the enemy trapped them in this unforgiving place, but he kept his horrible thoughts to himself.

They made their way through the gap, which took all morning. Around noon, they encountered Yankee infantry, so they fired at the Federal soldiers who marched by. The column of passing footmen was massive, spreading from north to south as far as the eye could see.

Scouts reported that every road in the area was filled with marching Union soldiers. With no other recourse, General Stuart decided to fall back into the mountains for the night.

Rain fell throughout the following day. The Rebel troopers circled southeast, and found a clear path near Fairfax Court House, where "Fighting" Joe Hooker's Union headquarters had recently been located. That night, they camped southwest of the courthouse.

David was called to picket duty once again, so he dutifully mounted up. Riding out into the darkness, he heard a fiddler softly playing "All Quiet Along the Potomac Tonight." The song, about the death of a picket, caused a chill to run down his spine.

Riding far from camp, he met up with a few other pickets. Soon, he wandered away and came to an appropriate, lone position.

"Whoa," he said in a low, soft voice.

He gently pulled back on Renegade's reins. A cool breeze rustled through the trees. The moon above cast long, dark shadows across the ground. It was deathly quiet; not even a cricket chirped.

David shivered. Deciding to move around for warmth, he slid from the saddle, but stumbled in the dark. He noticed a round, white rock, so he knelt down and picked it up. Oddly, it was much lighter than a rock. He turned it in his hands. Empty eye sockets bore into him, and the bony teeth grinned at him from death. Impulsively, he screamed, and tossed the human skull away in a panic, which sent it flying over the field. Horrified, he suddenly became aware his surroundings.

Long white bones stuck out from mounds of dirt that at one point must have served as makeshift graves. Weathered woolen uniforms and knapsacks, still intact, clung to the skeletal remains. Cannonballs sat scattered about, an eerie reminder of what had happened here.

Realizing he was in a terrible graveyard, he shuddered. For some reason, the Yankee whose head he'd lopped off popped into his head. He glanced around, expecting the headless soldier to ride out of the darkness and attack him. An owl hooted. David nearly jumped out of his skin. Anxious to depart the frightening scene, he hurried back to Renegade, mounted, and prompted his colt to trot.

For the rest of the night, David walked Renegade along the side of a road, and carefully avoided the horrible scene of death. He had no need for coffee. His fright kept him wide awake.

When he returned to camp the next morning, he told Custis what he'd seen, and how he had held a dead man's skull in his hand, just like in a scene from *Hamlet*.

"Oh, that must be what's left of those poor fellers who fought over yonder last year. We're right close to Manassas. You didn't know that, did you, Summers?"

Wide-eyed, David shook his head.

Custis giggled. "Reckon you got a good scare, then!" He guffawed.

David scowled and strode away. He wanted to get some sleep before the orders were given to march again, so he managed to doze for a few hours before the alert came through the camp to proceed north.

General Hampton's brigade led the way toward Fairfax Station. General Stuart, in his usual regal grandeur, galloped past them. He soon returned, ordering a charge, and the cavaliers followed their *"Beau Sabreur"* with unquestioning devotion. They encountered a Yankee detachment of cavalry, and captured the entire regiment. Learning the Bluebellies hailed from New York, David asked one of his captives what the state was like.

"It's the most beautiful place you'd ever care to see," the Yankee informed him. "The trees turn the brightest colors in autumn, and the girls are all pretty and eager to keep you warm during the cold winter months!" The young man in blue smiled, seemingly unconcerned he was a prisoner, which caused his captors to scoff.

"Well, maybe I'll git up there someday," David said, "because I wouldn't mind seein' those pretty girls!"

They exchanged chuckles.

The captives were taken to the back, but were later released on parole. David understood then why the Yankee soldier had been so unconcerned about his capture. He had known he wouldn't be a prisoner for long.

The cavaliers rode to Fairfax Station. Upon arrival, they were allowed to help themselves to the abandoned sutlers' shacks. In a flurry, they swarmed down on the goods and devoured them eagerly, indulging in ginger cakes, lobster salad, wine, ale, and whiskey while their horses grazed. It was the first real sustenance they'd consumed in quite some time, since both passing armies had already trampled and used up the land David and his comrades traveled over. The Rebel riders found gloves, hats, and shiny new boots as well, and immediately put them to use.

They resumed their march, continuing on into the night. Exhaustion forced them into more frequent stops and slowed their forward progress.

Around 3:00 a.m., they reached the Potomac River, crossing at Rowser's Ford. The wide, ominous river roared at them.

"Gentlemen," one of the officers commanded. "Dismount and lead your animals across."

The horsemen obeyed. They waded out into the black water. David did the same, but as soon as he set foot in the rushing water, shockwaves ran through him. The icy water was much colder and deeper than he had imagined. Mimicking the other troopers, he held his ammunition above his head while he made his way across. The water threatened to rush up over his shoulders. He glanced back at Renegade, who held is head high to avoid the water. One man ahead of David was nearly swept away by the current, but he managed to free himself and get across. Some of the mules brayed in complaint but quieted under the roar of the rushing water. Finally, David reached the opposite bank and struggled to keep his footing. He comforted Renegade, and wondered if either one of them could endure much more. Shivering, drenched and dripping, he watched the rest of the cavalry follow. Braying mules lurched and strained. Some were nearly pulled into the current. The ambulances, after much difficulty, lumbered across. The guns almost went beneath the water, but the mules managed to pull the heavy artillery up and through the river. Amazingly, after over an hour, Hampton's brigade succeeded in crossing the wide river without any loss of men or munitions.

The troopers were now in Maryland, on Yankee soil. Following orders, they burned barges and mutilated boats. David didn't mind, since they belonged to the Yankees. The men set about their destructive task with all seriousness, for they knew they could be attacked at any moment. After they carried out their orders, they were allowed to sleep for a few hours before resuming their march.

While they traveled, the commanding officers passed the word to be on the lookout for free and escaped slaves, and to capture blacks they came across. Freedmen, or contraband, were to be returned to slavery. In accordance with President Davis' declaration on May 1, several weeks before, black soldiers who were caught fighting for the Union side were to be taken as prisoners of war. The declaration authorized their punishment; even their deaths.

The Confederates rode into Maryland. Along the route, they pillaged fields and knocked down telegraphic links connecting the army with the capital. They came upon the Chesapeake and Ohio Canal, and wrought as much damage to it as they possibly could. A few hours later, they tore up the Baltimore and Ohio rail line leading to Frederick. By mid-afternoon, they passed through Williamsport, and captured several wagons and teams from the enemy they encountered.

They reached Rockville. This being Sunday, the townsfolk were dressed in their church-going finery. As the cavalry proceeded through, sympathizers to the Southern cause waved Confederate flags, and cheered from upper windows and side streets. Hampton's brigade came upon an all-girl seminary. David and his comrades found themselves immediately surrounded by pretty young ladies in brightly-colored dresses. The cavaliers graciously accepted the girls' admiring glances. Many of the young women waved small, improvised Confederate flags, sheet music, and handkerchiefs, while others requested souvenir buttons from the soldiers' uniforms.

The butternut coat David wore wasn't equipped with elaborate brass buttons. Disappointed none of the fair maidens noticed him, he could only watch while they chatted, flirted, and pinned ribbons on the uniformed troopers while asking where they were from. Some of the horse soldiers exaggerated, claiming to be from various Southern states, thus convincing the young ladies that they represented every state in the Confederacy.

A girl in a lavender cotton dress with purple ribbons in her long, dark brown hair walked over to David.

"We are so very proud of you boys," she said, flashing a smile so radiant his heart melted.

Returning a shy smile, he replied, "Why, thank you, miss."

Custis and John snickered, amused by his reaction.

The girl held her hand up to him. "My name's Rebecca. Pleased to make your acquaintance."

He hesitated for a moment, then gently took her hand and kissed the back of it. "I'm David," he half-whispered, causing his comrades to chuckle even louder.

"I was wonderin', Mr. David, if you'd be so kind as to cut me off a piece of your hair." He gave her a questioning look. "As a memento, of course," she added. She brought her other hand from behind her back and handed him a pair of scissors.

Remembering the character from *Ivanhoe* of the same name, he wondered if this Rebecca was also a sorceress, and what intentions or spells she had in store for his hair. He could certainly see how brave men would fight for her honor. Grinning bashfully, he took the scissors from her and politely snipped off a lock.

As though reading David's thoughts, Custis asked Rebecca, "Whatcha fixin' to do with it?"

Rebecca looked over at him, still smiling. Custis' quizzical expression faded, and a slight, enchanted smile crossed his lips.

"Why, I do believe I'll make a bouquet with it, frame it, and hang it up in my bed chamber."

John raised his eyebrows, the corners of his mouth curling beneath his beard. He and Custis both looked at David, as did Rebecca, who flashed her same disarming smile at him. David could feel his face blushing. Once again, the other two soldiers chuckled at his reaction.

"Thank you kindly, dear David," Rebecca said. She handed him a sweet before pursuing another long-haired cavalier.

David sat stunned atop Renegade. For a moment, he couldn't hear anything but his own heart thumping in his ears. A trooper from the 2nd South Carolina rode in, bringing David back to reality.

"There's a supply train comin' this way," the trooper alerted them. "Sent from Washin'ton City. We reckon it's intended for Hooker's army."

The horsemen quickly pulled themselves away from their admirers and spurred after their quarry. It wasn't long before they caught up to the wagon train. Hungrily anticipating a feast, they whooped, screamed, and gave the Rebel yell. The surprised Union teamsters started to flee in panic. Some turned off onto side roads, while others at the end of the wagon train quickly reeled around and thundered back toward the capital. The raiders descended upon the frightened wagon masters, kicking up dust as they ran. They slashed their reins, produced pistols, and proceeded to gun down the teams and drivers, whose terrified mules galloped with such fury that the teamsters lost control. As a result, their wagons overturned, spilling their contents and flipping the mules onto their backs. Other wagons behind them collided, causing a pileup, and making it much easier for the Rebels to surround and contain them. The teamsters ahead of the collision lashed their mules mercilessly, and barreled back toward Washington, but the Confederate cavalrymen pursued.

As Renegade thundered ahead, David leaned down from the saddle and slammed the butt of his Enfield rifle on the ground to pack the powder, shooting at the retreating wagons as he came upright. Once again in the race, Renegade's gait was quick and smooth. For a moment, David marveled at the phenomenon. It was almost as if his little horse could fly. He nearly caught up with the end wagon before reaching a ridge. Pulling back on the reins, David abruptly forced Renegade to stop. The wagons escaped, and vanished down the road to the capital.

From the hillcrest, David and his fellow cavaliers could see the unfinished dome of the Capitol Building, and all of Washington City around it. They were too close to enemy territory. David made a sharp turn and galloped back to the captured wagons. The others followed. Troopers from Chambliss' brigade were already raiding the wagons of ham, sugar, bread, bacon, and whiskey. David and his comrades managed to filch some of the ham before being run off.

Stuart's cavalry proceeded to take inventory of the newly-acquired bounty. The U.S. Army wagons were brand new, the harnesses were in use for the very first time, and the mules were fat and sleek. Of the 150 wagons they had chased down, 125 of them had been captured, along with 900 mules and 400 teamsters.

The Yankees were paroled that evening, and released after they vowed not to return to duty as Union soldiers. The Rebel troopers fed their own horses the oats they had obtained, righted overturned wagons, and burned damaged ones. At sundown, they resumed their march north, but constant drizzle, compounded by the added hindrance of their captured wagons, made the journey painfully slow. As the Rebels traveled twenty miles to Cooksville, exhaustion ate away at them.

"Destroy the enemy's main war artery," General Stuart commanded.

His cavaliers demolished six miles of track, rolling stock, and station buildings belonging to the Baltimore and Ohio Railroad. By the time they were finished, the oppressive summer heat bore down on them.

A train rumbled toward them. The troopers heard it and ran for their horses in hopes of capturing and destroying the engine, but the alert engineer noticed danger ahead of him, so he pulled on the brakes.

The locomotive screeched until it came to a halt. Reversing direction, it disappeared around a bend before the Rebels could catch up to it. Several other trains appeared, but those engineers also observed trouble and escaped.

The cavaliers continued on to Sykesville, where they burned a bridge and cut telegraph wires. They resumed their march, bivouacking that night near Westminster.

David shared the ham he had acquired with his messmates. While the men settled in, worn out and dusty, his mind began to wander. He thought of Jake, and how he would have reveled in the day's excitement. Exchanging flirtations with the young women at the school would have delighted him, no doubt, and the Rebels' merry chase in capturing the wagon train would have had him talking about it for days. Instead, David was alone with his feelings, for it was difficult to speak about personal things with his fellow troopers, even with John and Michael. It just wasn't the same as confiding in his best friend. His heart ached with the realization Jake had been gone for nearly two months.

Pulling the pocket watch out, he clicked the cover open. There was Callie, staring back at him, radiant as ever. The sight of her face gave him some comfort. Hopefully, she was waiting for his return. He wondered if she had received his letter by now, informing her of Jake's untimely death. He wished for some word from home, but knew it wasn't likely to happen, since they were on the march. Lying down, he choked back sobs, and closed his eyes. Exhaustion quickly overtook him.

He was aware of bright sunshine surrounding him as he rode Renegade along an unfamiliar road, but he couldn't feel heat from the summer sun. Only its brightness was apparent. Turning a bend, he saw two girls, one taller than the other. Both had long flowing blond hair that glistened and sparkled with golden rays of sunshine. Their dresses glowed with vibrant, soft colors, like a rainbow, but brighter somehow. They were standing beside the road, clutching bouquets of purple, pink, and yellow wildflowers, and they looked up at him as he approached. Renegade came to a halt. The taller girl faintly smiled at David, and then the two girls fluttered, and turned into doves. They flew up into the sky, their bright colors fading to white as they disappeared into the clouds.

A horse whinnied. David awoke with a start. Realizing it had all been a wonderful dream, he rolled over onto his side, thought about the ethereal angels that had visited him, and pondered his vision's meaning. Gradually, his mind fogged over, and he eventually fell back to sleep.

The cavalry moved out early the next morning, June 30. Because Hampton's brigade was now responsible for protecting the captured U.S. Army wagons, they were positioned to the rear of the cavalry procession. Their equines wearily plodded along, dust billowing up around them in the sweltering heat as they traveled.

David and his fellow comrades learned from an officer that the Union army had replaced General Hooker with General Meade, and that they had crossed into Pennsylvania.

"Looks like all the farms have been abandoned," Michael observed as they rode.

"See how all the fences are made of big rocks cemented together?" John pointed out.

"I wonder why they call Pennsylvania the "Keystone State?" David asked.

Michael shrugged. "I wonder if'n the girls are as purty here as the ones in New York are rumored to be?"

"Girls in New York are purty?" asked John. "Where'd you hear that?"

"I don't recall. Someone back home, I reckon."

David wondered to himself how long he would be in this alien state, a sojourn itinerant in a foreign land. He didn't understand why the Confederates hadn't attacked Washington City when they were so close, or why the infantry hadn't appeared by now. The war was dragging on for much longer than anyone had anticipated, and to him, three months felt more like three long years. He admitted to himself he was ready to return home, for the possibility that he might soon be joining Jake in eternal repose daunted him.

Suddenly, he realized what was actually taking place, and his heart leaped. He was truly in Yankee land now. There was no turning back. The forbidding unknown that lay ahead terrified him. His palms started sweating. His heartbeat accelerated, pounding in his ears. An unwelcome thought crossed his mind: he might not live to see another day. He might not live to see home again.

If we oppose force to force we cannot win, for their resources are greater than ours. We must substitute esprit for numbers. Therefore I strive to inculcate in my men the spirit of the chase.

Confederate Major General J. E. B. Stuart

Chapter Ten

The Confederate cavalry crossed into Pennsylvania. By the time they reached Hanover, the troopers were gasping for breath. The warm, humid evening air, as thick as molasses, made David feel like he was breathing through a damp cloth, and he reckoned the temperature was nearly as high as it had been during the day. Swarms of annoying insects, attracted to the sweaty men and equines, relentlessly bit them and flew in their faces. David was no exception. He swatted at them, but they persisted without yielding.

Hampton's men lagged far behind Stuart's. More than once during the trip, the mules appeared ready to drop in their traces, forcing frequent stops.

Gunfire erupted ahead. A courier rode up and reported General Stuart had been captured. General Hampton ordered his panic-stricken Confederates to burn the captured wagons in case they were attacked. He led the Jeff Davis Legion up to the front of the cavalry. They galloped furiously and charged, hollering with such ardor that they took the Yankees by surprise. The cavaliers sought cover in the woods, dismounted, and fired at the Bluecoats, keeping them at bay.

David grabbed the Enfield rifle he'd found at Chancellorsville. He tore open a paper cartridge with his teeth, poured the powder and encased ball down into the muzzle, and rammed the entire contents down to the bottom of the barrel. He cocked the rifle, placed a percussion cap on the lock, and squeezed the trigger. All of this took a few minutes, but he got quicker at it with each shot. While he struggled, he noticed a trooper next to him who repeatedly rammed in charges.

Fool's fixin' to blow his damned head off.

"Reckon you've got ten or more in there already," David commented.

The young man gave him a questioning look.

"You have to bite off the end of the paper and pour it in or the powder won't ignite."

The nervous trooper hesitated. "Oh, yeah!" he responded. He emptied out the barrel and started over. This time, he managed to fire off a blast.

David hit what he aimed at until darkness fell. Veiled by the black cloak of night, Hampton's stolen wagons pulled out. Once the wagon train was at a safe distance, David and his fellow comrades rejoined it and escaped north. Following the skirmish, the Confederates learned from a courier that General Stuart had not been captured after all, but had escaped when his big blooded mare, Virginia, jumped over a fifteen-foot wide gully, leaving the pursuing Yankees behind.

The Rebels rode on throughout the night.

Slouching over Renegade, David's eyes drifted shut. He slumped over onto the horse's withers, pulled his hat back on his head, and grasped onto Renegade's mane to keep from tumbling off. Each time he succumbed to sleep, Renegade reared slightly, startling him awake.

"Are you doin' that on purpose?" he whispered to his horse. Whatever the reason, he remained in the saddle, unlike many others.

The horses plodded along with their eyes closed. Some of the drivers fell asleep. Their drowsy mules walked off the road and into ditches, pulling the wagons behind them. Some bucked, brayed, and kicked in protest of their hunger and fatigue. Several assigned soldiers rode up and down the line in the dark, looking for delays, but they were barely awake themselves. A few men slept while their horses jumped over fences, sending them sprawling, but even then they were too tired to awaken. As the hours passed, some of the men slid from their saddles, landing on the dirt road with a thud. David's messmates slightly snorted, but he was too tired to even grin. He didn't see any smiles on the faces of the others, either, although hysterical laughter would have greeted antics like this at any other time.

At last, dawn approached. General Stuart cantered alongside them, singing his battle song at the top of his lungs. His obedient soldiers, happy to see their commander alive and well, stirred themselves to sing along.

"Well, we're the boys that rode around McClellian,
Rode around McClellian, rode around McClellian,
We're the boys who rode around McClellian,
Bully boys, hey! Bully boys, ho!

"If you want to have a good time, jine the cavalry!
Jine the cavalry! Jine the cavalry!
If you want to catch the Devil,
If you want to have fun,
If you want to smell Hell,
Jine the cavalry!"

The lyrics inspired and rejuvenated David and his comrades. The troopers began conversing amongst themselves in every effort to stay awake. Gradually, the sky grew brighter, but the sun failed to appear. It remained hidden behind thick clouds, and once again, the cavaliers wondered if they would be riding through a rainstorm.

"Wish there was somethin' to eat besides dust," Michael complained while their mounts trudged along behind the wagon train.

"I surely could go for a dunk in a lake right about now," said John.

"And I wouldn't mind gittin' me some new boots," Custis added. He pulled one of his feet from a stirrup and held it in the air, revealing a hole clean through the sole. "These here are plumb wore out, and I weren't lucky enough to snag me a pair back in Culpeper."

"Well, if'n we ever git paid, I'll buy me two pairs of socks from the quartermaster, or from some lucky feller who got them from home," said Peter Smith. "Then I'll keep a pair, make the other one into puppets, and send them to my daughters."

David snickered at the thought of Peter drawing puppet faces on his socks.

"Seems the only one of us with any money is Summers," Michael noted. The men all looked over at David. "Whatcha fixin' to do with the grayback you won in that race?" he asked.

Hesitating for a moment, David realized he was the only one in the group who had been capable of earning rewards by racing and writing letters home, even though the practice of reciprocation had been outlawed by General Lee sometime before his enlistment.

"Well, I was thinkin' of savin' it up for college," he casually replied.

The other troopers laughed. He gawked at them, astonished by their reaction.

"Son, you'll be lucky if'n that gits you two cords of wood by war's end," John said. "Sorry to be the one to inform you."

David sighed. Even though his hope of going to school was just a pipedream, he held onto it as tightly as he did the $100 note. Against his desires, it seemed inevitable that he was destined to be a farmer all his life, and the thought made him heavy-hearted.

The horsemen reached Dover. It was the first day of July, and a hot one at that. They took time out to rest. The clapboard houses lining the street seemed lifeless.

Custis pointed out a broadside attached to a telegraph pole. "What's it say?" he asked David, who read it aloud to his fellow troopers.

THE ENEMY

IS APPROACHING!

I MUST RELY UPON THE PEOPLE FOR THE

DEFENCE of the STATE!

AND HAVE Called THE MILITIA for that PURPOSE!

A. G. CURTIN, Governor of Pennsylvania.

THE ENEMY OF SERVICE WILL ONLY BE WHILE THE DANGER OF THE STATE IS IMMINENT.

Custis chuckled and said, "Reckon we gived them a run!"

"I wonder how they like our way of comin' back into the Union!" Peter chortled. His black mare neighed, as if laughing along with him.

"Haven't encountered any militia," Alfred Crawford observed. "Could be we caught them unprepared."

John scoffed. "Oh, I doubt that. We'll be seein' those Yankee scoundrels soon enough."

Major Conner selected troopers to scout the area, choosing David and two heavily-bearded men David knew only from roll call as Cain and Evans. He tried not to stare at the long scar across Cain's forehead when he spoke to the man. Ordered to confiscate any horses they came across, except for those ridden by female travelers per General Stuart's explicit command, the three cavaliers rode off west of Dover. They took three bay horses from nearby farms and paid the farmers with Southern scrip.

"I'm hungry," Cain said after they'd ridden several miles.

"So'm I," Evans said.

David nodded in agreement. "Maybe there's vittles at that there farmhouse." He pointed at a small place not too far off. "Might be a chicken or two left in the henhouse."

They spurred their horses toward the little white house, eager to capture any discovered livestock. Suddenly, a shotgun blast rang out, whizzing a few feet past them.

"They're a-shootin' at us!" Cain exclaimed.

David sprang from the saddle and dragged Renegade behind a stand of trees for cover. The other two men did the same.

"Where's that comin' from?" Cain asked.

"Reckon somebody's in the house," David said. "There's chimney smoke." A second volley of buckshot confirmed his suspicion. "Let's get up there while he's reloadin'."

Leaving the horses, the three men ran for the small front porch. Pistols drawn, they entered the dwelling. David pointed to the fire still burning in the fireplace and placed a finger over his lips. The main room contained a small pine table and two wooden chairs that stood against one wall. Against the opposite wall was a sideboard with enclosed cupboards sitting on top of it. They crept through the tiny two-room house, but failed to detect any Yankee sympathizers.

"Musta skee-daddled," Cain said, opening cabinet doors. They discovered the cupboard was full of flour, sugar, and salt, so they snatched up its contents.

"I'm headed for the henhouse," said Cain. His boots clomped on the hardwood floor as he left.

"I'll check the smokehouse," Evans volunteered, and followed Cain outside.

"Careful..." David shouted after them, for he had the eerie sensation that whoever had been shooting at them was still in the house. He swung around on his heels and cocked his pistol. Slowly, deliberately, he walked across the room, his boots clunking against the floor. He reached the small bedroom. Pausing near the doorway, he held his breath, listening carefully for a sound. The room had a double bed in the center of it, and against one wall stood a walnut chest of drawers. A round mirror hung from another wall. Tiny azure flowers decorated the wallpaper.

A slight whimper, like that of a puppy, came from under the bed. David's heart leaped. Curiously terrified, he knelt down, and gingerly drew up the worn patchwork quilt. A young black woman gazed out at him, her wide, dark eyes bulging with fright, and her hand clamped over her mouth.

David frowned. Rising to his feet, he commanded, "Come on out of there," and braced himself for the worst, just in case she was armed. The woman hesitated. "Come on," he repeated, this time more gently.

He heard her rustle under the bed. Slowly, she emerged, and stood up on the opposite side. Her delicate features accented her small frame. She wore a brown gingham dress, and her curly black tresses hung down to her shoulders. She appeared to be young, maybe sixteen or seventeen at best. David noticed her belly bulging out from beneath her dress.

"Please, missa," she whispered. "Please don't hurt us. We'll give you anythin' you wants. Jus' leave us be!" She motioned him away with her slight hands like she was using them as two little brooms to sweep him out.

He looked at her, bewildered, but held his Colt Army steady. "Are you in a family way?" he asked.

She nodded, seemingly embarrassed by the question.

There was a commotion outside. Cain entered, holding a rope and the shotgun David assumed was the weapon that had fired at them. He was followed by a tall black man. Evans brought up the rear, concentrating his pistol at the man's head.

"Lookee what I found out yonder with the chickens!" he exclaimed.

Cain came across the bedroom to the young woman.

"Well, what do we have here?" he asked, reaching out to touch the young woman's cheek.

She abruptly turned away. Cain snorted at her reaction. Turning back toward the black man, he proceeded to tie the man's hands behind him. The young woman let out a sob.

David felt a twinge of pity for her, but swallowed the emotion. The order about capturing any free Negroes still stood. Going against regulations could result in his own death.

Cain tied another rope around the freedman's neck. He led his quarry outside, and the others followed. Evans brought over the horses. Sniggering, he climbed up onto his mount, took the rope from Cain, and tied the loose end to his saddle.

"Let's see if'n it works!" he said, grinning.

He spurred his horse, forcing the man to fall to his knees, and dragged him for a few yards.

Amused, Evans yelled, "Git up, fool! You've got a long walk ahead of you!"

The man obeyed, choking on dust and the rope. He gazed sadly at the young woman, who stood quivering beside David.

Cain climbed up onto his horse. "Summers, hand her up to me," he ordered.

David looked at the young woman, whose eyes had filled with terror. He bit his lower lip and motioned for her to do as instructed. Tears rolled down her cheeks as she walked over to Cain's horse. Returning his pistol to the holster on his hip, David hoisted her up.

Grinning sadistically at the woman, Cain grabbed her thigh. She gasped, turned her head away from him, and stared at the ground.

"She's with child," David growled at him, revolted by Cain's salacious assault.

Cain smirked. "Well, then some lucky slave driver will git two for the price of one, won't he?"

Evans glanced over at David, and barked, "Go fetch a few chickens for us to take along."

He tugged on the rope around his captive's neck. The black man flinched. Evans laughed at him, but his face quickly contorted into a scowl.

"Reckon this whole entire war is your fault," he snarled. "You do realize that, don't you, nigger fool?"

The man said nothing.

His fists balled up so tightly they hurt, David turned and walked into the henhouse. He caught two pullets, and twisted their heads. He wanted to do the same to Cain and Evans. The birds flopped spontaneously while he carried them out by their feet and tied them to his saddle. Renegade shied, craning his head around to look at the dying birds fluttering against his flanks.

The young woman let out a keening howl.

David looked up as Cain pulled her head around toward him, forcing a kiss upon her face. He considered a confrontation, but if he told Cain to leave the poor thing alone, he would undoubtedly have to endure never-ending ridicule. He wondered if the scar on Cain's forehead was given to him by some other poor wench who had resisted his attack. Looking away in revulsion, he climbed up into his saddle.

The troopers headed back toward their brigade, with Evans in front, pulling the newly-captured slave. Cain followed, riding just close enough so the captured man could see Cain fondling his woman. David rode after the other two, with the three geldings behind him. He tried not to glance up, but couldn't help himself. From under the brim of his hat, he looked up to see the woman glaring at him, tears still streaming down her bronze cheeks, and he wished he was anywhere but where he was. He stared down at the earth passing beneath Renegade's hooves, but he felt the woman's unwavering gaze. He clenched his teeth, knowing he was incapable of saving her. If he tried, the other two men could easily overpower him, and he would surely be court-martialed. He had heard of other soldiers defying orders and being executed for their disobedience. Regardless of his disapproval, he wanted to see home again.

Once they returned to the cavalry, he handed the confiscated horses and dead chickens to another trooper, and the two bearded soldiers turned in the captured couple. Eager to distance himself from them, David rode back toward the wagons. He found John crouching near a stream, so he dismounted and allowed Renegade to drink.

"Well, did y'all find any horses?" John asked with a smile. He splashed water on his face, which beaded on his thick beard and ran off in trickles.

"And then some." David heard the sadness in his own voice.

John raised an eyebrow. "What happened?" he asked.

Expelling a sigh, David said, "We found a couple of darkies, but Cain, he...he tried to..."

John shook his head, like he knew what his messmate was trying to tell him. "Some fellers will take advantage of any situation." He straightened. "Son, this is war, and terrible things occur. It's jist the way God intended, I s'pect."

David frowned. John's words didn't give him any comfort, nor did they help him understand the events taking place around him. Explaining it away as God's divine intervention was too convenient. The concept was far too mysterious for him to grasp.

The men prepared to ride out. After taking fresh horses from the citizens of Dover and leaving their worn-out mounts behind, Stuart's starving Confederates continued on their journey.

Even though General Lee had issued *Order #72*, which forbade the theft or seizure of private property, the cavalry pillaged every field and farmhouse they came across.

"It's fair treatment for the havoc the Yankees wreaked on us at Fredericksburg and Chancellorsville," reasoned Michael.

David agreed.

The Rebels took chickens, hogs, garden vegetables, and fruits from the Northerner's orchards. They raided their bee gums of honey, emptied their smokehouses, gorged themselves on their cherries, and plundered their wheat fields.

By the time Hampton's brigade reached the ravaged fields, most of the spoils had been taken.

"It looks like the raiders ahead of us set the fences on fire," observed John.

"They likely gorged themselves on everything they could find," Peter grumbled.

"Every horse and wagon in their wake has been acquisitioned," said Michael. "Which leaves nothin' left for us."

David frowned as his stomach growled.

By mid-afternoon, the sun was a scalding red ball in the sky. All of the prepared rations had now run out. The men, not only hot, thirsty, dusty, and exhausted, were forced to deal with their hunger as well.

Upon reaching Carlisle, the cavalry learned from a messenger that they had to detour east and then north, due to the Federal infantry's hindrance of their passage. After discovering the buildings in town were filled with Yankee sharpshooters, General Stuart ordered the Union soldiers to surrender. They refused, so Confederate artillery retaliated by sending a bombardment, and set several buildings on fire, including the U.S. cavalry barracks.

Word of what had happened filtered back to Hampton's brigade. They rode past the smoldering town, staring in wonder at what remained. General Stuart's cavalry rode around the Union infantry, cutting telegraph lines and destroying more railroad track at every opportunity.

As darkness encroached, a full moon slowly emerged from behind the horizon, illuminating the sweltering earth below it. The cavaliers embarked on their fifth all-night march in eight days. David barely noticed the men around him, who were again falling asleep in their saddles, since he was doing everything in his power to prevent his eyelids from drifting shut. Even the distant sounds of barking dogs and gunfire didn't faze him, for he was saddle sore and weary. It felt like he had been riding for months on end with no rest to speak of, and with no apparent end in sight.

The exhausted troopers trudged over Yellow Breeches Creek, through Mount Holly Pass, and across rolling farmland. At dawn, they finally halted to rest.

David promptly tied Renegade. Completely worn out, he flopped down onto the ground and fell asleep almost as soon as his head fell against the lush, dew-covered grass.

"Private Summers!"

Major Lewis rousted him awake. David sat up too suddenly, causing his head to spin.

"General Hampton would like a word with you." He motioned for David to follow. "Bring your horse."

David pried himself up and untied his colt. The two soldiers walked to the front of the brigade where General Hampton was waiting for them. They saluted their superior officer.

"Private Summers," General Hampton acknowledged in a gruff, powerful voice, "I have a message for you to deliver to General Stuart." He handed David a sealed envelope. "He's somewhere near Hunterstown by now, so you'll have to ride quickly. And be on your guard. The enemy is all about."

"Yessir!" David enthusiastically replied.

Saluting the general, he sprang into the saddle, and spurred Renegade into a gallop, leaving the rest of his brigade behind. At long last, he was asked to perform a daring mission. His heart raced. Comparing himself to Paul Revere, he rode like the wind, hell bent for leather on his perilous flight.

Renegade galloped for several miles before slowing to a rapid trot. No Yankees presented themselves, and for that, David was thankful. Even though he craved excitement, his head throbbed from lack of sleep. Rounding a bend, he saw the officer's staff ahead of him. He spurred his colt, cantered up to the entourage, and found the general, who turned to see the approaching horse and rider.

"General Stuart, sir," he gasped as he saluted.

The general smiled, returning the gesture.

"I have a message for you from General Hampton."

He handed the envelope to the general, who nodded. The black ostrich plume on the back of Stuart's hat bobbed up and down. David stifled a grin. The sight was nearly comical, but he was so tired that anything would have seemed funny. Regardless, he couldn't help but feel deep admiration for his commander.

"Thank you, Private," the general responded. He tore open the envelope, pulled the letter out, and read it silently. "Very good."

Glancing around at the other officers, David thought they appeared to be just as weary as he was. He looked back at the general, who scrawled something on a piece of paper, placed it in an envelope, and handed it to him.

"Make certain that General Hampton receives this personally. And tell him to be prepared for a major confrontation."

"Confrontation, sir?" he asked, realizing as soon as he spoke that he might be overstepping his bounds.

"Yes, Private," said the general. "We shall gallop toward the enemy, but we will trot away."

Awestruck by the general's confidence, David exclaimed, "Yessir!" with a salute.

General Stuart put his gloved hand to his brow, releasing him. Feeling a bit awkward, David turned Renegade and started back in the direction he had come.

"Private Summers."

He pulled back on the reins, taken by surprise that the general remembered his name. "Sir?"

"There is danger ahead of you, so travel with caution. I'm certain your steed will carry you through." The general produced a wide grin from under his thick, red beard.

David smiled in return. "Yessir!"

He spurred Renegade, who bolted into a gallop. Some of the officers hollered after him in delight. Hoping for another chance to race his little colt in order to impress them even further, David daydreamed about it, and rode at a canter for a few miles before slowing to a walk.

The road meandered over hills and through valleys, and the hot summer sun bore down, distracting him from his mission. Deciding he and his horse were due for a drink, he disobeyed orders, and led Renegade off the road for a few miles until he reached a stream. He dismounted and allowed the colt to suck in deep gulps of water, partaking in the cool refreshment himself. Once they had finished, he climbed back into the saddle.

Curiosity compelled him to ride eastward along the stream, so he led Renegade up onto a parallel road, temporarily losing track of time and his surroundings. Looking out across the fields, he observed heat radiating off the crops, reflecting like a wavy mirage. He continued to ride, staring at the road while he fought off sleep. Insects in the ditches made rapid, clicking noises. Butterflies fluttered over milkweeds, sumac, wildflowers, and goldenrod. The calls of meadowlarks and red-winged blackbirds filled his ears. He swatted away a fly and looked up. Bewitched by what appeared before him, he pulled Renegade to a halt.

Two girls, one taller than the other, stood not ten feet in front of him, their hands filled with wildflowers they had picked from the ditch. They gawked at him. He stared back in awe, and the recognition hit him: they were the two visions from his dream. The girls stood frozen, their heads covered with bonnets, their long golden hair flowing down around their shoulders, and their pale calico dresses fluttering in the faint breeze.

Stunned, he gazed at them in disbelief. Unable to breathe, he expected them to take wing at any moment. The taller girl faintly smiled at him, which shocked him even more.

Suddenly, he heard men yelling behind him, and the sound of thundering hooves approaching on the road. The tall girl held out her arm, pointing toward the woods across the road from where they stood. David spurred Renegade in that direction. He led his colt onto a deer trail, hid behind the cover of trees, and watched the taller girl direct several Union soldiers down the road. The Bluecoats galloped by and disappeared. Waiting until he thought it was safe, he led Renegade out of the woods and back onto the road. The two girls were still there, picking flowers. They turned to look at him as he returned.

"Ladies," he said meekly, touching the brim of his hat. "The Confederate cavalry is headed in y'all's direction. I recommend hidin' y'all's valuables and livestock." He grinned bashfully.

The little girl grinned back.

He heard the enemy dragoons returning from where they'd been sent. Spurring Renegade, he galloped as fast as he could to avoid the impending Federals. Four pursuers soon turned into ten, then twenty. They fired at him while they screamed and cursed.

"He's getting away!" one Yankee yelled.

"He's like a streak of lightning!" another one hollered.

David prompted Renegade by slapping the reins. The colt glided farther ahead of the pack. David turned onto the road toward Hampton's brigade, and rounded a bend with the Federals in hot pursuit. Before they had a chance to realize what had happened, they were led directly into the Rebel troopers, who immediately captured them. David galloped past his surprised comrades, who were traveling south. The Rebels let out a whoop when they understood what had happened. Sergeant Williams from Rooney Lee's brigade observed the ruckus, and caught David's eye by waving at him.

"Sergeant?" David called out upon seeing him. "What are you doin' here?"

"I'm deliverin' a dispatch," the sergeant replied with a smile. "But my ride wasn't nearly as adventurous as yours!"

Williams followed behind on his mount. David rode up to General Hampton, saluted, and presented General Stuart's envelope to his commanding officer.

"I presume you delivered the dispatch?" General Hampton asked.

"He not only did that, General, but I'll be damned if he didn't capture two dozen prisoners as well!" Sergeant Williams joyfully proclaimed.

General Hampton faintly smiled. "Well, for that, Private Summers, you'll be up for a promotion. Followin' this expedition, that is."

"Yessir!" David exclaimed.

Grinning gleefully, he saluted. After thanking the sergeant, he rode back to find his messmates, and excitedly told them of his adventure.

"You caught how many?" John asked with a chuckle.

"You saw what?" inquired Michael.

"I reckon they were angels," David said, referring to the two blond girls who he had just described. "One even helped me git away," he added with a sigh.

John and Michael laughed with amusement at his response.

"Too bad for you she's a Yankee," said Michael, who smirked at him. "It ain't likely you'll ever see her ag'in, anyway."

"Wonder what it all means?" John said, scratching his beard.

David sighed again. He wasn't sure if it was immaculate design. He only knew the angels had been there to guide him, and he wondered if it was a sign sent to renew his Christian beliefs. But why had his loved ones been taken? The whole episode left him confused. His weariness caught up with him, and his head whirled.

By two o'clock, the cavalry was a mile south of Hunterstown. Suddenly, Yankee cavalry appeared on the road. The cavaliers took shelter behind stake-and-rail fences. Sharpshooters fired from both sides. A squadron of Federal cavalry galloped toward them. The Rebels blew their attackers apart. Some of Hampton's men chased after them, but they were shot at with shells and bullets, forcing them to retreat, and a stalemate followed. The Confederates escaped, and continued their march.

David noticed how Renegade seemed to be favoring his right front leg, so he dismounted to inspect the hoof, and found a crack that spread down from the horse's coronary band. Alarmed, he notified Major Lewis, who told him to ride up to the regimental blacksmith. The Irishman, Michael O'Byrne, examined Renegade's hoof while David looked on, concerned for his colt's well-being.

"Oh, this doesn't look good," Blacksmith O'Byrne observed.

Becoming more worried, David asked, "What should I do?"

"Well, the best thing for this wee fellow would be to rest and stay off of that foot, but since that's not likely to happen, you'll be havin' to make do by rubbin' this ointment on his hoof three times a day." The gentleman handed him a small tin jar. "It would be best if you could wrap it, but since that's not likely to happen either, you'll be havin' to hope for the best."

David took the tin from the blacksmith, opened the lid, and looked at the creamy gray substance. Taking a whiff, he winced before replacing the lid. "What's in it?" he asked.

"Oak bark, chickweed, pine tar, dandelion root, and beeswax. 'Tis me own construction," the blacksmith announced proudly. He glanced back at Renegade's feet. "'Tis it true you've been havin' him shod every three or four weeks?" he inquired.

"Yessir," David replied, nodding.

Well, sometimes their feet get worn out from all the travelin'," the blacksmith said. "I'm afraid that if we're engaged in a battle, he won't be long for this world. That crack will split right open, and he'll be lame. And then he'll have to be put down."

David couldn't bear the thought of having to shoot his beloved little horse. Hopefully, he could spare Renegade from any strenuous activity until the crack healed.

By evening, they had delivered the confiscated wagons to the army's commissary officers, and Hampton's brigade learned they were four miles northwest of a town called Gettysburg. Finally allowed to rest, they were awakened at dawn the next morning. The hot summer sun appeared over the horizon as a flaming blood-colored ball. At the ominous sight, a feeling of impending doom came over David. From the comments of those around him, he wasn't alone in his premonition.

David rubbed the pungent ointment on Renegade's hoof, giving it four coats. He brushed his horse down with a curry comb, pulled some of the burrs out of his tail, and checked the colt's back for sore spots before inspecting his legs. Renegade nickered softly. David led him around in a circle, watching to see if he limped. Showing no sign of impairment, Renegade pranced behind him. David grew confident that he would recover, so he saddled him, mounted up, and joined his fellow troopers who congregated on the road, waiting for the command to march forward.

"I seen you lookin' over your horse," Custis said as David rode up to the assembled cavaliers. "He's all right, ain't he?"

"I reckon so," David said, forcing a smile. "Mr. O'Byrne gave me some ointment to put on his hoof."

"Well, I surely hope he'll be fine, because I never seen a man so attached to his horse afore," Custis teased.

Custis spoke true words. David was too attached to his horse. They had come a long way together. He only wished for the young stallion's recovery. The two of them had a bond no other horse soldier seemed to share with his mount. Although the other soldiers looked after their steeds with compassion, none of them seemed to have a problem replacing them or putting them down once they were worn out. But David and Renegade understood each other somehow. He loved the little colt. He could never replace Renegade. The Cherokees were right: his horse was special.

The Rebels assembled into columns on the road. At last, Charles W. Peters blew his bugle with the command to march. They rode throughout the morning. The farmsteads all appeared deserted. The every quiet unnerved David. Not a single bird chirped. It seemed like all the creatures on earth knew well enough to run away or hide. There wasn't a cloud in the sweltering July sky, which gave the hot sun a greater opportunity to scorch.

The band of brothers exchanged pledges while they rode, promising that if one of them came up missing at the battle's end, the others would search for him, assist him if he was wounded, protect his belongings, and notify his family if he was dead. David made the same solemn vow. He rode in silence. Some of the cavalrymen around him chewed relentlessly on plugs of tobacco, reminding him of the pouch in his saddlebag that had once belonged to Jake. He considered pulling out a twist and popping it in his mouth to relieve his anxiety, but decided against it. The tobacco might be better used for barter, like Jake had intended. Sorrow and uneasiness overwhelmed him, but regardless of his exhaustion, he also felt a pang of exhilaration.

Through the humid haze, David saw billows of smoke in the distance, and understood the smoke clouds were coming from both infantry's cannons. As he and his comrades drew closer to town, shots rang out.

"Should we take cover?" asked Michael.

"Naw," said John. "The perpetrators are too far away to cause us any damage."

The Rebels rode quietly, barely saying a word to each other, for they had been informed of a cavalry battle already taking place. David assumed everyone else was as nervous as he was, and thus, couldn't find their voices. The men were also told that the infantry had been fighting for two days. Finally, General Stuart's cavalry had arrived to assist them. The moment now presented itself for the Confederates to take control and overpower the Yankee tyranny. David and his messmates had discussed what they hoped would happen: they would vanquish the Army of the Potomac, capture Washington City, and put an end to this terrible war, once and for all.

The cavaliers were now three miles northeast of town. General Hampton's men arrived behind a ridge with Fitz Lee's brigade. David saw before him a wide field, and indeed, a battle already in progress. It was midday. The sun beat down so fiercely that he could scarcely breathe. Sweat trickled down his temples and back. The horses panted from the terrible oppressiveness. It seemed as though every horse and rider anticipated what was about to take place, because no one said a word; they all just stared out at the field.

A cannon boomed. David jumped. He felt the ground shake. Hoof beats thundered as soldiers on the field thrashed. Shots popped in rapid succession. Some bullets found their targets. Horses and men screamed in agony. The pungent smell of carnage reached David's nostrils. He winced. His heart raced faster, and his breathing quickened.

For some reason, the tall girl with golden, flowing hair appeared in his mind. He wondered if it was an omen, if the angel he had seen would soon be coming to take him. But with all the moral crimes he'd recently committed, he doubted it. He was certain his destination was eternal damnation. Perhaps his angel was really the Devil in disguise. He dwelled on that concept for a moment. Despite the oppressive heat, the dreadful thought made him shiver.

I could see the desperate and hopeless nature of the charge and the hopeless slaughter it would cause... That day at Gettysburg was one of the saddest of my life.

Confederate General James Longstreet

Chapter Eleven

Battle haze engulfed the weary Rebel troopers. Their regimental flags drooped in the sweltering heat, and their horses panted from the weighty, oppressive humidity. The soldiers sat at the crest of the ridge and gazed down at the terrific contest taking place in the field below them. Cannonade rumbled, belched, howled, and roared. Smoke-filled air glittered with red flashes from black powder explosions. For only a moment, a gust of wind moved the smoke away like the stroke of a giant hand, giving the new arrivals a glimpse of the viscid scene. Men in combat screamed, slashed, and cursed. Bullets whizzed, and thousands of hooves thundered.

The din surrounded David and his comrades. His own fear and nervous anticipation was etched on the features of every Confederate cavalier. Each man had to wonder if he would come out alive.

Major Conner surveyed the cavalry battle. After returning his spyglass to his pocket, he rode up and down the brigade, inspiring them to fight with valor.

"Comrades!" he bellowed, so that all could hear him. "We are now confronted with the enemy and must compel him to retreat. Focus on this fight for your loved ones. Your mothers, sisters, wives, and children are dependin' on you today. Remember the glorious land of Dixie, and prove that you are of noble race and lineage. You must show yourselves worthy of the women of the South, whose loyal devotion to you has never ceased!"

Galloping down the line on his horse, Butler, General Hampton ordered his men to move out to the left. Along with Fitz Lee's brigade, they supported General Stuart and the dismounted troopers of Chambliss' and Ferguson's brigades, consisting primarily of Virginians. In front of the woods near a farm, the Rebel artillery had unlimbered and aligned several guns, including Parrotts, Howitzers, Napoleons, and rifles. Smoke from the cannons rolled out of the valley like thousands of acres had been set on fire. The trade-off of artillery shook the ground. Fitz Lee's men charged into the swarm of dismounted Union cavalry, and the Federals retaliated.

The men below David thrashed, shouted, and fired upon each other as dust billowed all around them. The Yankees broke through a fence to chase after the retreating Virginians. Fear coursed through David's body, making him tremble. He would soon be amidst the conflict. Just as the thought crossed his mind, the Jeff Davis Legion was called up, along with a regiment of North Carolinians.

"Keep your sabers, men!" an officer shouted. "Keep your sabers!"

And then the command came.

"Charge!"

David's brigade swarmed down the ridge. They galloped onto the field, the Rebel yell bursting forth to release their pent-up apprehension. They tore into the attacking Bluecoats, slashing and shooting at them. The Yankees' startled horses stampeded. Panic ensued.

A bugler signaled retreat. The Union dragoons withdrew, but the Rebels were none too eager to give up the fight, so they chased after them. The Virginians joined in the pursuit and pounced on the Yankees, who fell back from the fence line.

David spurred Renegade and chased after the retreating Federals. The sun's scorching heat fueled his fury. Any exhaustion he felt before had now completely left him. Along with his fellow cavaliers, he got caught up in the chase, and shot at the enemy with his Colt Army while hollering at the top of his lungs.

The Confederates pursued their opponents too far and found themselves confronted with the fire of four Union regiments. The warriors swirled in a melee of confusion. Suddenly, General Hampton appeared.

"Follow me!" he shouted.

His struggling troopers obeyed and fell back into the woods, but after a respite, they were once again ordered to make ready. The brigades of Wade Hampton and Fitzhugh Lee aligned themselves in long rows, one regiment next to the other.

An officer belted out, "Battalions forward!"

With their heads held high and their sabers glistening in the sun, the mounted Rebels emerged from the woods. Starting out at a walk, they accelerated to an imperial trot. A murmur of admiration came up from the opposite side as the Yankees watched the advancing cavaliers. The Confederates spurred to a gallop and came at the Federal line with the Rebel yell rising up from hundreds of throats.

David shrieked with his fellow comrades. His entire brigade whooped from fright, exhilaration, hatred, nervousness, and a dash of devilry combined. The charging Rebels raced toward their aggressors. Their horses galloped like calamity unleashed. Hooves thundered upon the ground like thousands of battle drums.

A blast of Yankee artillery blew into the lines. Horses somersaulted and riders flew. Screaming in agony, some were hit with shell and shrapnel. The Rebels filled in the gaps and kept on coming, while the Nationals continued their assault on the advancing line of Graycoats with artillery fire and sharpshooters. They hurled single and double doses of canister, shot, and shell, but each hole in the line that the murderous weapons produced was immediately filled with charging Confederates.

A bugle sounded. The Union cavalry came out onto the field, riding toward them, and chanting, "Hurrah," in unison. A bizarrely-dressed officer led the Federals. He was adorned with long, blond, curly ringlets, a red cravat, a black jacket, and a wide-brimmed hat. David thought the officer looked like a rider in the circus with his gaudy trappings.

"Come on, you Wolverines!" the gaudy Union officer shrieked. He raised his saber and charged.

The Federals advanced and cantered four lengths behind the officer. Both sides rode toward each other with increased velocity until they collided together with a tremendous crash, like a tidal wave hitting a rocky cove. The incredible impact sent horses tumbling, falling, hurling their riders, and crushing some beneath them. Their tremendous bodies landed with a thud atop screaming soldiers. Men tore at each other, attempting to pull their rivals from their mounts. Thirsty for blood and revenge, troopers on both sides fought hand-to-hand, slashing, shooting, shouting, and screaming.

"Surrender or be shot!" one roared.

Another cried out in agony as a saber slashed into his side, spilling his entrails.

"Give up now and your life will be spared!" hollered another.

Cannoneers on both sides fired shell and canister into the melee. Some of the balls were misdirected into the Rebels. David thought the spectacle nothing less than gruesome. They attempted to avoid their own men, but found the grisly undertaking was nearly impossible.

Swerving around oncoming horses, Renegade galloped through the smoke, dust, and haze. David tightly grasped his saber in his left hand with the leather sword knot wrapped firmly around his wrist, and slashed at imperiling sabers while wielding his sword for protection. All around him, men cursed and screamed, damning each other to the depths of hell. Bullets buzzed in every direction, like the Rebels had ridden into an angry nest of hornets.

Just as he loaded another round into his pistol, a whistling shell came at him. It exploded on his left side. The impact sent a shower of dirt clods flying. Renegade was hurled to his knees. He threw David off into the dust, shrieked in a shrill whinny, and ran off into the smoke.

Stunned, David sat up, and saw the insanity swirling around him. The rapid fire of a gun he had never heard before made his heart leap with horror. Trying not to panic, he regained his composure and stood, but struggled to balance himself. He squinted through the dust and smoke. Renegade was nowhere to be seen. A Yankee dragoon approached, so he fired at him, and avoided another's saber attack. Gasping for air, he put his fingers in his mouth and blew a strident whistle. Several more enemies attacked, so he fought them off as well.

Through the clouds of dust, Renegade appeared, and galloped toward him. Responding by instinct, David threw himself up into the saddle. He spurred his mount into the fray, and in one graceful move, ran an oncoming Yankee through with his saber, shot another, and slashed a third across his forehead.

Urging Renegade ahead, he saw General Hampton in front of him. The general raised his saber in both hands before he sent it crashing down on a Federal's skull, whose head split apart, exposing his brain tissue as he fell from the saddle in a heap.

Another unhorsed Bluecoat who had apparently run out of ammunition furiously hurled rocks at his attackers until he was shot down from several angles at once. All around him, David heard demands for surrender amidst slashing and shooting. The cannonade thundered, sending concussions through the ground beneath. Men triggered into chests and faces, and intentionally shot horses out from under each other.

A Union officer rode toward David on his right. It was the same man he'd seen before, the one with unusual uniform trappings who had led the Federals out onto the battlefield. With a demonic gleam in his penetrating eyes, the curly-haired Yankee approached him. David scowled back. Both cavalrymen raised their sabers and raced toward each other. Another Rebel trooper attacked the Yankee from behind.

The Union officer slashed at the charging Confederate, who vanished amidst billows of dust. Renegade galloped past in the opposite direction.

Glancing back, David saw nothing but smoke. His eyes burned, his throat ached, and his throbbing left ear rang from the explosion that had thrown him from his horse. Turning Renegade, he came upon Custis, who was fighting off a heavily-bearded Yankee. Their sabers clanked together as both men struggled to avoid death. Without thinking, David fired into the Bluecoat. The soldier cried out and fell. Custis blankly looked at the casualty, then turned his awestruck gaze toward David, who rode past him to slash at another oncoming combatant. That Northerner also screeched out in pain. David looked over to his right and noticed Sergeant Williams kneeling on the ground, but he was unable to assist, since Yankee assailants were all around.

John rode toward him, wielding his saber.

"Behind you!" he bellowed.

David turned to see an enemy dragoon coming at him. Without hesitation he reacted, spurred Renegade to a gallop, and fired into the Yankee's chest. The man slid from the saddle and hit the ground with a thud. Taking a moment to catch his breath, David pulled back on his steed. Several feet away, a Confederate flag bearer caught his attention. The color-bearer lowered his flagstaff at an attacking band of Federals and drove it into a Union officer's face. The Yankee fell to the ground, senseless, with his jaw ripped apart. Another Rebel soldier a few feet away stood over a fallen Federal, screaming at him to surrender, but the man resisted arrest by turning the gun on himself. He pulled the trigger, fired, and blew a hole through his own head. The Rebel soldier gawked at his victim for a moment. He looked at David, who came to his senses, quickly turned his horse, and rode toward another charging adversary.

He thundered through the gagging dust, and again came upon General Hampton. This time, however, the general had been badly injured. Blood oozed from his head wound and ran down his face. Several of his comrades dismounted, coming to the aid of their commander. They eased him down from his saddle and carried him off the field. David watched in distress, unsure of what to do next. A group of Nationals cantered past. One of them held a flagstaff, and attached to it was the Southern Cross, which fluttered out behind. David chased after the captured regimental flag, but two Union soldiers attacked him at once. Furiously slashing at them, he warded them off and outrode them.

Union cavalry bore down on the cavaliers from three sides, nearly surrounding the Confederates. Attacking Bluecoats tore through their columns and proceeded to drive them apart. With no other recourse, the resisting Rebels fell back to the ridge. Every Federal who chased after them got caught up in the current of retreat and was instantly captured. Ordered to withdraw, the Confederates galloped toward a cluster of farm buildings. Their adversaries reluctantly gave up the chase.

A Southern color-bearer mounted on a gray steed stopped near one of the buildings. David smiled as the flag bearer turned back toward the Yankees and waved his flag at them in defiance, as though daring them to come and take it.

At last, the battle came to a weary end. Smoke hung like a heavy blanket in the thick, humid air. The Rebel troopers departed from the field exhausted, dusty, and dry, just as dark clouds began to gather above the waning turmoil.

A few cavaliers filtered back onto the field in search of their fallen comrades. Several soldiers from David's regiment congregated near one of the outbuildings. Unable to find his messmates, he wandered out onto the field. Before long he came upon Sergeant Williams, who was still in the same place David had seen him before, slumped over.

"Sergeant Williams?" he asked.

The sergeant looked up at him, his damp eyes filled with pain. David saw that he was hovering over his brother, the same soldier whom he and Jake had met when they'd first joined up. The man was obviously dead, and his spectacles were missing. Sergeant Williams looked back down at his slain brother, holding him in his arms while he rocked back and forth. He mumbled something inaudible, but David knew what it must be, for he had experienced the same painful horror not long ago.

At a loss, he rode further, and noticed how some troopers, who seemed to be unscathed, staggered around the sward in a daze. A few were crying. An officer walked up to one, gave him an order, and slapped him hard across the face to make him obey. The trooper glared at him for a moment, saluted with a trembling hand, and stumbled off the field.

A Yankee soldier assisted his fellow dragoon. The wounded Federal leaned on his comrade and hobbled toward an ambulance, his right leg crushed, and his expression blank from shock. What was left of the Yankee's horse lay a few feet away. The battlefield, covered with dead and dying equines, and with dead and dying men, smelled of blood. The odor filtered through the hazy air and mixed with the putrid stench of gunpowder.

Holding his arm over his nose and mouth, David discovered his dusty jacket reeked strongly of gun smoke. He noticed a young soldier who was having difficulty controlling his panicky horse, so he led Renegade over.

"Twist his ear," he told the young man.

"What?"

"Let me show you." David reached down and gently twisted Renegade's ear. "Like this. Give it a good yank."

The young Rebel did as he was told, and his horse immediately settled down. "It worked!" he said. "Thanks for the help. I thought Sergeant McDonald was fixin' to shoot him if I didn't get him under control."

"It's a trick I learned back home," said David. He forced a solemn grin. "Glad I could assist. And save your horse."

Turning Renegade, he continued on with his search to find anyone he might recognize. It wasn't long before he found what he was looking for. Peter Smith, the brave man for whom he had written letters, the young man with a wife and two little daughters, lay dead on the ground, his body twisted, and one boot missing. David stifled a sob. He dismounted. After withdrawing a pencil and a piece of paper from his saddlebag, he collected Peter's personal effects, and jotted down the information pinned to the inside of his jacket, taking note of his address. Peter's black mare was nowhere to be seen.

David vowed softly, "I'll git your two daughters those puppets, Smith. I promise you that."

He looked down at the tintype he had retrieved from one of Peter's pockets. Two young girls stared out at him from the photograph. His throat tightened as he realized that they would never again see their father, just like he would never again see his. Placing the dead soldier's bowie knife, coin purse, and tintype in his own saddlebag, he mounted back up. Heartache welled up inside him. His eyes stung and began to water, so he blinked several times. Hesitating, he gulped, and went on with his search.

Most of the fallen soldiers on the field were being attended to by litter bearers or by their own messmates, but he noticed a lone, struggling Yankee, so he led Renegade over to him. The man looked up with fear in his eyes. Compassion inexplicably replaced David's heartache. He handed down his canteen.

"Thanks," was all the Union officer had to say. He grabbed hold of the metal container with both hands and took several swigs before solemnly giving it back.

Without saying a word, David clicked to his horse and rode to another section of the field where he had fought. The sound of artillery blasts still penetrated the air, along with the cries and sobs of injured men, whose pitiful wails rose up in clashing harmonies all around him. The twisted corpses, most of which were covered in blood-splattered dust, looked like strange dirt creatures with bodies almost unrecognizably human.

Reality of the brutal confrontation made his head swirl. He heard men screaming in various registers, like orchestrated instruments blasting out of tune, or like bawling sheep, but with more anguished urgency. The sorrowful symphony dulled to an echo, giving way to the ringing in his left ear, which grew so loud it overpowered the hullabaloo surrounding him. He put his hand up to it, as if rubbing it would make the ache go away, but the pain became more excruciating.

A group of Rebel troopers huddled together, so he led Renegade over. Three men stood around another soldier, who lay on the ground.

David vaulted from Renegade's back.

"Chase!" he cried, falling to his knees beside his messmate. Both of John's legs had been blown off: one at the knee, and the other at the ankle. David gasped in revulsion.

John looked up at him and smiled.

"Reckon I got too close to that cannon blast," he muttered. His blue eyes twinkled for a moment, but then he grimaced in pain.

"We'll git you fixed up, won't we, fellers?" David asked the other cavaliers, trying to disguise his alarm.

One of them started to answer, but David looked up with anguish in his eyes.

"Won't we, fellers?" he repeated, and the men murmured their agreement.

One of the troopers who had tied off the bleeding from John's right leg now finished the tourniquet on his left. "Let's git him off the field," he said.

All four men lifted John carefully, and carried him to an ambulance wagon.

"You'll be jist fine," David assured his friend, attempting to be optimistic. But in his heart, he knew his messmate wouldn't be fine at all.

John smiled, patted David on the arm, and closed his eyes.

The ambulance trundled away. David mounted Renegade. His gaze followed the rolling, rumbling wagon across the cluttered field to one of the farm's outbuildings, which now served as a makeshift hospital. Turning away from the sight, he made his way over to a group of his comrades who were sprawled on the ground near the farm's well. He told them about John's injuries, as well as the deaths of Peter Smith and Corporal Williams, and he gave Peter's belongings to Alfred Crawford, for he knew the two of them had become close.

"I'll make sure these git sent home to his wife," Alfred said solemnly.

The horror of what they had been through left David stunned, and he saw that the same was true for his friends. He blankly stared at the artifacts, unable to come up with anything further to say.

Without a word, David returned to the shed where John had been taken. He found John inside, lying unconscious on a pile of hay. John's lower body was concealed by a blanket, and David wondered if the poor man could possibly survive his wounds. Moaning soldiers surrounded him, but he could only concentrate on John. After lingering for a few moments, he walked back outside, where he gaped at the ground in shock, unable to move or feel. His mind and body were numb.

"Summers."

Jolted by the sound of his name, David looked up to see Custis standing in front of him.

"We're ordered to roll call. Come with me."

David followed Custis over to where the Jeff Davis Legion had assembled. Major Lewis instructed his troopers to line up, and sadly informed them that their commander, Major Conner, had been killed. The men all moaned in unison. He then told them the infantry battle in Gettysburg, which had lasted for three days, was now over, and the Confederates were claiming victory. The major proceeded to read off names. By the time he'd finished, David realized that Custis Kerr, Alfred Crawford, and himself were the only ones left of their little group who had survived the battle intact. Michael was nowhere to be found.

Following roll call, David told Custis he wanted to return to the field to look for Michael.

"It's my impression that he's flanked the sentinel," Custis whispered through his straggly beard, and grinned.

David looked at him, aghast. The army frowned upon desertion. So did David. But Custis merely winked at him, chuckled, and walked away.

Artillery exchange continued past sundown. To David's dismay, Renegade's hoof had split even further from the coronet. Fearing it would cut into the stallion's sole, he pulled out the unguent and applied several coats in hopes that his little colt would finally have a chance to recover.

After dark, General Stuart ordered the surviving troopers to mount up. They rode out to the York Pike. Once again, David was commanded to perform picket duty. He considered protesting, because Renegade's hoof had become a serious impediment, and David wanted to remain near John. But he followed orders.

At least the Yankees have retreated into Gettysburg for the night, he thought.

He wandered from the other pickets like he always did, and headed southeast toward Granite Hill, positioning himself near the edge of the woods. Even though the sky was overcast, it was unusually bright. A slight breeze rustled through the trees. He was so tired, he barely noticed his own exhaustion. There wasn't any delectable coffee left; he had shared the remainder with his messmates during their long journey into Pennsylvania. The thought of poor John lying crippled in a field hospital entered his mind, which deeply disturbed him. It occurred to him that nearly everyone he knew was dead, dying, or missing. He wondered if some kind of curse had been placed on him, one that would cause immeasurable suffering to everyone who dared get close to him.

It all started with Tom Caldwell.

With much effort, he shook the daunting thought from his mind.

Like an infection, the realization of what he'd experienced during the past few weeks took hold of his heart. All of the death, horror, and destruction he had witnessed slowly permeated into his soul. The more he dwelled on it, the sicker he became, until his nausea was so intense that he thought he might vomit. He was thankful for the lack of provisions, since he had been unable to eat all day. Thinking a drink might help, he put the canteen to his lips, but barely a mouthful of water came out. The Yankee he had generously given it to had nearly drained all of the contents. Resentfully, he regretted his kind gesture, and spat out the remaining mouthful. With a sigh, he returned the empty container to his saddlebag. Now that he had no water, his thirst intensified, but he decided not to venture out in search of a creek just yet. Instead, he amused himself by softly singing a song his sister, Rena, had taught him, called "Aura Lea." Renegade propped his ears back as David sang.

> *"When the blackbird in the spring on a willow tree*
> *Sat and rocked, I heard him sing, singing Aura Lea*
> *Aura Lea, Aura Lea, maid of golden hair*
> *Sunshine came along with thee, and swallows in the air."*

He removed his slouch hat, shoved it into a saddlebag, and ran his long fingers through his thick brown hair in an effort to untangle it. His left ear rang incessantly through his weariness. He put his hand up to it, but covering it only amplified the annoying ping. Fortunately, the pain was starting to subside. He hadn't noticed any blood leak out of it. Perhaps that was a good sign.

Sitting motionless atop his steed, David's tired eyes gazed around in the darkness. Time moved so slowly it seemed to be at a standstill. His eyes drifted shut. He yawned several times before his head drooped down, and his breathing became rhythmically steady.

Renegade abruptly bolted. He whinnied and spun around. Startled awake, David saw a Union soldier canter toward him on his left side. The ringing in his ear had been louder than the intruder's approach, and had drowned out any noise. Hastily, he drew his saber and spurred Renegade toward his foe. Like opposing knights, the two pickets rode at each other. The Yankee swept his blade across, his weapon swishing through the night air. It sliced the side of David's right thigh and cut through Renegade's right rein at the same time. David cried out in anguish, but then, his fury seethed. He pulled his Colt Army and turned Renegade toward the Yankee, who had his pistol pointed at him. David fired. The pop of his handgun echoed in the stillness. The Yankee groaned and swayed on top of his horse. Slowly, he slid off, hitting the ground with a dull thud. His sorrel mount screamed and galloped off into the woods.

David stared at his attacker, lying in a heap on the side of the road, the pistol still clutched in his hand. Returning his own handgun to its holster, he felt a warm sensation on his chest and looked down. A dark stain spread across his shirt, rapidly growing larger. The pain came as abruptly as the realization.

"Oh," he uttered in stunned anguish.

He dropped his saber, along with Renegade's left rein. His left shoulder bled profusely; the stabbing pain was agonizing. There wasn't anyone around for miles who could help. The sudden comprehension that he was about to die assaulted him with terror, and he sobbed in panic.

"I've been hit, Renie!" he cried out. He moaned, feeling himself start to slide from the saddle.

Renegade turned his head and looked directly at his master, his greenish-brown eye glistening. He started to trot, then suddenly bolted and ran at a dead heat, forcing David to grab onto the colt's mane with his right hand. His left arm wouldn't work at all, so he held it close by his side.

"Renie, whoa!" he commanded, but the horse kept running.

Since one rein had been severed with the Yankee's saber, and the other was flowing out behind, he had no way of pulling the horse back. He tried to grab the loose rein, but the pain in his shoulder pierced through him, causing him to cry out. With no other option, he held onto Renegade's mane. The horse ran in a frenzy through unfamiliar countryside, galloping like he was in the race of his life. Outrunning unseen competitors, his body stretched, propelling him further with every long stride.

"Renie, stop!" David yelled. "What are you doin', you crazy horse?"

Renegade thundered ahead. He galloped off the road and through a field, jumping ditches and fences as he flew. David groaned in agonizing pain each time his horse landed, but he managed to stay in the saddle. His left foot slid through the stirrup. He knew if he tumbled off, he would be dragged behind his horse to certain death. With no idea where his colt was headed, he realized that he'd rather go wherever Renegade took him than expire out in the middle of a field unnoticed and unburied, so he clutched tightly onto the horse's mane, wondering how Renegade had the stamina to keep going. The little colt raced ahead, foaming at the bit.

Racked with pain, David hollered at him. "Where are you takin' me, Renie? Renie!"

The horse ran for miles through the dark, unknown, forbidding Northland. A bullet whizzed past David's head. He realized he was being chased, but there was no way for him to direct his steed. The little horse grunted, panting with each stride, his hooves beating down upon the ground in faster repetition. Finally, his pursuers gave up the chase. David wondered how much longer his colt would run before he fell dead from exhaustion.

For what seemed like hours, Renegade continued to gallop while David clung on for dear life, although he could feel that life seeping from him with every passing minute. Renegade abruptly turned onto a lane and slowed to a rapid trot.

Squinting through the darkness, David tried to distinguish what was on the road ahead. He could barely make out a farm. As they neared, he saw flickering candles in the windows, which gave him a warm sense of welcome, but he knew his hopes were false, for he doubted the occupants would be happy to see him. Fireflies glittered from surrounding trees, and the sounds of chirping crickets filled the muggy night air. A large draft horse, watching from behind corral posts with his ears pricked, nickered at them.

Renegade slowed to a walk. His gait became staggered as he limped through the barnyard. David noticed, but was too blinded by his own pain, and he knew there was nothing he could do. The double doors to the barn were open. Renegade went inside. His hooves clomped on the wooden floor until he came to a patch of straw and stopped. The interior enfolded David in its dark mustiness; the smell of freshly-cut hay lingered in the warm, stale air. Two cows looked up from their provender at the unknown soldier and his mount who had entered their dwelling. The bovines mooed softly, staring with large brown eyes as they casually chewed their cuds.

"This ain't no time to be thinkin' about food, Renie." David grunted, maneuvering his foot to free it from the stirrup. "That's why we're here, ain't it?"

He slid from the saddle with great difficulty. His feet hit the floor, but his legs gave out from underneath him, and he tumbled sideways into the straw. Landing on his left hip, he groaned a few times while waiting for the pain to subside, and then struggled to pull off his jacket. Slowly, he eased his left arm out of the sleeve, but cried out in agony as he did so. Blood saturated the entire front of his shirt. He balled up the jacket and placed it over the wound in his shoulder in an effort to plug up the hole.

Dogs' excited barking mingled with the music of a piano playing. David assumed the music was coming from inside the house. The melody sounded like "The Star Spangled Banner," but he couldn't be sure, because the pianist repeatedly played a few bars, plunked on a wrong note, and started over. The song reminded him that tomorrow would be the 4th of July. David remembered how his fellow cavalrymen had told him they were engaged in the second War for Independence. Somehow, it all seemed irrelevant now.

Renegade turned and looked straight at David, his nostrils flaring, his sides heaving in and out. His eyes rolled with fright. Foam frothed from his mouth. He snorted, grunted, lifted his head, and gave a shrill whinny.

"I'll be all right, Renie," David reassured him, trying to sound calm. "Jist leave me here...to...die." He closed his eyes, the pain so tremendous that he felt himself losing consciousness.

Renegade whinnied even more loudly.

David's eyes opened to mere slits. Renegade stomped his injured foot. The cracked hoof, split halfway down the middle, bled faster than David's shoulder.

"Oh, Renie," David sobbed. He tried to sit up, but his head was too light, his body too weak. With a moan, he fell back against the soft bedding of straw.

Renegade whinnied again and spun around like he was uncertain of what to do next. David wished he could understand what his horse was trying to tell him, but he was too light-headed for cognitive thought. The colt pranced, circled, and ran out of the barn.

Tilting his head back, David tried hollering after him, but he couldn't muster the strength for more than a whisper. He grimaced, trying his best to tolerate the pain.

His thoughts turned to home. How he wished he was there with his mother and sisters. If he'd had a choice, he would have preferred to expire under their loving watch, but if this was how he was intended to die, he supposed it was as good a place as any. At least he had given his life in protection of his homeland, which, to him, was for a just and worthy cause.

The thought crossed his mind that he should pray for his own salvation, but he dismissed it. After everything he'd done, he was certain God would never forgive him. Tears trickled down his cheeks in self-pity. He closed his eyes, heaved a heavy, sobbing sigh, and resigned himself to his fate. More than anything, he wanted to join his father and Jake, wherever they might be. Feeling the essence of his being ooze out of him, he listened in wait of his passing as the "Star Spangled Banner" accompanied him to impending death. Like an ocean wave, a strange sense of calm washed over him, and he knew that, although he was in a foreign place, it was all right. What was happening was supposed to happen. It was all as it was. It was all as it should be.

Death and Casualty List

Battle of Fredericksburg—Infantry
Union (under Burnside) Killed—12,653
Confederate (under Lee) Killed—5,309

Battle of Chancellorsville—Infantry
Union (under Hooker) Killed—16,792
Confederate (under Lee) Killed—12,764

Battle of Brandy Station—Cavalry
Union (under Pleasanton) Killed—81; Wounded—43; Missing—382
Confederate (under Stuart) Killed—51; Wounded—250; Missing—132

Five Days of Fighting: Aldie, Middleburg, Upperville—Cavalry
Union (under Pleasanton) Killed—between 613 & 883 (conflicting reports)
Confederate (under Stuart) Killed—510

Battle of Gettysburg—Cavalry
Union (under Pleasanton) Killed—254
Confederate (under Stuart) Killed—181

Battle of Gettysburg—Infantry
Union (under Meade) Engaged—88,298; Killed—3,155; Wounded—14,529; Missing—5,365; Total losses—23,049
Confederate (under Lee) Engaged—75,000; Killed—3,903; Wounded—18,735; Missing—5,425; Total losses—28,063

Three million fought, and an estimated one million died. This was two percent of the entire population. One-fourth of all Southern men were killed.

About the Author

J. D. R. Hawkins is an award-winning author who has written for newspapers, magazines, newsletters, e-zines, and blogs. She is one of a few female Civil War authors, uniquely describing the front lines from a Confederate perspective. Her "Renegade Series" includes "A Beautiful Glittering Lie," winner of the 2013 John Esten Cooke Fiction Award and the 2012 B.R.A.G. Medallion. The sequel, "A Beckoning Hellfire," is also an award winner. "A Rebel Among Us" is the recipient of the 2017 John Esten Cooke Fiction Award. These books tell the story of a family from north Alabama who experience immeasurable pain when their lives are dramatically changed by the war. Ms. Hawkins recently completed a nonfiction book about the War Between the States titled "Horses in Gray: Famous Confederate Warhorses." She has also written another sequel to her "Renegade Series."

Ms. Hawkins is a member of the United Daughters of the Confederacy, the International Women's Writing Guild, Rocky Mountain Fiction Writers, and Pikes Peak Writers. She is also an artist and a singer/songwriter. Learn more about her at http://jdrhawkins.com

www.ingramcontent.com/pod-product-compliance
Lightning Source LLC
Chambersburg PA
CBHW030252200626
46816CB00002BA/610